SAFARI

Also by Keith C. Blackmore

Mountain Man
Mountain Man
Safari
Hellifax
Well Fed
Make Me King
Mindless
Skull Road
Mountain Man Prequel
Mountain Man 2nd Prequel: Them Early Days
The Hospital: A Mountain Man Story
Mountain Man Omnibus: Books 1–3

131 Days
131 Days
House of Pain
Spikes and Edges
About the Blood
To Thunderous Applause
131 Days Omnibus: Books 1–3

Breeds
Breeds
Breeds 2
Breeds 3
Breeds: The Complete Trilogy

Isosceles Moon
Isosceles Moon
Isosceles Moon 2

The Bear That Fell from the Stars
Bones and Needles
Cauldron Gristle
Flight of the Cookie Dough Mansion
The Majestic 311
The Missing Boatman
Private Property
The Troll Hunter
White Sands, Red Steel

MOUNTAIN MAN

BOOK 2

SAFARI

KEITH C. BLACKMORE

Podium

*Special thank you to Donna Beck, Ken Maidment, and
Rob Richter for help with those little things.*

All rights reserved. No part of this publication may be reproduced, stored in a retrieval system, or transmitted in any form or by any means electronic, mechanical, photocopying, recording, or otherwise without prior written permission from Podium Publishing.

This is a work of fiction. Names, characters, places, and incidents are either products of the author's imagination or used fictitiously. Any resemblance to actual events, locales, or persons, living, dead, or undead, is entirely coincidental.

Copyright © 2012 Keith C. Blackmore

Cover design by Podium Publishing

ISBN: 978-1-0394-4415-7

Published in 2023 by Podium Publishing, ULC
www.podiumaudio.com

Podium

SAFARI

Prologue

Jackman froze on top of the wall when Puller and Screech blew apart.

Only a moment earlier, the first three men had jumped the wall and dropped behind it. Shots exploded, and they started wailing from the other side of the barrier. Jackman, Puller, and Screech answered the calls for help. They had leaped off the hood of the pickup to breach the gate and wall, avoiding the nails, scrambling up and over when Puller and Screech practically exploded.

Something slammed into Jackman with the force of a truck and flung him back, where he crashed onto the frozen ground. He landed flat on his spine and gasped for air, knowing for the first time what it was like to have the wind knocked out of him. He gasped, straining to get his diaphragm working, but the air merely trickled into his chest while his brain screamed for more. His side sparkled with distant pain, but what was really funky, even better than the trips on mushrooms, was watching the fishbowl slow motion of the rest of the group rushing to get over the wall. From where he lay on the snow-covered ground, feeling the cold creep into his back, Jackman heard Jonathan rage at the men and women to get their asses over the barrier and rush the house. Roxy was in there, and even though Jackman knew Roxy was with Jonathan, he still would not have minded being the one to save that beautiful ass, possibly making her grateful.

Gunshots, like dreamy fireworks, perked his hearing. He struggled to a sitting position. Something was wrong. Something was slowing him down. He looked down at his body.

His lower right side seeped blood in the area where a kidney might be. His coat covered the wound, but the bullet had made a jagged hole in the material just before biting a chunk out of him. A big chunk.

Gasping, he tried to stand. He rolled over, finally getting air into his lungs and feeling nausea taking his guts into a rinse-cycle ride. After another gasp, he got to his knees, grimacing and swaying. More gunshots behind him. Screaming. Jonathan wouldn't be too happy if Jackman didn't get his ass into the fight, but his ass had been *shot*. How the hell could he fight when he was banged up? He pressed a gloved hand to his wound, and the contact took his breath away again. He swooned and saw black stars for an unknown amount of time. Getting a hand up via the tire of the nearby pickup, he stood and leaned heavily against the vehicle. He was all alone on this side. The sky blinded him. How had the sun become so bright?

And why was it so quiet all of a sudden?

A feeling of dread washed over him, and he felt the need to retreat, to beat his ass back to the city. If the others were still alive, they'd be hollering. But they weren't. And *damn* if his side wasn't really starting to sing. Blood ran down his leg and spattered the snow, frightening him with its bright thickness.

Taking deep breaths, Jackman considered the pickup he leaned against. He wouldn't drive it, however, because it was Jonathan's rig. All told, five cars and one motorcycle were parked along the wall. Three of the cars had their tires punctured by nail-studded planks set into the ground. Jonathan had stayed on the mountain road, bypassing the crude, but effective trap. Rup on his motorcycle and Cleaner in his Dodge pickup had hung off Jonathan's ass all the way up to the wall, avoiding the damage as well. The pair of empty trucks were lined up before the gate as if expecting it to open.

With blood soaking through his glove enough to make it feel squishy, Jackman lurched to the second pickup. He opened the door and hauled his bleeding body in, taking great gulps of air to fight off the nausea. He thumped his forehead against the wheel and let out a muffled curse. He cringed when he inspected his wound again. It was bad. Really bad. But if he could drive away, all would be fine. He had no real proof that things *would* be fine, but he felt it. He turned the key and the engine started. The door remained open, but that didn't worry Jackman. He pressed his wound again, not bothering to look at it. With great concentration, he put the truck into reverse. Blood ran down his side and covered the seat. He made the first of a two-point turn and heard the tires abruptly hiss and deflate as they rolled over more of the nails. Groaning, he shifted the truck into drive and eased the machine back down over the road. The door bounced, but didn't close.

Not sure how he did it, he reached the bottom of the mountain. In a daze, he slowly drove through the gate they had found and smashed through earlier. He turned right and kept his speed constant. Jackman peeked up over the leather-bound steering wheel, his forehead tapping the wheel's upper curve in a slow cadence. He took a breath, and the pain made him bare his teeth. Every movement seemed heavy, and he barely had the strength to turn the wheel. The truck moved on for meters, slowing as Jackman had to concentrate on pressing on the gas. Seconds later, he wasn't sure if his foot was on the accelerator or not. His wound didn't hurt so much anymore, but he felt cold. In fact, he was freezing. He reached out to close the door, missed, and tumbled from the cab of the truck. Sparkly white rushed up to meet him. He broke his nose on the cold pavement, a quick *squish* like an eggshell mashing on one side. A second later, the rear tire missed crushing his heel by a hair. Somewhere, a soft crunch of metal on metal reached his ears, and he wondered what it was.

Tired, Jackman thought. So tired. He lay on the road and took a breath, tasting the asphalt tar. Groaning, he rolled himself over onto his back and stared up at the sun.

The sunlight made him shut his eyes, and the darkness pulled away his consciousness. Images flooded his mind, of coming to Nova Scotia with the gang of self-styled road warriors, looking for sparsely populated areas and a safe place to live.

A sound, like the soft expulsion of air from a tire, came from somewhere near him. The noise didn't rouse Jackman enough, however, to open his eyes. Blackness dragged him away again, and he relived times in the camp, sitting around open fires, talking and joking with the others.

Something nudged his boot.

Jackman opened his eyes and snarled against the light. Dark figures stood like shadows around him.

"Hey." Jackman sighed, still feeling someone messing around with his boot. "Hey, help me out will ya?"

The shadows stood for several moments before one dropped to its knees. Jackman detected a smell, rancid and breathtaking. Who *were* those fucks, and what had they bathed in? That thought made him smile.

Fingers brushed his face, and the kneeling shadow lowered its head. A solid grip formed about his chin.

"Don't need no mouth to mouth, man," Jackman moaned. "So just—"

The shadow descending upon him opened its jaws. Gray skin flecked with black. Shards of teeth gleamed. More hands touched Jackman's body. He felt his coat being ripped open, exposing his wound.

"Da *fuck?*" Jackman blubbered in a growing panic, wincing from the overwhelming stench of decaying flesh.

A mouth found his gunshot side and bit into it. He felt teeth and fingers claw into his wound, widening it, making the blood bubble up. The new pain shoved his senses back into his skull, and Jackman had a final, terrifying moment of clarity. Zombies were on him. A *lot* of zombies. He tried to move, but they were on his legs and on his arms, pinning him to the ground. They crowded in, blocking out the sunlight, covering him in rancid-smelling shadows. They jostled with each other for a piece. Jackman glimpsed ever-widening jaws as one of the creatures lowered its face to his. Filthy hair swung into his eyes. The zombie's maw covered Jackman's mouth, muffling his screams, before finally biting down on his tongue.

1

Gus could watch Roxanne for days, feeling her naked form pressed against him under the sheets, her hair splayed out behind her like a wild, overflowing river. He studied the smooth curves of her face and her long lashes as they fluttered in dream. Listening to her little breathless snores, Gus felt a twinge of happiness. He was one lucky bastard. He'd had to become the last man on Earth in order to find her, but she was worth the wait. He reached over and caressed her cheek. The space between her eyes momentarily wrinkled, and he smiled. He touched her again, and she moaned.

The moan became a scream.

Roxanne's eyes flew open, and her hands pawed at his face. He wrenched away from her just as she threw back the blankets. Two bloody holes in her body drooled blood, soaking the sheets. He panicked and reached for Roxanne's rapidly paling face. She snarled and bit on his forefinger—

With a violent shiver, Gus opened his eyes. Darkness filled the living room. He blinked, feeling the savage ache where Roxanne, the real one, had smashed him in the mouth, face, and body. The alcohol daze had deserted him, and the pain gnawed on his nerve endings like little fangs. He hitched a breath, regretting it instantly as the cold air once again pricked his broken teeth like needles. Lifting a hand to his face, he realized he still held a bottle of Jack Daniels.

"Uncle Jack," he muttered, keeping his lips close together to keep the air out of his mouth. It was a lost cause because his nose was still clogged with a combination of blood, bone, and mucous. He moaned wearily and looked around the room. Bodies lay like dark and gruesome lumps of coal. The wind sang through the broken door, a lonely sound that rose and fell.

Roxanne. He felt a bolt of loss skewer him through his core. True, the bitch had tried to kill him, had succeeded in kicking the living shit out of him, and had brought the rest of the gang to his doorstep. It hadn't been a fair fight. He had superior firepower with the Ruger pistol and the Benelli shotgun. They only had, at best, ordinary hunting shotguns. They'd had the numbers, though, for all the good it had them.

Gus had killed them all with no regrets.

The funny thing was that he had never thought he had it in him to kill another living human being. Killing the dead was scary, but they weren't living people. They were *unliving*, and as frightening as they were, it still felt somewhat *noble* to put them down for the last time, as though he was releasing them from some unspoken hell of reanimation.

Sadly, he felt only a lingering guilt about putting down the living. He thought he should feel more—*Thou shalt not kill*—but the truth of it was that he didn't. They'd tried to kill him first. Maybe that had something to do with it.

Or maybe he had just stopped caring after the fiasco with Roxanne.

A deluge of images filled his head, painful memories, all ending with her knee smashing into his face. If he had the choice, he would take the physical pain over the ache she'd left him with, a cocktail of loss and yearning with a generous dollop of betrayal. It wasn't as bad as losing Tammy, but it was the most . . . recent.

Grunting, he got up off the sofa, hearing the slosh of Uncle Jack in his fist. Gus paused and studied the bodies scattered about the living room. They were still there. That was a good sign. He knew they were living, breathing people when he killed them, and they stayed where they were put down, so that was one variable to rule out from the ongoing puzzle of the disappearing dead. Only the *un*dead seemed to vanish.

The living—once killed—did not.

Or at least, not yet.

Gus gently rubbed his forehead, very careful not to touch the bandages straightening his broken nose. He took a deep breath and grimaced upon expanding his rib cage. Sparkles of pain caused him to straighten, and he paused, a shaking hand to his chest. Broken ribs. Had to be. Just fucking great. Roxanne had been one helluva dancer. Too bad her stage had been his face and body.

In the darkness, he spied a glint of metal—the Ruger. He picked it up from the sofa and shambled into the kitchen. He retrieved a two-liter jug of water from the fridge. The chill of it on his broken teeth would kill him, but he would want it later.

He climbed the stairway to his bedroom. Once there, he placed the water near the bed, kicked off his boots, and without bothering to undress, crawled underneath the thick blankets. Like some great wounded bear about to hibernate, he closed his eyes and let the dark roll in.

The last thing he heard was the comforting creaks of the house settling.

Buried in blankets, Gus woke up in darkness the next morning, lips smacking in want of water. Pushing back the covers, he swung his legs off the bed and reached for the jug on the floor. With his eyes squinting at the daylight, he drank straight from the bottle, stopping when the pain of his teeth became too great.

He'd have to do something about them.

Plopping the jug back on the floor, he gingerly fingered the empty sockets in his mouth, drifting to the two places where only stubs of enamel remained and stung like live wires. He wondered if the nerves would eventually die, which brought on another question: Should he leave the roots in his head?

"You wouldn't happen to know a dentist, would you?" Gus asked the bottle of Uncle Jack perched on the nearby nightstand. "No? Well . . . shit."

Gus emptied his bladder in his room's bucket, then wandered into the upstairs bathroom. He stopped in front of the mirror and beheld a reflection that showed a bruised and bloody fright of a man, complete with swollen, bloodshot eyes and nasty-looking cuts. He inspected his wounds, hissing at the amount of damage he'd sustained. He bared his teeth and thought he looked like an old style hockey player who had stopped one too many pucks with his face. He poked a finger at the raw edges of white enamel just barely visible below the gumline, and hissed.

"No dentist," Gus said with a sigh. Those jagged nubs couldn't possibly stay in his mouth. The pain would kill him each time he drank or ate something. And who knew how long it would take for the nerve endings to die, if ever. He was no dentist. In a moment of dark clarity, he figured on what had to be done and left the bathroom.

Minutes later, he returned and, on the white granite countertop, placed the half empty bottle of Uncle Jack, a full bottle of Captain Morgan dark rum, his Bowie knife, two pairs of pliers—one needle-nose and the other the regular stubby kind—a bottle of peroxide, and a threaded needle. He spread a dark towel next to his makeshift surgery kit.

Gus shook his head. He couldn't believe what he was about to do. There weren't any painkillers stronger than aspirin in the house, and he didn't know what kind he should use if he went looking for some. That left the old-fashioned, plain stupid-assed way. Dry-mouthed, he took a pair of steadying shots from the whiskey bottle. He glared at his reflection, thinking of Tammy, Scott, and Roxanne. Another shot of booze and he focused on his terrible eyes, bloodshot and miserable-looking. He thought he heard Roxanne whispering from beyond the grave, her voice teasing him in the back of his head. After another shot of whiskey, the whispers seemed louder.

Gus didn't want to think about Roxanne. Not ever again.

Three more swallows of whiskey went into his belly, and his senses began to swim. He picked up the Bowie knife and considered its formidable foot-long length. He sprinkled some peroxide along the tip of the blade, hoping it would do the job of disinfecting it. Heating the knife occurred to him, but in his current state, the notion vanished, and the peroxide seemed to be enough. The booze started to hit him, and he struggled with a drunkard's senses to stay cognizant of what he was attempting. He would make the initial cuts and then shave back the gums just enough to get a grip on the enamel knobs with either the needle-nose pliers or the stubbies. He figured he'd try the stubby pair first. The surgery was going to hurt. It was going to hurt like unholy *fuck*, but he didn't see how he could leave the roots of the broken teeth in his mouth to torture him with every breath.

The tip of the knife gleamed.

Gus wondered if he would pass out.

Hello, pain, my old friend. He drew back his lips, snarling at himself in the mirror. He gripped the gums he wanted to cut, found them slippery, and rubbed the corner of towel around them for a better hold. He panted and brought forth the Bowie. He inserted the blade and felt it prick his flesh. The angle had to be just right. If not, he could picture himself driving the tip of the blade through his upper lip. Once he angled it appropriately, a part of his mind, that disbelieving sober part that realized he was truly going to go through with it, screamed, *No, no! Don't! Dear Jesus, don't!*

He dug in.

2

When morning arrived, Gus found himself face down on the bed, his head resting on a towel soaked with blood seeping from his tortured mouth. During the night, when the ferocious aching had awakened him despite draining Uncle Jack and half of the rum, he'd swished water and spat it onto the floor. He'd eventually stopped spitting and simply downed the bloody water, cringing at the oddly metallic taste.

With a groan he sat up, swayed on the mattress until finally stabilizing, and hesitantly tongued the stitches in his tortured gums. Wrenching those two stubborn knobs of white from his head and stitching the holes up afterward had been the single most painful and time-slowing experience of his entire existence. He wondered if the booze had even helped any, remembering how his mouth had felt as if spiked rockets had detonated inside it. The blood had made things not only slippery, but difficult to see as his gums had oozed constantly. Sometime during the process, while he was huffing and practically squealing with pain, Gus was certain a piece of his sanity slipped. He'd started giggling at himself in the mirror, pausing at the sunspots of agony in his head and the wide, dark droplets of blood dappling the porcelain sink. The endorphins his laughter released were perhaps the brightest part of an otherwise very dark and long process.

In the end, he'd stayed conscious throughout the entire surgery, not wanting to ever do such a torturous procedure again and wanting very much to shake a dentist's hand.

Gus got out of bed and used the bucket in the corner, not daring to brave the chill outside. His mouth ached like fingers being repeatedly slammed in a door, but once the bleeding stopped, that would be it. At least he hoped. He finished his business, picked up his boots, and plodded down the steps to the living room. Corpses still littered the floor, and a distinct smell lingered on the air. There was a lot of work to do after breakfast.

With dark thoughts, he wandered into the kitchen and fixed a bowl of cinnamon oatmeal with brown sugar. He warmed it up and consumed it with the utmost care, glad that he didn't have to bite anything. There was going to be a lot of soft food in his future for the next little while. After breakfast, he wandered back into the living room and put on his boots. The morning light shone in from the ruined sliding door, and Gus paused on the threshold, gazing out over the snow-covered lawn and deck. Roxanne's body lay out there, face up and seemingly staring at the sky.

Under the glare of the sun, Gus marched over to Roxanne's body. Snow partially covered her face, sparing him from looking at it. He grabbed her ankles and pulled her to the edge of the deck. Without a word, he flipped the body over the railing. Roxanne fell forty feet to land with a muffled thud at the bottom of the mountain, her limbs splayed out at awkward angles and her blood staining winter's first snowfall.

She was only the first. He went back to the sliding door and lugged one of the raiders onto the deck. He propped the man atop the railing, dumped him over the edge, and watched where he landed. The body half-landed on Roxanne, and it made Gus glad that an arm partly covered her face.

Staring down at them, Gus realized he was moaning. He straightened and frowned. *He* wasn't moaning.

"What the Jesus . . . ?" he trailed off and walked toward the house. Footprints circled the house and trailed away to the outer wall. He followed them and, with each step, heard the moaning even more clearly. Stopping at the corner of the house, he peeked around it, becoming increasingly aware of the horrible cacophony of sound from beyond the wall.

"What the fuck?" He ran through his living room and stopped in the kitchen to gaze out one of the windows. All was still clear within the wall, but the moaning droned on. Lurching back into the living room, he gathered the Benelli shotgun where he had discarded it the day of the attack and checked the magazine of his sound-suppressed Ruger. He went about the house, arming and armoring himself as quick as his aching body would allow. The Nomex coat and pants he had taken from the fire station went on over his frame. Elbow and knee pads were hauled into place. When he put on his helmet, he shivered in pain from the nudge against his nose.

He went out through the front door, the length of the stone wall filling his vision. The barrier lay ahead, ten feet high and surrounding the house from mountainside to cliff's edge. Gus thanked God above for whoever had built the thing. He walked past the bodies he'd shot two days ago. The thin snow layer concealed the gore.

Shotguns lay near the bodies, and Gus made a mental note to gather them up later—if he was able.

The gate shuddered, but the beams bracing it held firm. The sight and sound of the gate trembling stopped him dead in his tracks. He placed the skeletal buttstock of the Benelli against his shoulder, fingers flexing on the pistol grip. The moaning rose in volume, and he even heard something hissing.

How did they find me? He had no answer. He also had no way of looking up and over the wall. Thoughts of what to do zipped through his mind before the answer became obvious. With a huff, he turned and ran for the garage. Five minutes later, he parked the beast as close to the stone barrier as possible. With a thump, he jumped out of the rear and hauled the ladder from the back. He placed the ladder against the van and climbed with shotgun in hand. He had perhaps less than a foot of clearance between the side of the beast and the wall.

What lay beyond took his breath away.

"Holy shit," he whispered.

Though he had to lean forward to discern what was piled against the gate, he had no problem seeing what occupied the grounds in front of the wall. He stood on the roof of the beast and beheld a solid, writhing mass of corpses pressed firmly against the stone. Cars and trucks were trapped in the tide of reanimated flesh. A dark pickup was parked closest against the gate. Deadheads in the rear of the mob mashed up behind the ones against the walls, while stragglers from the road stumbled forward, drawn to the pitiful howling. Many of the unliving somehow sensed him above the wall and raised their arms accusingly, their voices rising in urgency. Faces in the horde turned up, and mouths split open. Some immediately attacked the section of the wall below Gus.

"Well . . . *shit*," he breathed. The scene resembled a huge mosh pit, but if he had to jump into it, he knew he'd be torn apart like so much greasy leftover chicken. He guesstimated at least two hundred, perhaps even as many as three hundred, were just outside his wall, laying siege to his home. The question reared up in his head again as to *how* so many found their way to his secluded house.

As he watched, the zombies crowded around the pickup parked in front of the gate and began squirming up onto the hood of the truck, as if they *knew* that was the best way to get to their meal. Some slipped and fell back, but the dead were so tightly packed that the more determined ones managed to get onto the hood and stay there. Others used the initial bodies as handholds and gripped legs to pull themselves to the top of the heap. Some of the dead were beaten back, but the rising swell of corpses did not relent. Three zombies eventually got to their feet and faced the gate.

One wearing jeans and a t-shirt moved unsteadily forward and placed its feet onto the many shoulders wedged between the front of the pickup and the gate. The zombie fell forward, but his hands caught the brim of the gate and held on.

Gus brought up the Benelli, sighted the corpse through the scope, and fired. The shell punched the zombie through the midsection with enough force to fling it back onto the press of bodies, where it thrashed as if floating upon a stormy sea.

Others stepped up onto the hood of the pickup.

"Mother... *fuck*..." Gus took aim and promptly exploded the heads of two besiegers. Their bodies fell and were absorbed by the mass. Gus didn't like that either. By attrition alone, a ramp of unmoving bodies would soon allow the others to breach the wall. And if he did nothing, they would eventually scale the top. A spike of dread made him straighten his back.

Setting his legs wide and picking the next target, he commenced firing at those on the hood of the truck. A woman with a ponytail had her face sheared away. A teenager in a collared shirt lurched over from a head shot. An overweight business type took two shells before his skull popped from his shoulders and his body slumped to the hood, oozing over one side and out of sight. Each shot bucked the shotgun against Gus's shoulder. The jolt travelled down his side to his broken ribs and gave them a punishing grind, forcing him to take frequent, shallow breaths. The Benelli soon emptied, and he stepped back to shove more shells into the weapon. Eight rounds went into the shotgun, and Gus took a steadying breath to control his mounting fright. He blew the head off a priest and winged a teenager. A blast took the face off another businessman. Another round bent a woman's head back over her shoulders as if she'd been kicked in the chin. The bodies continued to fall, and Gus believed some of the zombies closest to the wall were actually getting *taller*.

More of the dead wormed their way onto the hood of the truck. Gus shot the ones managing to hook their arms over the gate before they could hoist themselves up, but his earlier sense of dread swelled. His chest burned with pain, even though he struggled to ignore it. He pulled extra shells from his bandolier, jamming them into the weapon's breech.

"Jesus *Christ.*" Gus unleashed another shit storm of lead upon the climbers. The Benelli brutally punched several off the truck, only to watch them be replaced by more. He was thankful there was only one truck against the wall, but the growing ache in his ribs informed him that he couldn't maintain the pace forever. He dropped to a knee and reloaded the shotgun, noting that he would soon run out of shells.

Without warning, the world went dark, and the moans became distant echoes. A crash, and he saw only gray.

As if in a dream, something informed him that he'd just passed out and landed on his back. Cold sweat broke out on his forehead, and his stomach fluttered. His chest burned with pain, enough for him to set his jaw. A jolt of fright went through him. He was relieved a second later when he realized he still held onto the shotgun.

With a grunt, he pulled himself to a sitting position. *At the walls.* They were at the walls. They were *waist high at the gate.*

Snarling, he took aim once more, destroying the ones closest to climbing over the top. Each shot flung a zombie back from the wall. He glanced beyond the mass of dead things and wondered if more were approaching on the road leading up from the highway. Nothing but empty space lay beyond the army pawing at the walls, and for that, he was grimly thankful.

His fingers buzzed as if they'd fallen asleep, but he forced them into reloading his weapon. The sky darkened. The irregular *pop-pop-pop* of the Benelli perforated the air. Gimps moaned, limbs flailing above their heads and reminding him of a river teeming with drugged eels. Gus put down a highway linesman, a cook, and then a nurse, wondering where the hell she had come from. He killed an old codger bent over like a cane, taking off the top of his head like a detonated firecracker. An overweight woman dropped and slid down the hood, disappearing into the savagery of the corpses slamming their hands and arms against the gate and allowing some of them to get a little higher. A few could touch the top of the barrier and, if he let up for a moment, would be able to swing their legs over the top.

He ran out of shells.

"*Fuck!*" Gus dropped the Benelli to the van roof with a clatter. He pulled out the Ruger SR-9 and switched to his other knee, holding the pistol with both hands. Squinting down the sights, he started squeezing off rounds. The greater magazine capacity of the sidearm was just the thing needed to push the tide back, as he didn't have to reload as often. The Ruger coughed and stopped the zombies from climbing up over the gate.

The initial rush and spark of hope that he might be able to defeat the army at his walls dissipated. The ones Gus killed sloughed to the bottom and continued to pile up. Worse still, dizziness wobbled the edges of his senses. Anger at the situation began to take hold, enabling him to fight back his giddiness. He fired and killed, controlling the urge to hurry his shots. He waited seconds between the kills on the truck's hood and the ones crawling up to replace them. During that time, he altered his aim and fired into the mass, causing heads to snap back when the nine-millimeter shells entered them. The recoil of the Ruger was less than the Benelli, and Gus didn't feel the pain as much when he fired. Shifting targets, he mowed down gimps further back from the wall.

He fired round after round into the mob, ignoring their stubborn drive to breach the wall. The Ruger's magazine went dry. Gus popped it out and replaced it. That left four full ones; he hadn't replenished all six magazines after the shootout with the pack looking for Roxanne. He hadn't thought he'd be under attack so soon. And how the *fuck* did the zombies find him anyway? Did the firefight attract them? The smell of the recent bodies?

Gus continued firing, pacing himself and wondering if the sound suppressor could overheat from continuous use. He emptied the magazine and popped in another. Three remained.

He cursed whenever he missed a shot. The dead continued to pile up at the gates until the tallest ones could press their pelvises against the top. At those times, the lead zombie probably felt a rush of accomplishment just before its brain was splattered into daylight.

The magazine emptied with a click that Gus barely heard over the noise. He loaded in the second to last magazine and fired into the side of a young teenage boy's head. Black fluid sputtered out the other side of the thing's skull as it fell away from the ramp of unmoving flesh. The incline at the gate became broader. Four more pulled themselves up, climbing as if they realized they were very close to breaching the defenses. Controlling his breath, Gus aimed and grimly picked off the top four.

"You're shit," Gus told them. "You're nothing but shit."

He killed until he shoved the last remaining magazine into the weapon, then decided he would save that one. He needed to get back to the garage for more shells. He'd have to give up the wall to do it, but he had no choice. He shoved the pistol down his boot, picked up the Benelli by its warm fluted barrel, and climbed down from the van. He bared his teeth at each step and breath, feeling the grisly rattle of his ribs. Once at the bottom, he staggered a little ways and placed a hand to his chest before finally stopping and bending over to catch his breath. The moans of the dead swarmed his senses, making him glance up to see two corpses flipping over the top of the gate. As Gus watched in stricken horror, the first zombie, dressed in stained beige pants and a polo shirt, fell into the compound with a thud. The creature pushed itself up off the ground, gray arms flexing with sinister strength, and spotted Gus. With an eager hiss, the thing dragged itself toward him, and Gus saw that the dead fucker had shattered its ankle in the fall. It eventually stood up, gleefully intent on the living, and placed its flopping foot down, slowly puncturing the flesh and sinew at the joint with bone splinters. Off kilter, the thing limped forward. The foot hung off the splintered stump by strands of ligaments, dragged along like a sack of boneless flesh. Behind the gimp, the second intruder fell to the snow-covered ground.

"You bastards." Gus dropped the shotgun and drew the Ruger.

The zombie with the broken ankle got a bullet between the eyes, the back of its head bursting violently. It dropped to the ground as if the earth had sucked it down. The second deadhead rose, hissing, and Gus put a shot into its right eye, spinning it off its feet.

Panting, Gus grabbed the shotgun with his free hand and jogged at his best speed to the garage. Once inside, he slapped up his visor and peered back the way he had come. Four more of the creatures hung off the gate, falling like shit out of a horse's ass.

Leaving the garage door open, Gus went to his locker and pulled out a box of twelve-gauge shotgun shells. He reloaded the Benelli, shoving the shells into the weapon while swearing under his breath. The bandolier got filled and draped over his shoulder. The thought of getting his old twelve-gauge from the kitchen popped into his head, but he decided against it—too much to carry around. He yanked out a blue tackle box full of loose nine-millimeter shells. With his hands surprisingly steady, he pulled the spent magazines from his pockets and began to reload them. He spotted his bat in its sheath and smirked. If he tried swinging the thing, he'd only rip his ribs apart.

Behind him, the sounds from the dead grew louder. Closer. They were inside the wall. How many, he had no idea. He ignored them, concentrating on getting bullets into the magazine. Sometimes his fingers became contrary, and he dropped a red-tipped brass casing; sometimes he picked up the bullet wrong and had to switch it around before thumbing it down inside the magazine. The moaning seemed nearer. He thought he heard something scuffling along the frozen ground. He refilled the second magazine and jammed it into his pocket. Not bothering to look over his shoulder, he went to work on the third one.

He got it halfway full when he heard the hissing.

Gus spun around, bringing up his Ruger in a two-handed firing stance and zeroing in on a zombie about to cross the threshold of the garage. The dead thing had a huge swath of ashen skin ripped from the top of its jaw to its lower right eye, giving it a permanent smile. *Pewp-Pewp*. A jawbone boomeranged from its head, and the creature crumpled to the ground. Gus walked over, and when the dead thing raised its jawless head, he put another bullet into the back of its skull. He saw more Dees climbing over the wall, but he put them from his mind and returned to the magazines. Sounds of the undead reached his ears, somewhere behind him and in the distance. A muted crash made him grimace—a body falling over the gate and no doubt slamming into the others at the base. He finished loading and went to work on the last two magazines, feeling the seconds tick away. A nearby hiss made him jump. He dropped the magazine and whirled to find three undead shambling toward the garage.

Steady, he willed his nerves and racked the slide. Taking aim, he fired on the first deadhead and missed. He adjusted his aim and shot the thing through the forehead, taking it off its feet. Two slim female zombies closed the gap, moving with macabre sensuality, and almost entered the garage before having their heads blown apart three seconds apart from each other.

Gus got back to work, setting his jaw and moving as fast as his fingers would allow. When he finished filling the magazines, he stuffed the extra ones into his pockets. He zipped up his jacket and placed three boxes of twelve-gauge shells in the pockets. With no more time to lose, he went and stood on the threshold of the garage bay. He thought about the container of gas he had positioned on the slope at the far end of the wall, but getting to it would kill him. Even if he were able to reach it alive, he didn't want to set the front on fire. The raider's pickup on the other side would be useful. He wanted to save it.

Inside the gate, about two dozen of the living dead feasted on the dead men. Gus watched as the deadheads tore into the frozen bodies with a feral intensity that momentarily stunned him and made him shake his head. It appeared frozen meat wasn't beyond the dead's appetites. He wanted nothing better than to take a bat to the works of them.

Cautiously, he stepped away from the garage and closed the distance. Another corpse fell over the gate and into the compound. The deadheads inside paid no attention as they pulled on dark red patches of flesh stretched as far as the elasticity would allow. When Gus was close enough, he raised the Benelli and sighted the back of the head of one gore-splattered reveler. He fired, slamming the zombie forward. Dull white brain matter sprayed the other feasting friends, who didn't even pause in their meal. The sight bewildered Gus for a moment. They seemed oblivious to his presence, thinking only of eating the dead men.

He'd make them regret that mistake.

Two minutes later, he'd executed them all.

Reloading the shotgun as he walked toward the van, he glanced at the top of the gate. Dark torsos and filthy hands missing fingers appeared. Gus knew he had four boxes or so of shells in the rear of the beast, but he would use what he had on him first.

A pear-shaped woman—probably once a mother—straddled the gate. Gus stopped, sighted her face through the scope, and blew her back over the wall.

SAFARI

Once at the van, he climbed up the ladder, huffing and straining, to the roof of the beast. With a heave of his shoulders and feeling the stab of his ribs, he regarded the pack. They milled at the barrier, limbs waving in drunken fashion. They gripped at the top of the wall only to be pulled back by one of their own kind. Three had fallen inside the gate and were struggling to regain their feet. The entire scene made him pause—*so many*, even though he figured he'd put down at least a hundred of the things. Fear had left him, and he felt only pain and weariness, having perhaps that in common with the latest round of attackers. His discomfort armored him against the dread he'd once felt at facing the undead.

"All right, you undead cocksuckers," Gus bellowed.

A chorus of wails answered.

"Time to shut you up."

He commenced firing.

3

The last bullet shattered the remaining deadhead's skull with an almost dusty crack, just as the sky began to darken. Heavy clouds drifted in from the north and pelted everything with a light snow. Exhausted, Gus gazed at the mindless dead things sprawled over his property. Outside the gate lay a slope of unmoving zombies, arms sticking out and hands crooked with hooked fingers.

On the second trip back to the garage, after he had emptied all of his shotgun shells into the mob and used up all of his magazines for the Ruger, his hate for the things had slipped into a fatigued pity. He had been in no danger of being overrun toward the end, but he had only thought of the steady reloading and firing, and the constant shudder in his arms with each discharge. He had expected either firearm to stop working, or to jam, but neither did, and with growing prejudice, he put down everything hissing and moaning.

A breeze blew past, chilling him despite his heavy gear. He ached all over. The Ruger had less of a kick than the Benelli, but in his weakened condition, the only real threat near the end had been passing out once more and falling off the roof of the van. He figured he'd put a significant dent in his ammunition stores, but as large gauzy snowflakes fell around him, he felt the tired rush of victory. He also felt a stab of loathing over the amount of bodies he would have to remove from inside, and especially outside, the gate. Gus studied the pickup truck parked just beyond the wall. Fallen zombies, with their arms and legs sticking out like frayed wiring from a blasted fusebox, were piled between its grill and the gate. More sprawled over the hood, kept there by the bodies heaped up on either side of the vehicle. He would back that one up and perhaps burn the mound of flesh where it lay. The thought of throwing the gates wide open and dousing the whole lot of them with gasoline appealed to him.

Oh, yes. He *liked*.

"That's right, fuckers," he shouted, hurting his ribs and breaking the graveyard silence. "That's *right*."

Nothing moved.

Gus descended the ladder and walked unhurriedly back to the garage, holding his ribs and wincing. Ignoring the unmoving zombies around the front of the bay, he entered the dark cave, made a beeline for his locker, and found the rum on the top shelf. He drained it in two heartbeats and cracked open his spare. The fiery goodness made him gasp and lower the bottle to study the label with newfound fondness. He'd have to bring more up from the basement.

Sniffing only slightly to spare himself the pain in his ribs and nose, he grabbed a gas container and, with both hands, lugged it back toward the bodies lying inside the wall. Halfway there, he stopped to rest, swearing a few inspired words at his gimpish invaders. After a moment, he continued to the spot where he intended to burn the whole goddamn bunch. Some of the dead were splayed out away from the main pile, and he grabbed the stragglers by pants, legs, and arms. Holding his breath so he wouldn't have to smell the worst of them, he dragged the gimps into a low pile, one at a time, and doused the works with gasoline. Each movement made his ribs ache, reminding him of his recent asskicking at Roxanne's hands. He didn't have the energy to go over the wall to get at the rest outside or to retrieve the pickup. That would be something for another day.

He fished out a pack of matches while taking shallow breaths that still hurt.

"Y'bastards came here to die," Gus said as the snowflakes thickened and turned his Nomex gear white. "Know that now. And I'm the one who put the whole goddamn mob of you down. On this mountain, I'm the man. I'm the *king*. Dead fucks."

He hunkered down and shielded the match as he lit it. The flame hissed into existence, and he held the match for a moment, appreciating its pureness. Before it burned out, he dropped it onto the mound of bodies, and a sheet of flame flared up, high and crackling. The fire flashed over the unmoving figures with ravenous intent, and the stink of roasting flesh accosted him. He lifted a hand and almost touched his nose before he remembered it was busted. Making a face, Gus backed away from the growing blaze, but the flames mesmerized him. The wind fanned it from the north, and the snow thickened even more. He figured on winter coming in earnest for some time, but he had mixed feelings on its early arrival. He had no snow tires on the beast.

The fire burned, devouring skin and cloth alike and turning the bodies into blackened lumps that crackled and sizzled. The warmth felt good on his face, and that heavy weariness came back, causing his shoulders to slump. Gus felt exhausted from the day's killing. The sky continued to darken, and snow pelted his face. He took a breath and felt the sting in his stitched gums and chest. *Work.* Still had a lot of work to do. It wouldn't be soon. All he wanted was to eat something, get drunk, and sleep. Or at least just get drunk. He'd need to be good and shitfaced to take off his goddamn helmet.

The cold took a hold of him as he left the fire. Grunting with each step, he made way back inside the house, leaving the dead to burn.

Gus woke up in an even harder condition than the one he had gone to bed in. His upper jaw ached dearly, and he made a face upon prodding at his gums. The booze he'd consumed the night before had numbed the pain enough for him to wrench off his helmet and eventually get to sleep. His arm dropped away from his mouth, and he simply lay there, tangled in the blankets, still dressed in his Nomex pants. He eventually swung his legs out over the bed. At some point, he had gone to bed fully clothed, not giving a shit.

He took a shallow breath to test his ribs. Still hurt.

"Roxanne . . ." Gus rubbed his legs. Women would be the death of him. Probably faster than the alcohol, which was another cause for concern.

"Not now, brain." He staggered to his feet. Realizing he still had his boots on, he clumped toward the piss bucket stationed in the corner. He assumed the position and let go, sighing in morning relief and wondering why he didn't keep the bucket in the bathroom. With a lingering scratch at his balls, he wandered out into the hallway, breakfast occupying his mind. Nothing crunchy and nothing cold. Soup it would be. He needed to eat, needed to keep up his strength, so he could heal.

Gus smacked his lips. He also needed a drink.

Wincing with almost every movement, he boiled water and made coffee, ignoring the shaking of his hands. He opened a tin of vegetable soup with a contrary can opener and emptied the contents into a small pot. Once he got that going, he settled down with his cup of instant and put in two fingers of rye whiskey just for taste. He ignored the dead men splayed in various poses on the floor of his kitchen. The time for dealing with them and their smell would come after breakfast. He sat down at the island and slipped into a morning death stare. Minutes later, Gus managed to get down his food, snarling from the pain of his extracted roots and gasping at how good the soup tasted. Afterward, he wandered into the living room, picked up his Nomex coat, and struggled into it as he went out into the garage. At his locker, he grabbed the bottle of Captain Morgan he'd started the day before and gulped down two swallows of confidence.

Then, he got to work.

Dark clouds continued to cover the sky, flicking snow at Gus, as if daring him to say something or pick a fight. He dragged all the bodies from out of and around the house to a red wheelbarrow, which only held one body at a time. He stopped often, favoring his aching ribs, nose, face, and jaw. By afternoon, he had dropped a total of fifteen bodies over the railing and cliff, piling them on top of Roxanne and the others.

He held onto the last body for a moment, taking out his Bowie knife and slicing off a long strip of denim from the dead man's leg. Gus eyed the pale white limb, feeling sour inside, before pushing the corpse over the railing. He lugged a gas container to the deck and dipped the length of cloth inside, soaking it with fuel. He poured the rest of the contents over the railing onto the lump of corpses forty feet below his deck.

He looked down and thought once more of Roxanne lying under the whole bloody bunch. Then, conscious of the time and his pain, he struck a match, lit up the length of denim, and let it drop to the mound below. A ribbon of flame came to life as it fell, writhing in the air like an exotic snake. The cloth landed on a belly of one of the raiders and the gas did the rest.

Gus watched until the smoke irritated his senses, then he turned away.

Gus positioned two ladders against the wall: one to take him up and one to take him down the other side. Climbing up took longer than he expected, and swinging his legs over the top made something twist in his torso which momentarily froze him on the wall. Once the sensation had passed, he climbed down the other side, stepping on the very last rung before letting go of the ladder. With a huff, he lifted the Benelli and turned about, feeling somewhat exposed while standing outside of the wall. He strained to listen, but heard only the white-line buzz of silence in his own ears. He paid attention to where he stepped, wary of the defenses he'd set long ago—the planks studded with nails. The nail-studded strips of wood had claimed three cars in front of the wall, puncturing their tires and no doubt surprising the hell out of the drivers. That thought brightened an otherwise gloomy Gus. Looking past the cars, he eyed the far-off treeline and the road that sloped down and out of sight.

All empty.

"Hey!" he called out, Benelli at the ready with his fingers flexing on the pistol grip. "Hey! Dead fuckers! Yeah! I'm fuckin' here, man! I'm fuckin' *waitin'*! Come on!"

Nothing stirred from the shadows. Nothing slinked from behind the cars.

Gus grunted and stalked to the mess of zombies piled against the gate and over the black pickup. Just behind the truck, a perfectly good motorcycle lay on its side, the noisy bastard that he'd heard cutting through the city. He pulled the thing upright and inspected the body. He knew nothing about bikes, but he recognized an electric starter. He patted the gas tank and, for a moment, just admired the crumpled curves of the machine. Bruised and dented, the outer shell reminded him of the beast. The name *Kawasaki* lay over the fuel tank in scratched chrome. The number *900* was stamped on another part of the lower engine. According to the speedometer, the thing could reach a hundred and eighty kilometers an hour. He depressed the starter button on the right handlebar, and the machine growled into life. He had the presence of mind to keep a grip on the clutch of the bike. He thumbed the button a second time, and the bike powered down.

Not bad.

A bike could be helpful in the summertime, but he'd have to take the time to learn how to ride it, which was something he wasn't keen on. A cousin of his had broken his neck on one of the things, prompting Gus to swear never to ride one. No, he'd stick to four wheels if he could, and a bicycle if he couldn't. He pushed the motorcycle to the side of the road, mindful of the nailed planks hidden in the snow. He couldn't see a kick stand, so he laid the bike on its side again.

He regarded the truck and the dead around it. The snow covered everything in white fluff, filling open mouths, empty eye cavities, and the nooks and crannies among the tangle of limbs. Gus walked to the rear of the truck, noting suitcases were piled in the back. The Ford hybrid had a four-door extended cab. When he opened the driver's side door, he saw that the keys hung from the ignition.

"That's what I like to see." He threw the Benelli into the passenger seat and got aboard. A foul smell lingered in the interior, and torn instant noodle wrappers littered the floor. The door to the glove compartment was missing, and a great set of fuzzy dice dangled from the rear-view mirror. He checked the rear-view mirror and blinked. All clear.

"All right then," he muttered and started the truck. The dead shuddered and slid off the hood, their frozen limbs tipping upward as they fell, reminding Gus of dark jagged ice. He twisted around in the seat to see where he was going, and once he had enough space cleared between the log jam of zombies, he stopped and placed the truck in park.

He got out of the vehicle and studied the mound of dead and the ones littering the ground. Mulling it over, he finally decided to burn what he could of the pile at the gate. The ones around the wall didn't concern him so much, but he needed to get rid of that ramp of flesh. With that intention, he climbed the ladder, perched atop the wall, and pulled the ladder up after him as he climbed down the other side. The effort made his ribs scream and left him bent over and wincing for seconds.

He scuffed through the area where he'd burned the corpses. The fire had eaten well, ravaging most of the bodies down to stark, soot-spotted bone. His ribs continued warning him with bell-like chimes of pain as he labored with the gate, taking down the wooden beams bracing it. He took several breaks—saying, *"Goddamn it"*—every time until he was able to open the gate. He doused the corpses on the other side with gasoline and readied a match. He sheltered the flame with his hand and dropped it on the bodies. A huff and the fire quickly spread, feeding on the dead with a focus as single-minded in purpose as the corpses had been when animated.

Gus straightened and watched the funeral pyre as it grew, lighting up that section of the wall and pushing back the encroaching gloom of the storm. Larger flakes of snow swirled, dancing on violent air currents. Shreds of black ash joined in above and around the growing blaze. He looked up at the darkened sky and wondered where the day had gone. He figured there was no way to close the gates, not with the fire going, so he would leave it to burn away as much as possible and close the gates in the morning.

If anything, dead or alive, found him during the night, he'd let his new best friends, Benelli and Ruger, do the talking.

Gus woke up to discover two inches of snow had fallen during the night, and the heavy cloud cover suggested more was on the way. He got up and sleepily checked his wounds. Everything still hurt. The holes in his gums had stopped bleeding and, while looking bruised, didn't seem to have any signs of infection. He thanked God for that, but cringed at the face in the mirror, still battered and bruised in a harsh display of red, purple, and yellow. Long lines of blood-crusted scabs marked the trenches Roxanne had clawed in his face, and Gus wondered how the hell she hadn't permanently blinded him. The woman could fight.

He rinsed his mouth with an antiseptic and went about the rest of his morning routine, feeling how cold the house had become from the broken door.

That, and the lack of human company.

After breakfast, he suited up. He studied the motorcycle helmet and thought of his nose. Missing that important piece of armor didn't set well on his nerves, but he shuddered at the thought of trying to get the helmet over his nose again. He tried slipping on his ninja hood, but the pressure on his nose made his eyes water. Swearing, he elected to go without anything on his head. The wind chilled him as he wandered out to the gate, his bootprints marking the way in the snow. The fire had died during the night, and the mound of bodies still hadn't burned completely. A light coating of snow covered the remains, and knobs of charred bone and bent knees rose above the mess. Gus arched his back, feeling the creak and crack there, and adjusted the Nomex coat. He had to do two things. He had to get building supplies—planks of wood and sheets of plastic in particular—and seal up the ruined sliding door in the living room. Then, he had to clear the gate and seal the wall. The scale of the assault wasn't lost on him—he'd shot hundreds—but others could arrive at any time. The cold would slow them down, but wouldn't stop them. The wall was the first and best defense in keeping them at bay, and he needed to secure it.

Periodically muttering to himself, he hauled out another gas container and doused the leftover dead. He lit the pile once more and howled at the height of the flames. Gus peered over the fire, through the gate, and saw the dark husk of the pickup. He didn't want to chance driving down the mountain road with the beast. The beast was a summertime animal. The pickup was his best bet in winter.

He retreated to the garage and readied his weapons. The aluminum bat got slipped over his shoulder, but he hoped he wouldn't have to use it. It would probably kill him to swing the thing.

After getting the ladders back in place, Gus went up and over the wall. His heavy, steel-toed boots squeaked over the snow as he made his way to the road leading up to the gate. He got to the pickup and remembered the suitcases in the back.

"Might as well . . ." He got back out and proceeded to haul them from the rear of the truck. Gus opened the stylish blue one first and quickly dismissed it as belonging to a woman and containing only clothes. The two black ones were filled with an assortment of men's and women's clothing. He didn't see anything useful, so he left them in the snow, open and exposed to the elements.

Grunting, he got aboard the pickup and gave the dangling fuzzy dice a slap for luck. His bat and shotgun went into the passenger seat with a warning of 'Be good.' He turned the key, and the engine rumbled to life. The fuel gauge informed him that he had three quarters of a tank, plenty for what he wanted to do.

As he drove over the snowy road, huge flakes splattered against the windshield. Moments later, the lower gate came into view, and he frowned. Roxanne's raider friends had smashed through it and left it ruined on warped hinges. That was another job that would have to wait. Shaking his head, he pulled onto the highway and turned in the direction of Annapolis.

A huge Dodge pickup sat in the middle of the road, snow covered and as dead as the corpses he'd only just burned.

"What's . . . ?" Gus slowed and stuck his head out the window. He pulled ahead of the dark truck and saw the driver, a man, splayed out on his back in the road. His torso had been gutted in a fashion that reminded Gus of someone perhaps eating a meat pot pie, face first and leaving only the crust about the edges. The man's clothes had been shredded. Frost coated the jagged edges of the corpse's abdominal cavity while a trail of guts snaked from the body, frozen to the asphalt, and congealed into a gruesome lump a few feet beyond. It almost seemed as if a zombie had scooped out a generous dollop of intestinal tract, left the other undead feeders, and dropped it for some unknown reason.

"Sucks to be you." But he shifted the truck into park and studied the remains.

He had to make sure.

Reaching down and pulling the Ruger from his boot, he switched the safety off the weapon and racked the slide. The cold air gusted in as he opened the door and struggled from the vehicle. Lumbering like a deadhead himself, he reached the side of the devoured corpse and stared down at the ravaged face. Gus felt his stomach turn. They had clawed the eyes from the poor bastard's head and chewed the flesh from his face, gnawed right to the bloody bone. Distaste smoldered within Gus's core, and he aimed the pistol, straight-armed, at the forehead of the corpse.

"Hey," he said.

No reaction.

"I said *hey*, you stupid rat fuck bastard."

Still nothing.

Gus considered the man's legs. The thigh and calf muscles had also been gnawed to the bone. The guy wouldn't be rising even if it could. The undead hadn't just feasted; they had eaten the man down to nothing.

The body at his feet moaned.

From its ruined throat came a hollow sound that startled Gus and caused him to step back. The head turned slowly, shaking as if about to detach itself from the few tendons fastening it in place. The eyeless sockets seemed to track him. The jaw opened, and Gus had the unfortunate pleasure of seeing a gaping hole where the tongue should have been. The corpse continued hissing, and Gus stood away from the new zombie, once again awed by the sinister life force that animated the dead even when nothing was left on the bones. The thought entered his mind that the newest zombie had somehow been responsible for the army of deadheads at his front door. At his feet, the zombie tried in vain to lift its head. Strands of a few remaining tendons enabled it to open its jaws a little more, as if it were attempting to scream.

Gus shot it through the forehead, the sound of the suppressed Ruger sounding strange on the snow-covered highway.

He'd lingered too long. There was work to do.

4

Gus circled the Home Hardware superstore in his new pickup, keeping at a steady thirty kilometers per hour and giving the few deserted cars left in the parking lot a wide berth. The sky remained overcast and sprinkled snowflakes as if seasoning a soup. Snow blanketed the ground and candy cane shaped streetlamps, giving the scene a Christmas-like feel. He rolled behind the shop and saw that the loading bay doors were all closed, which was a good sign. Sometimes gimps lucked out and got a door open, especially if it meant pushing a lever instead of a turning a knob.

He circled the store once more and studied the ground for signs of tracks. There weren't any that he could see, but the sound of his tires creeping over the snow-covered lot plucked on his nerves.

"Shit." He should have gotten half-drunk before venturing into town. That was a mistake he felt in his face and ribs. Painkillers. He needed painkillers as well as building supplies, but he didn't know any of the stronger brands beyond the more generic ones, nor did he have any idea of dosage.

He brought the truck around to the front, then turned it so the rear faced the entrance of the Home Hardware. Once in position for a quick getaway if needed, Gus stared ahead for a minute and mentally readied himself. He reluctantly got out and felt the cold air brush across his devastated features. The bat went into the scabbard across his back, and a full bandolier of shotgun shells crossed it. The weight of the bat pulled uncomfortably against his ribs, but he kept it there. Wishing again for the pain dampening buzz of whiskey or rum or whatever, he checked the Bowie knife in his left boot and the Ruger pistol in his right. Satisfied, he hefted the shotgun and placed the butt against his shoulder, hoping to God he wouldn't have to use it.

"All right. Let's get shopping, Captain." The name drew him up short for a moment. He didn't have a bottle of Captain Morgan with him, but the idea that the foppish sailor accompanied him in spirit was comforting.

Gus marched toward the main entrance, flakes attaching themselves to his battered brow and eyelids. The snow crunched with each step, and he tried to look everywhere at once. He reached the dark maw of doors and noted that they were intact. He rattled one in its frame before realizing he was pulling when he should push. Placing his shoulder against the glass, he eased inside and scowled at the gloomy interior. Shafts of daylight periodically stabbed the darkness from skylights high above, but it was too far to illuminate anything deep inside the aisles. Gus paused, standing before a turnstile and chrome sensor used to deter shoplifters.

"What do you think? Hmm?" he asked the captain's spirit and eyed the deep recesses of the hardware store. After a moment, he clanged the barrel of the Benelli against the metal sensor. The echo rang out in the store, and Gus shifted the skeleton butt against his shoulder, his fingers flexing on the grip.

He didn't have to wait long.

From somewhere deep inside the store came a loud crash, as if a small mountain of cans had toppled. Gus turned to his left when he heard the rapid thudding of bare flesh against the floor, like a drummer warming up to really lay into the skins. Footsteps. The feet came closer, and he hunched over, shotgun ready.

The patter of bare feet sped up, closing in, coming from his right. The thing had altered its course. Gus shifted and looked over the scope of his shotgun. The clamor became louder, as if the person who had just entered the main aisle was gathering steam.

"Shit," Gus whispered.

He heard the maniacal wheeze and moan of the runner before it burst into sight, and even though he had known it was coming, seeing the tall, lanky corpse with both of its arms chewed off at the shoulders startled him. The dead thing spotted him, and its eyes brightened with famished delight. It slammed into a cash register, buckling its upper body over the counter and knocking a rack over in its clumsy haste. It lifted its head up frantically, checking to see if its meal was still in sight, and when it sighted Gus again, the jaw dropped open in a jagged grin.

It turned the corner of the checkout counter, and Gus shot it in the face, the spent red shell-casing spitting out the side of the weapon. The blast flung the armless deadhead back, crumpling it over a packing station. Bare, filthy feet went up and shivered in the air for a brief moment, like something stretched out before snapping back into shape, then flopped down out of sight.

"Right on," Gus said, not lowering the Benelli and feeling the lingering punch of the recoil. Then, he heard the rustling of debris, of things being pushed aside with no consideration of silence, coming from different directions, and knew he'd come upon a nest.

Backing through the doorway, Gus retreated to the pickup and tossed the shotgun into the rear. He drew his pistol, switched off the safety, racked the slide, and checked the surrounding area before finally settling his attention on whatever was about to spring from the hardware store doors. He had a killing field of perhaps ten feet. If there were more Dees than he had bullets, it would be a challenge to get into the truck and away before they swarmed him. He wasn't as spry as he used to be.

Shadows slowly solidified into shambling husks of long-dead shoppers and red-shirted staff. They spotted him and charged, crashing against the glass door.

With a sigh of disdain, Gus remembered the door opened inward, yet the monsters were intent on pushing. Shaking his head, he cut the distance in half and put a bullet into the first zombie that stayed still long enough. A splintered hole appeared in the surface of the glass with a harsh tinkle at the same instant he squeezed the trigger. Faces smeared themselves against the pane, mindlessly tracking him as he moved. He shot the second one a moment later, then put down the remaining five, riddling the glass without regret.

Afterward, he kicked out the crinkled glass in one door and stepped inside. The smell of the decomposing bodies hit him like a mallet, fouling his mouth and his wreck of a nose. Snarling, he pulled the corpses back, clearing the way, and used a couple of them to prop open the door.

"Stay," he warned the mound before turning around and heading back into the store. Once past the powerless shoplifter sensors, Gus readied his pistol two-handed and yelled, "Anyone else want some of this? Huh? Anyone? I'm right here, you sorry sons-a-bitches."

He made an effort to keep his upper lip down over his gums, to shield them from the cold air. Hearing nothing, Gus shouted again, a nonsense bellow of noise that failed to attract any attention.

He stepped over to a rack near one of the checkout counters and picked up a handheld, rechargeable flashlight. He squeezed the handle, powering up the device, and after a few seconds, the bulb emitted a dull light. Holding the flashlight in his off-hand and keeping the Ruger ready, he proceeded into the hardware store, stopping once to reach for a shopping cart and wonder if there might be any specials. The thought made him chuckle.

The light from the flashlight wobbled as Gus steered the cart down the main aisle. Listening to the gentle rattle of the cart, he soon found himself leaning over its push bar. Surprisingly, many of the shelves hadn't been looted. He passed painting supplies and remembered a career long gone with some nostalgia, and actually stopped and considered the prices. Next, towels and facecloths appeared, along with a supply of miscellaneous kitchen goods. He spotted a shelf full of small tents and grabbed a box, dumping it in the cart. The noise made him pause for a moment, listening once again for any reaction.

He rattled past aisles cluttered with debris of all kinds—hockey sticks, cans of motor oil, plastic water bottles, coolers, even children's preschool toys. Some sections had been gutted, especially the firearms and stores of ammunition. Gus had come there perhaps a year ago looking for weapons, only to find that everything had been taken. He pushed the cart to the building supply section and quickly found boxes of three-inch nails. A few of these went into the cart, as well as several boxes of short ones from another nearby bin. He wheeled up another aisle and came across a dark set of patio furniture, which made him think of the deck.

And then Roxanne.

He pushed her face from his thoughts and forged ahead, ignoring the sour smell of decayed sweat on the air. Cans and other fallen items on the floor clattered as the cart's front wheels shoved through the debris. Weaving through the dark maze, he eventually located several large pallets of wood. Switching the safety on the pistol, he holstered it in his boot and inspected the planks. He figured each piece was about an inch thick and at least three inches wide. He took one piece from the pile and guessed it to be cut at least eight feet long. The pallet itself had wheels, but he wasn't able to haul the raw building material anywhere. Fumbling with a plank, trying to make it fit in the cart, he piled up several pieces length-wise across the top, spanning the front and handle bar and wrapping an arm around the ends of the planks for stability. It took some effort to get moving, and he plodded down the aisles, the wood jutting from the front of the cart as if he were about to joust. He returned to the truck, unloaded the wood, and made the first of several trips back to the pickup. He didn't know exactly how much he needed, so he decided to haul back as much as the truck could handle, just to be sure.

Once he finished storing his scavenged supplies in the pickup, Gus noticed the temperature had dropped. He badly wanted to sniff, to clear his sinuses, but he knew the pain wasn't worth it. Gus turned around, sensing something sneaking up on him, but the parking lot remained as snowy and stark as an Antarctic plain.

He looked up, taking in the huge yellow lettering of the store, and kept his eyes on it for a moment before slowly turning his attention to the distant tops of houses and buildings fencing in the lot. The idea of making one more search of the store hit him, as he wasn't certain he had an electric saw back at the house. He had a handsaw, but there was no way he could take that kind of motion. It would rip him apart. He'd need an extension cord as well, the heavy outdoor kind. While thoughts on where exactly to find the needed items filled his head, he took the keys from the ignition.

Just to be safe.

On the final trip inside the store, he found the extension cord he wanted, and something he hadn't thought of, even though it was that time of year.

Christmas lights.

His gums were aching by the time he returned to the truck. More snow was beginning to fall in lazy, fluffy chunks. Tossing his newfound items into the cab, Gus started the machine and drove home.

For the rest of the afternoon, Gus made repairs to the house. In the garage, he cut the number of planks needed per his measurements, carried them to the smashed sliding door, and nailed them into place, boarding up the hole to the best of his ability. He placed caulking around the edges and hoped that would keep some of the cold out. Once the door was sealed, he draped a section of tent canvas over the bare wood and nailed that into place as well. He had no insulation for the new wall, and he had no idea of where to look for it. He then went to work on the windows in Scott's old room, wondering where the dude had gotten himself over the last little while and hoping he was okay.

While he worked, Gus sipped on Jack Daniels straight from the bottle. The alcohol helped the pain. He even brought out a bottle of Captain Morgan, the same bottle that had survived the gunfight. The foppish sailor on the label grinned from where Gus placed him in the snow, and he looked back at the captain every now and again. He swore the bottle was watching him as he worked.

"What do you think?" he finally asked once he hammered in the last nail.

Looks good, the captain replied.

Gus nodded. He knew the voice was inside his head, but damn if it wasn't as clear as a bell. "Not much of a carpenter," he added, eyeing the bottle.

You did good. Better than I would have.

That was probably true.

"How come you weren't saying anything before?" Gus asked.

Because, lad, you weren't listening right.

"Oh." Somehow, that made sense to him.

He stopped when it became too dark, with the intention of finishing everything the next day. He had one more task to do before retiring and becoming comfortably shitfaced. Gathering up the captain, he took the bottle upstairs and pulled down the trapdoor in the ceiling; the folding steps were the same style as the ones he and Scott had used in another house not so long ago. He unfolded the steps, smelling dampness, and climbed up into the attic. A single skylight illuminated one section of the attic in silver, and Gus easily found what he wanted.

Within an hour, he had the tree covered in lights and decorated with Christmas bulbs of red, blue, green, and gold. He placed the tree directly in front of the sliding door to conceal the bare wood, and the addition brightened the room considerably.

"Whattaya think, eh?" Gus asked the captain.

The bottle lay on the sofa, facing the tree. The officer grinned.

"It's nice, ain't it? Now, wait for it . . ."

Gus stooped and picked up a cord from the floor. He flipped the switch, and the tree blazed warmly. He stepped back toward the sofa, getting out of Captain Morgan's view, and simply stood and gawked at it in merry, shitfaced fashion.

"Nice," Gus said with a satisfied smile.

The captain agreed.

Nodding, Gus took another sip of Jack Daniels. He had a case of Irish Cream in the basement and thought that he would go about drinking some of that for the rest of the evening. He'd probably be sick enough to wish he was a deadhead in the morning, but that was the morning—a long time away. The dead outside had been consumed enough by flames to allow him to close the gate for the night, and the glow from the festive lights lifted his spirits. He could probably spare some electricity and turn on the upstairs stereo as well and maybe play a CD of Christmas music if he could find one.

After changing into warmer, fresher clothes, he dug into a can of beef soup, chasing the meal with whiskey.

The captain had mysteriously appeared on the kitchen island to watch him eat.

Gus regarded the bottle and couldn't remember moving it. Oddly enough, the captain's appearance didn't bother him, nor did the staring.

You okay? the captain finally asked.

Gus nodded. "I'm fine. I'm home. My goddamn gums hurt. My goddamn ribs hurt. And allow me to point out, just in case you haven't noticed, that my goddamn *face* hurts, too. I'm gonna check the goddamn bucket tomorrow just to see if I shit out that goddamn lucky horseshoe of mine. If I do, I'm staying inside for the rest of the goddamn winter. If I don't, well . . . I don't know what I'll do. But it'll probably have something to do with the—" He suppressed a burp. "—the windows in the rooms here. Gotta board that up. Just consider us lucky that them bastards never shot the place up that bad. Could've been a lot worse, buddy. A *lot* worse," he ended with another spoon-jab at the sailor.

You need to fix them doors.

"That's right," Gus agreed. "Good point. I'll get on that tomorrow too. Definitely . . . maybe."

He went on eating, studying the grinning features of the officer until the captain spoke again.

You need to finish the house, too. Pronto.

"Don't be an asshole," Gus warned. "I got other bottles with pictures on 'em down below. Just my luck you had to be a dude. Why couldn't you be like a chick in a bikini or somethin'? Topless even."

You mean like Roxanne?

"Bein' an asshole." Gus shook his head. "Don't mention her ever again. Okay?"

That time, the captain kept his thoughts to himself.

"Better," Gus grumped. "After this, I'm gonna get me some of that Irish Cream from the basement. Yeah, that's the shit. Get me some of that and get all comfortable on the sofa. Howzat sound? Good, eh? I know."

He took half of a deep breath before his ribs warned him not to go all the way. "Christ, I'm a mess." Leaving the empty bowl on the island, Gus took the captain by the neck and carried him into the living room, the multi-colored lights warming it better than solar power and doing much for his overall state-of-smashed mind.

"Nice," Gus muttered. He put the captain down on a nearby sofa chair, facing the tree. He saw no need to deprive the old sailor of such a sight, despite the guy's being a nagging prick at the supper table. The Irish Cream resurfaced in his mind, so he went downstairs, brought up two large bottles of the liqueur, and placed them on the coffee table in front of the sofa. Gus then sat down, exhaling wearily, and cracked open one of the bottles. He drank straight from the bottle, luxuriating in the creamy coffee taste of the drink, his eyes slipping shut in drunken appreciation.

"Nicer," he said, noting that his hurts weren't hurting so bad at all anymore. It had to be the booze. And the Christmas tree.

"And the company," he said to the bottle in the sofa chair, and the captain grinned back. Gus's attention rolled back to the tree and its hypnotizing glow.

Christmas, he thought in drunken wonder.

How the hell had he forgotten *that*?

He drank a toast to the memory of the season. Somewhere between the first and second bottle of Irish Cream, the Ghosts of Christmas Past appeared. The smell of a roasting turkey wafting in from the kitchen made him smile. More memories unlocked themselves from Gus's mind, of parents and friends no longer with him, yet his smile did not fade, and as time went on, the more intoxicated he got. He toasted them all and drank to the New Year, hoping for all the best. A sense of wellness flowed through him, relaxing him more with each sip, and did not diminish.

When he finally passed out, he escaped to a dream where the captain played his fiddle. Clapping hands accompanied the old sailor's tune while ethereal toes tapped on bare wood floors, accompanying Gus into the dark.

Gus woke up to a predawn, ash-coloured morning and wished for death. His head ached so badly that he thought a mini-zombie might have wormed into his ear during the night. He opened his mouth, which felt as if someone had filled it with wood glue. Tasting his own morning breath, he almost grossed himself out to the point of puking. He hoped his gums weren't infected and that the smell was nothing more than an after-effect of not brushing . . . for how long? How long had it been since he had flossed? The answer to that grossed him out even more. He remembered Tammy once giving him a hard time about not flossing; she'd vowed never to kiss him again unless he started doing so on a regular basis. That threat had been enough to get him started on it, but after a while he stopped again. Then, he had to pay a visit to Doctor Hool. The young dentist delighted in displaying what he had hooked from between his gums, magnified to stomach-turning clarity under the light of a microscope. That sight had been enough to make Gus start flossing and using mouthwash every day.

Grimacing, he staggered upstairs to the bathroom and plopped down on the bucket. There was no way he was going to freeze his ass getting to the outhouse. Finishing his business, he made his way back downstairs and eventually slunk into the kitchen. The captain was on the island, smiling in sympathy.

"Fuck off," Gus growled, but then stopped in his tracks. How the hell did the bottle get into the kitchen? He studied the bright sailor for a moment before looking back toward the living room, as if it might jar his memory of bringing and leaving the bottle on the island. He couldn't recall doing any such thing, but scoffed at anything else.

"Anyone in here?" he yelled. "Hey! Anyone?"

He waited. If anyone was in the house, they would surely pounce soon, while his head felt like a cavity and his stomach rolled like a bad sea at night.

On the table, the captain beamed merrily at him.

"Whatever," Gus said to the bottle and shuffled to the fridge to get a jug of water. He guzzled it down and felt it light up the stitches in his mouth. He took the jug with him as he moved into the downstairs bathroom. Once there, he grabbed a bottle of anti-septic mouthwash, and for the next minute, he soaked and gargled. Flossing came next, in and around his molars, and he took great care not to disturb his stitches.

Feeling like a lazy tide had a hold of him, Gus drifted back into the living room. The curtains were closed, but he could still feel a draft coming from the boarded-up section. He had to get a few little things done around the house, but first, he flopped down on his sofa. In a flash of memory, he saw the men who had attacked him lying dead on his floor, the smell of discharged weapons in the air.

One blink swiped the vision away, like a hand squeaking over a dirty windshield. Breakfast. He needed something in him before he got to work, but breakfast was out in the kitchen.

"Honey," he called out to the captain. "Make me up some scrambled eggs, will ya?"

No answer.

His strength sapped, Gus rolled over and lay on his side. He smacked his lips and, as easy as that, slipped into sleep.

He woke up with a jolt, feeling hands around his ankles. He kicked his bare feet out and used the weight to swing himself into an upright position. The movement made his ribs sparkle, and he hissed, placing a hand to the afflicted area.

"Shit." He took shallow breaths and looked around the living room. Melancholy light seeped around the curtains, and Gus took a moment to simply sit and have a morning moment in the afternoon. He reached for the water jug and drank a third of what remained.

Eventually, he decided to get something to eat. Things needed to be done, and they weren't going to do themselves, unless whatever the hell had transported the captain into the kitchen decided to help him out a little further.

About twenty minutes later, a can of chicken soup was ready, along with a drink of rum and coke, mixed three parts booze and one part cola. He ate his soup from the pot, staring off against the captain. The naval officer didn't seem too impressed with him this day for falling asleep when he should have been repairing and further fortifying his position, but Gus wouldn't let himself feel any guilt over the wasted morning.

"I'll get on it."

The captain smirked. I've heard that before. Some deadheads could be out there right now, about to bang on the front door. You'd sure as hell move then. Wouldn't you?

"Let 'em come. I ain't scared of 'em anymore."

The bright officer had nothing to say to that.

For the rest of the day, under a cloudy sky, Gus finished the repairs on the house. He couldn't do anything with the door knobs the raiders had chopped off when they penetrated the interior, so he braced the doors with two-by-fours. He boarded up the holes in the doors with planks and filled the creases with caulking, hoping to keep out any drafts. Fixing the house, he thought of the countless Science Fiction stories he'd read as a kid and felt a twinge of nostalgia. He was repairing his ship after successfully repulsing an alien attack. There were losses and he hadn't come away unharmed, but he was alive. That was a hell of a lot more than could be said for the ones lying at the base of . . .

He paused, standing in front of the main door and thinking about the mound of dead at the base of his mountain. His parents had taught him that he could do without religion as long as he stayed true to the ten basic rules the Lord had set down. The big one, the one he thought there was no going back from, was the "No killing" commandment. Killing the dead was easy. They were dead. It was a mercy to put them down, to release them from whatever hell they were experiencing.

Killing the living wasn't so easy.

Yet, he'd done it.

And he'd done it *well*. He held up a hand and examined it, noting the slight quiver. The shaking wasn't as bad, which was a small comfort, but on other days, his hands could be mistaken for divining rods, except they only became still when he drank.

Or killed, as he'd recently discovered.

Hell bound, *his mind told him*. You're Hell bound, buster. Big time. What's worse than killing those folks was the fact that you didn't even repent. No guilt whatsoever.

"I have . . . guilt," Gus muttered.

Oh no, you don't. You *say* you do, but who are you talking to here? Hmm? I'm the only thing rattling around in here, and I can sure as shitfingers say there ain't no guilt—nothing in here but us chickens. Don't know what's come over you, but you've gone different, Gus, ol' son. You've gone *bad*. Sad thing is you crossed the line without even blinking.

"They tried to kill me first," he said.

And that makes everything just cushy? Hmm? All square? Oh wait, you didn't just take a life, did you? You killed a *shitload* of people. I mean, Charlie Bronson would've been fucking impressed with the way you handled that shotgun! And it was all self-defense. That, and the booze, right? Lucky you to have all those excuses.

"Yeah."

You *know* what the good book says about killers.

"Yeah."

You're Hell bound, ol' son. No denyin' it.

"Guess not," Gus said. His cheek throbbed.

Anything to say?

"Yeah, fuck off."

To his relief, the inner voice shut up and left him alone. What was he supposed to do? Nothing? They had come to kill him—that was a certainty—but he killed them first. He supposed he was going to Hell, but he wasn't a bad person. He had taken in Scott and Roxanne without asking for anything in return. How would that measure up against his slaying of real people? Wouldn't that balance things?

It was something to think about, and Gus thought better about such things when he was drunk.

5

On the morning of New Year's Eve, Gus inspected the snowy mountain road and decided to chance driving into town in the pickup. He'd cleaned his mouth out with the anti-septic, then inspected the stitches, the scabs on his face, and his fading yellow-black bruises. The last few days were nothing more than a drunken blur, smeared and spotted with sound bites. Yesterday, he'd tried not to drink, but by early afternoon, his mouth was so dry and the *need* for a shot of *something* became so bad that he drank just to quell it. He chose amber rum and gulped it down like fiery tea, the taste leaving him shivering, but much better. He didn't even put any cola into it anymore, and that thought was enough to sober him up for all of an hour.

Then he'd *really* started to chug it.

As he suited up in the garage, he looked at the new bottle of Jack Daniels in his locker. He'd only just placed it there, but shaking his head, he pulled it out and opened it. He took two mouthfuls before screwing the cap back on and hefting the bottle. He still hurt in places, and the booze was the only painkiller he had. However, taking the bottle with him was only exacerbating another problem he was slowly becoming aware of. *Don't be stupid*, his mind warned, but he dismissed it. The only stupid thing he'd done in the last month was taking in Scott and Roxanne. Alone was best. When Scott left, Gus had been disappointed and actually missed the time-obsessed man.

"Yeah, he was all right." Christ almighty, he was talking to a rum bottle, and he knew that had to be cause for worry. Then, there was Roxanne. The bitch had not only tried to kill him, but also brought her gang to his house.

Just don't be stupid. Again.

"Don't you worry," Gus said. "Don't you worry one bit."

He took the bottle with him.

Another overcast sky and Gus believed that it had been a very long time now without any sunlight. It was as if Scott had taken the sun with him. Gus got aboard the pickup and dropped the ninja mask on the passenger seat, along with the bat and Benelli shotgun. His mission was simple in concept, but fucked up in execution. Painkillers. He needed painkillers, something besides the booze, but he didn't know what the really powerful ones were. Antibiotics would be helpful, too, but again, he simply didn't possess the knowledge to dose himself.

But he knew where to go to find out—Acadia University.

Located in the Wolfville part of the city, the school had been known for its business college and well-respected Arts program. The university had also opened an extensive school of dentistry on the compact campus. He was sure he could find a textbook listing what he needed. If the internet had been still functional, he could easily go online and find the information, but it wasn't, so he had to get old fashioned.

Gus peered through the open garage door at the frosty white that covered the land. It wasn't snowing, but it could start anytime, and there were certainly a few blizzards in store for the area. He questioned heading down into Annapolis at all, when he could just as well hole up for the month and just let time do its healing thing to his body. That would be the sensible thing to do. Guaranteed. There was a reason why he avoided the Acadia area of the city. Zombies were usually tidal, but some seemed to linger in places they felt a connection to—some ungodly attraction to certain places where they once had a daily routine they steadfastly adhered to when they were alive. Gus wasn't sure what to call it, a muscle memory perhaps? Perhaps a spark of yearning fed by some ghostly residue of life.

Or maybe it was just a good place to hunt.

Whatever it was, the few times he had driven through Wolfville and the main drag going by the university, he had always had to be on extra guard. Deadheads populated the place, and because the university didn't really possess a lot of material, scavengers like himself weren't attracted to the place. There wasn't much to take from there to increase survival of the apocalypse. As a result, the dead, left unchecked, seemed much thicker there. Acadia once had a student population of several thousand, plus the staff.

Gus rubbed a hand across his forehead. He intended to stay away from the residences and the science halls. The university library was just off the main road, and he knew a person could enter it through the Beveridge Arts Center, or the BAC as the student body once referred to it. He even remembered a better way to get in, away from all of the main entrances, just across an open field that blazed green and white in the summertime and exploded with color in the fall. The lower floor was comprised of a wall of windows, and no doubt some or all would be smashed. With luck, he could drive right up to the lower level and crawl in through a window. The cold weather would slow the dead, and if he did come into contact with any gimps, he had five full magazines for the Ruger, in addition to the one currently in the pistol. He mentally thanked the Lord for helping him find the extra weapons. They had served him well thus far. Perhaps when he was healed up and functioning better, he would find another cache of firearms in Annapolis. Perhaps even something better. Anything was possible.

He stared at the wall. Was he really going to go to Acadia? In the condition he was in?

To answer his own question, he put the truck in gear and drove out to the main gate.

The truck bounced and caused him some discomfort as he rattled down over the white road. He turned onto the highway and soon came upon the corpse in the road. The meat pie. He slowed and divided his attention between the highway and the body that reminded him of a frost-glazed, empty dish.

Under a blanket of snow, the carcass lay still. That suited him fine. He stepped on the brake, and he let the truck idle for a moment, while he considered getting out, dusting the guy off, and checking on him up close. But that little voice in Gus's head told him not to even think about it, to stay in the truck.

Gus heeded the voice and drove away. Thoughts lingered in his head, however, of doing another experiment to see what was happening to the dead. That mystery remained unsolved. He believed wild dogs were dragging them off and perhaps even feeding on them. What would that do to the dogs? Would it affect them somehow? Would they change into something other than dogs? Gus hoped to hell not, and knew that he would have to look into the matter in greater earnest sooner rather than later. He'd have to solve the mystery before it killed him.

The truck rumbled along the highway, past familiar landmarks and into the heart of the valley and Annapolis. The houses became more numerous, and he remembered a time when everything would have been covered in Christmas decorations. Snowmen, wooden reindeer, and waving Santas would have populated many a front lawn. In Gus's mind, nothing made a cold night warmer than the festive glow of Christmas lights. He envisioned kids rolling huge snowballs for winter forts or snow people, saw neighbours hanging wreaths and greeting each other, asking them to drop by during the holidays for a mug of apple cider or something with a little more punch.

All gone.

Feeling the ache in his cheek, he made the necessary turns to get to Wolfville's main street. He passed several antiquated bed and breakfasts and one or two larger hotels, the frames glazed in snow and appearing haunted. Roadside parks with frozen duck ponds and abandoned picnic tables and chairs came into view. The empty-looking houses, desolate storefronts with smashed out windows, and unkempt grounds could have been frozen by a nuclear winter. Christmas was over in the valley.

Something grabbed his attention . . . the lack of footprints in the snow.

That was a gift in itself.

Cold slowed them, Gus knew from previous winters. It slowed down the eaters of flesh to a point where the city merely appeared as a ghost town instead of a hunting ground. Gus made the mental note—once his ribs were healed, he'd go on a hunt. Winter was the time to kill the dead, to decimate their numbers and take back a little of what they had stolen. Even the ones inside houses were affected by the cold. The deadhead back at the hardware store was the first runner that wasn't chilled by the drop in the temperature, and that was enough to set him wondering why. Perhaps the zombie had been only recently turned.

Regardless, Gus figured the ongoing decay of the bodies factored in as well. It was a crime they didn't rot away into nothing, which would have made things much easier for the survivors. Instead, the dead seemed to rot to a point where they just shambled about, willing their bones into movement. Some were worse than others, but whatever the virus was that had killed and reanimated them, it would not allow them to crumble into dust.

Not until their brains were bashed in, anyhow.

He drove down the section of Main Street populated with savaged grocery and convenience stores, restaurants, and coffee shops. The once-vibrant avenue was as stark as a scorched rib cage. Glass windows were long since smashed out, and doors were either broken down or hung off hinges, just a touch away from dropping off their wrecked frames. A sign denoting a pharmacy caught his attention. The shattered front window allowed him to glimpse a looted interior, but he would still return and check it out.

An intersection loomed before him, with a dark church on the left and a service station on the right. The Beveridge Arts Center lay just beyond and stood like a four-story bunker. Made of red brick and steel, the center looked like a chunk of meat suffering from freezer burn. Gus drove past and spotted the building he'd come for, next to the BAC.

The library wasn't as robust looking as the Arts Center, but its brick and mortar construction still looked stout. The building was partially hidden by tall, thick trunks of elms, whose frosted skeletal limbs stabbed at the sky and made everything look all the more eerie. He edged the vehicle ahead until he spotted the utility road that split the university grounds. The tree limbs connected overhead to form a snowy tunnel of sorts, and the road went right up to the concrete foundation of the library.

The sound of crisp snow squeaking under tires reached his ears as he drew up beside the building and slowed to a stop. He turned the truck around so that it was pointed in the direction of the main road if a quick exit was needed. Gus got out of the truck, hefted his shotgun, and studied the broken glass of the lower windows. Inside, dark cubicles where students once parked themselves during library hours appeared scarred by the elements, and darker rows of bookshelves, still intact and full of books, could be made out past those.

That surprised him for a moment, but why would people ramshackle a library during an apocalypse? Fuel for fires maybe? Gus couldn't think of anything else. He put the bat in the sheath. God help him if he had to swing the thing. Even the shotgun seemed inappropriate, and he thought that the silencer—or sound suppressor, as Scott had once told him—would be better for a straightforward infiltration. Still, he brought the big gun along, drawing comfort from its weight and power.

Feeling the cold, he moved to a concrete loading area located near the corner of the building closest to the BAC. The snow under his boots squeaked with each step, cutting the silence and eventually grating on his nerves. The temperature had dropped further, and Gus noticed it most around his bare face and the way his sinuses seemed to seize up with every breath.

The white loading door leading into the library didn't have a knob and apparently opened from the inside, which Gus thought was fucking stupid. He climbed onto the platform and placed his back to the wall. Taking a shallow breath, he leaned over to peer through a broken window. Jagged fangs of glass lined the frame. The gloves he wore were his summer ones, and he frowned at his bare fingers. With a huff, he laid down the Benelli and took out the bat. He raked the bat the length of the frame, sending glass fragments flying. Once finished, he tucked the bat away, picked up the shotgun, and carefully climbed through the opening.

It was just as cold inside as out. The library contained six floors, if he recalled correctly. It had been a while since he was contracted as extra help in painting the interior of the building, but he had worked there for close to two months. Gus regarded a wall of green metal drawers. A co-worker had once informed him that they contained very rare and valuable microfiche. Numerous booths with viewers filled the room as well, but he moved past them to go through the open door on the other side of the room. Creeping down the hall, he peered around a corner and saw the door with a single horizontal bar. He figured that exit led outside to the landing. In the other direction, the corridor darkened, with one distant wall made out of glass. Placing the butt of the Benelli against his shoulder, he slinked toward the glass wall. He turned right, following the direction of the hallway, and saw rows of empty computer terminals just beyond the glass partition. A moment later, he came upon a door with a sign designating the room as the student computer lab. Gus didn't see anything of use inside, so he focused ahead on the deepening dark. The snow wasn't squeaking underfoot anymore, but the gloom still played with his fears of things unseen and nubs of rotting teeth eager for meat.

Gus crept further down the hall until he came to a beige doorway. He cracked it open and saw shelves of books draped in near blackness. A whiff of aging paper accosted him. Turning his attention back to the hall, he proceeded to a stairwell that went down another level as well as up several. Leaning over the metal railing, Gus saw a rash of daylight from above. Pointing his shotgun ahead, he moved toward it.

He stopped at what he remembered to be the main floor. He edged out of the stairwell into a room with sparse lighting coming from the far wall of windows. Long bookshelves divided the level into aisles, while in some of the more open sections, broad tables with books still on their surfaces cluttered the floor. Chairs covered in cheap vinyl faced the wall of windows, giving students a beautiful view of the university grounds. Gus stopped and stared out the window for a moment, seeing his truck two stories below. Beyond that, snowy trees lined the main road. The scene looked like a frozen oil painting. He listened, but heard nothing. The place seemed deserted.

It would be easy to find out if it wasn't. One yell was all it took to bring the dead out to investigate. However, he wasn't ready for a full-blown hunt. Not yet. But soon.

Pulling back from the window, Gus skulked toward where he remembered seeing encyclopaedias. Whether he could find anything of use in those books, he didn't know, but they were a good place to start. Moving past empty tables and chairs and feeling as if ghosts might inhabit the place, Gus entered the main entryway to the library and the front checkout desks. Offices were behind a long brown counter cut with slots for designated book drop sites. A dead elevator lay to his right, as well as another bank of computer terminals, but then he found the books he wanted.

He went looking for the volume with the letter 'P' on it. He pulled it from the shelf and took it to a nearby table. The paper smelled old, the scent hitting him in the face as he went through the pages.

Painkillers. Also known as *analgesics*. Gus smiled. Was it time for him to have some luck after all? He started reading the entry and soon found opiates, as well as an explanation for codeine. Codeine, Percocet, and Tramadol jumped out at him. Those names were enough for him. Gus regarded the heavy, cumbersome book. He tore out the page, the ripping noise cutting through the silence of the library loud enough to make him freeze. Tension-filled seconds passed while he waited to see if anything would appear, but nothing did. Not wanting to waste any more time, he stuffed the paper inside his coat and left the book open on the table.

Mission completed. He'd be lucky indeed if that drugstore he'd seen on the way in had any of what was on the page.

He moved past the front checkout counters and back into the main area.

He heard a squeak.

Gus brought up the Benelli and looked around, searching the spaces between the shelves.

Another squeak. Longer this time. Definitely movement.

And unquestionably behind him.

Gus turned around and looked at the doorway he'd just come through. The squeaking came from beyond, like a wheel that had grown cranky with rust.

When the cause of the noise came into view, Gus's jaw dropped.

6

The guy had died in perhaps the strangest position. The zombie, dressed in a shirt and pants, had crawled into the lower part of a book cart. Its legs trailed behind, at least, the ribbons of its pants legs did, shredded and dragging like filthy streamers. It pulled itself along in the cart, no more than three inches off the floor, black fingers clawing into anything that would give enough purchase. The eyes of the deadhead were milky cataracts, and its lips drew back in a permanent grimace. The thing reminded Gus of an ancient sea turtle, flippers working to pull its weight forward.

The squeaking continued, shrill and grating, like an old man whistling through ill-fitting dentures. It rolled toward Gus, keeping its eyes on him as if to mesmerize him. Gus wondered for a moment how to dispatch the thing coming for him. He could see the opaque knobs of the corpse's missing legs as they wobbled behind the cart. Poor bastard had to have been escaping something and crawled up into the lower shelf of the cart, then died there while something chewed off his legs. Or maybe it happened differently; Gus could think of a couple of ways things might've gone down for the man.

Gus placed his shotgun on a nearby table, drew the silenced Ruger, and took aim.

The dead fucker had closed the distance to where its black-tipped fingernails were only an inch from the toes of Gus's boots.

He shot the thing through the top of the head, stopping it dead on its wheels. The spent cartridge bounced with a tinkle on the tiles. The thing's arms flopped to the floor, and for a moment, Gus simply stood and studied the zombie. He'd seen so many of the dead come back to life that they all seemed mundane, but this zombie was something new. That it had managed to worm itself onto the cart made it different.

The sound of the shot hung on the air for just a second and he waited, listening. Nothing else approached, so he shoved the gun back down his boot and picked up the shotgun.

Then he heard it.

Moaning came from the direction of the stairwell, ghostly and ringing in the shaft like macabre dinner bells. Somewhere in the aisles, books crashed to the floor, startling him. He started for the stairwell, hunched over so that he could peer between the shelves. Shadows lurched over the uneven tops of books, making him wonder from which direction the corpses would emerge.

He rushed into the stairwell, all thoughts of stealth gone as the cries of the dead rang down from above. Leaning out over the railing and hazarding a peek upward, he glimpsed a collection of heads, shoulders, and torsos hanging over the railing. Zombies walked and stumbled down the stairs as if having one massive party. One hung precariously out over the railing and spotted Gus. Its hands came up, clutching, and its hiss of delighted discovery speared Gus's heart. He bolted.

He took the steps two and three at a time, each impact making his knees sing out in pain. He reached the bottom of the well just as the zombie crashed to the floor and exploded on the concrete in front of him. Gus threw himself backwards and turned his head in pure reflex, but that vase-like shattering of a skull was hard to get out of his mind's eye. He edged around the flopping form of the female corpse, squeamishly peeking at broken limbs in a widening pool of black.

Gus ran into the hall, hungry echoes tailing his boot heels.

The beige door he'd opened earlier thrummed with savage energy as he passed, shooting more adrenalin into his already overloaded system. The door stayed closed, but Gus increased his speed anyway. Beyond the glass wall of the computer lab, wraiths emerged from behind the dark lines of empty terminals, rising from their internet graves.

Gus turned into the home stretch.

He exploded through the outer door, letting it rebound hard on its hinges. He jumped down off the loading platform and raced to his truck. In seconds, he was behind the wheel. An instant later, the library shrank in his rearview mirror as he drove away. It disappeared when he made the turn onto the main road.

Lucky, he thought. So very lucky. And not a zombie on the road ahead.

Still too cold. Much too cold for the dead fucks.

Catching his breath, he focused on the next task on hand—checking out the drugstore. He hoped there weren't any surprises waiting for him there. He doubted his nerves could take it.

A minute later, he parked in the middle of the street, right in front of the drugstore. Two quick swallows of Uncle Jack steadied his hands and rattled nerves. Studying the ravaged store front, Gus shook his head. It looked as if people had gutted this one, searching for goods. Still, luck was potentially on his side, so he got out, determined to take a look. The shop contained five aisles, all running perpendicular to the entrance. Gus walked along the front, checking each aisle. Most of the useful items had been taken from the shelves. He'd already been in the store about a year and a half ago, and hadn't found much then either. Even the toothbrushes had been snatched. In the rear, a raised counter for prescription drugs lay partially obscured by darkness. The weaker drugs had been taken, but the stronger stuff—prescription-grade medications—might still be behind that counter. Debris covered the floor—torn paper, packaging, and various other half-crushed items. The smell of sour milk and something else he couldn't quite place lingered on the air, despite the smashed window.

"Hey," he called. "Any dead bastards in here?"

No answer.

He kicked at some garbage littering the floor and wished for a flashlight. Confident the place was indeed empty, he moved down an aisle, spotting shredded magazines, empty pop bottles, candy wrappers, and other items that made him think that whoever the hell had been through could've used more goddamn sense when shopping.

He found the waist-high gate to the prescription drug area and eased it open. The hinges squealed, making him pause. When no zombies popped out, he went behind the counter and let his breath out in a hiss.

"Can't see shit." He started sifting through the boxes and bottles still on the shelves. He brought several containers up to his eyes, reading what he could off the label in the scant light, and put them back. Most of them had words on them he could barely pronounce. The search stretched into the better part of an hour, the chill stiffening his fingers and face. The wind picked up, the sound of it as chilling as any dead thing at times, and blew across the front of the drugstore, sending up cauls of white and slowly coating the pickup. Gus stopped every once and a while to peer out toward the street, ensuring nothing else was in the store but him.

He finally came across ten small boxes of a drug called Tramacet. Taking them all, he went back to the pickup and inspected the little boxes, comparing the information to the page he'd taken from the library. Each Tramacet tablet contained thirty-seven milligrams of tramadol hydrochloride as well as three hundred and thirty-five milligrams of acetaminophen. He read the usual dosage amount and consulted the page. All of the drugs seemed to have some sort of derivative of the original, and a good feeling about what he had blossomed inside of him.

Gus threw the first boxes into the truck and went back to scrounge for more. He found a total of twenty-two and, after loading them, celebrated the discovery by taking three more mouthfuls of whiskey. He turned so that his back took the brunt of the wind and took in the empty Main Street of Wolfville. If he thought hard enough, he could envision the place before the fall, with students populating the sidewalks and a long pulse of cars moving on the road.

Then, he remembered he was close to his old apartment. Just behind the main drag lay Front Street, where he had rented a small two-bedroom apartment. He studied the afternoon sky and figured he had time for a little nostalgia. He drove to a side road and made the turn toward the bay. He made another turn and proceeded slowly until he stopped alongside his old apartment, which was on the bottom floor of a two-story house. The building didn't look any better than when he had lived there. Sky-blue paint colored the house, and a satiny green lined the trim. The front door going into his place was wide open, only kept in place by a small dune of snow. He could see directly inside so didn't feel a need to enter. Pleasant memories formed in his mind, of apartment parties raging out of hand and cheap, all-night poker matches where the pots never got any higher than ten dollars. He even remembered a time when he'd held Tammy's head up by her ponytail while she puked into a garbage can outside of the apartment.

Gus's attention centered on the nearby shed. The lock was busted. A snowmobile had been stowed there at one point in time, owned by Chris Russell, his landlord.

Putting the truck in gear, he inched the truck ahead and turned it around until its rear faced the shed doors. Gus got out with his shotgun, looking down the street for any zombies, and went to the shed. He widened the crack of the doors and peeked into the gloom.

The snow machine was still there.

Gus wasn't much for snowmobiles, as he had never been able to afford to maintain one. But things were different. In fact, a machine like the one before him was just what he needed. It was a Yamaha, a large red monster built for racing. A high fiberglass windshield provided protection for the driver, and saddle bags hung from a heavily padded backrest that gave support for an extra passenger. A set of red handlebar muffs were fastened to the handlebars, to keep the driver's hands warm while steering the machine. He stood there for a moment, simply admiring the vehicle for what it was. A moment later he spotted two planks that would allow him to drive the machine right up into the rear of the truck, so transporting it back to the house wouldn't be a problem.

He liked the idea, but felt a moment's disappointment when he couldn't find the keys. Russell's apartment was just above his own, and Gus remembered a key rack hanging just inside the doorway. Glancing around, he crossed the yard and climbed the steps to the second-story apartment. He hesitated at the closed door before trying the knob. The door opened with a tug and a frosty crack.

Stepping into the entry area and kitchen of Russell's place, Gus saw that no one had been living there for a long time. Hanging on a peg beside the stove was a set of keys. It was almost too good to be true. A smile spread across his face as he took the keys. Something bad was going to happen. Had to. The morning was going too well. He left the apartment and closed the door behind. Returning to the snowmobile, he inserted the key and pushed the electric start button. He hoped the motor would start. Battery longevity in all machines had been greatly improved up over the years, engineered to start under the most extreme conditions or after years of inactivity. Fuel quality had also been improved upon, and gas was laced with a chemical additive that maintained octane levels for extraordinarily long periods. Still, despite advancements in engine and fuel technology, some engines refused to start.

Like a monster waking, it rumbled to life.

With cold fingers, he threw the shed doors the rest of the way open and got the planks in place to drive the machine up into the bed of the pickup. He mounted the snowmobile, squeezed the throttle, and eased it up the makeshift ramp. A near-perfect fit.

He got down from the back of the truck and stowed the planks beside the snowmobile. He took another glance inside the shed and spotted a gas container. He grabbed it and gave it a shake. Not much, but some gas sloshed, so he tossed it into the back of the truck with the snowmobile.

Gus took one last look around, didn't see anything else he needed, and walked back into the street. Daylight seemed to have dimmed, and the snow was noticeably thicker. He regarded his old apartment one final time, saving the image in his mind, before getting aboard the pickup.

7

For the next few days, Gus stayed home, comfortably medicated. The Tramacet did the trick, staving off the greater portion of the pain while the booze kept him comfortably high. He was sure there was something wrong in taking the painkillers with the booze, so he spaced it out as much as he could, and only took the pills with water. The booze he drank straight, not even bothering with a mix anymore. What was the point? He drank because he enjoyed it, because it took the edge off, and a shitload of other reasons he couldn't articulate. At some point in time, when his senses were swimming and his limbs felt like slabs of rubber, he realized he didn't have to explain himself to anyone, so he drank even more.

Several mornings, he threw up in the bathroom bucket, heaving his guts out, waiting for the time when he would see blood in his vomit. Somehow, he finished the repairs on the house, kept an eye on the solar panels and batteries, and patrolled the grounds with the Benelli tucked in under one arm, as vigilant as he could be while half-drunk. The solar panels remained a mystery and a wonder, and he dreaded the day they ever stopped working. The snow continued to fall in great lazy clumps, and the days when it stopped, the clouds appeared as if they were merely gathering up wind for the next onslaught. Thus far, no more zombies had made it up the mountain and approached the wall, and the remaining dead scattered outside were buried in snow.

As time marched on, his face slowly healed. When he could stomach looking in a mirror, the progression was easy to see. The cuts healed into scars that lashed his features, as if he'd fallen sideways, face-down onto a hot grill. The once-brilliant purple explosions underneath his flesh had slowly receded and disappeared. His cheek still ached, but only as long as it took for him to down a couple of Tramacet tablets. His gums evaded infection, although there were a few mornings when he spat pus into the sink. The mouthwash helped clean it up, leaving him with the sense of having dodged one serious bullet. He wondered if the holes where the teeth had been would ever completely heal. Not that it mattered. His diet consisted of canned vegetables, stews, pasta, and dry noodles, and he cut any larger bits into smaller pieces. The stores in his basement were fine, and at the pace he was going, he figured he had enough food for a year, as long as it didn't spoil in the cans. After that, the old problem came back. There wasn't any fresh food anymore, and he still hadn't figured out a way to grow his own. It was a problem he had to get on in the spring. There were old apple orchards and farms in other parts of the valley, and those places would be a good place to start looking for wild growing produce.

Other than drinking and watching old movies, reading continued to be his sole entertainment. He read steampunk and fantasy paperbacks from authors like Jason G. Anderson, Eric Zawadzki, Jason E. Thummel, and Katrina Anne Jack, even some zombie fiction from Brian J. Jarrett. He read until he passed out, and when he awoke, usually to the sound of winds battering the house, he'd shiver, have a mouthful of rye, and forage for something to eat. The movies he watched were from all genres, but he grew increasingly fonder of the old George Romero flicks. There was a style about them that he enjoyed. The newer zombie action movies were fine, and he continued making a study of them, vowing not to do the idiotic actions some of the characters did when faced with undead hordes.

One evening, with the day darkening like the door being slowly shut on a frozen wasteland, Gus walked out to the wall and climbed the one ladder he'd left out there. He gazed over the top, a lone sentry on the battlements, and wondered when the next attack would happen, and if he would be awake when it did. The mob that had breached the compound wall made him think about what to do if it happened again. They'd been a stern test of his defenses, and he wasn't entirely happy with the results. The nail-studded boards were hidden underneath the snow, causing Gus to avoid walking anywhere off the beaten road. He couldn't complete his trench like he wanted to, delaying that particular project until the spring when the ground thawed. Giving Scott enough ammunition to protect himself had halved his store of shotgun shells, and after the assault on his walls, his ammunition supply had become even lower. He couldn't afford to blast away another couple of hundred deadheads. Explosives came into his head, although he didn't know where to get them or how to handle them if he did. There was a national armory in Halifax, but in his daily semi-plastered state, he didn't want to risk the drive. Chances were that anyone who did know how to handle explosives had probably already raided the storage facility. He thought of Scott again and wondered how the young man was faring. He'd been gone for three weeks, and Gus missed their banter. He then switched back to the state of his defenses and how to improve them.

Then, it came to him. Molotov cocktails. He'd already made a few, but the idea of making more appealed to him. The fire bombs would be just the thing, and they also gave him reason to drink more. He had plenty of empties around the house. The only thing he had to do was get the gas, plug the bottles with cloth, and stockpile them. The more he thought about it, the more he liked the idea of watching the dead walk until they were ashes.

The next day, he started producing firebombs. In the garage, he set up a funnel and gas container, made a line of empty whisky and rum bottles, and filled them in assembly line fashion, pausing only to take away full bottles and replace them with empty ones. After three dozen of them, he plopped down at a work bench and formed a secondary line. He sliced T-shirts into shreds with his Bowie knife and stuffed the strips into the bottle necks. The work made him feel quite pleasant, and occasionally, he would take a short break and reflect on his progress with a few straight shots from a bottle of vodka. Vodka was his choice of a morning drink, thinking it was time to put a dent in the stores of booze brands he hadn't even touched yet, stashed away like an alcoholic squirrel.

At one point he got up to stretch and listen to the garage and the house, hearing nothing but the slow dissolve of time. He turned to the captain, the same empty rum bottle he'd kept with him about the house, and stared at the foppish sailor. Next to him were about a dozen other rum bottles, each with their own sailors on the front, all standing at attention, brimming with gasoline, and ready for action.

"You're in charge of those assholes. Got it?"

The captain smiled.

"I mean it. If I ever have to throw them over the wall, you gotta be on them and make sure they burn. And I mean *burn* in fuckin' spectacular fashion. Light up some undead asses."

I'll take care of it. You can depend on my boys. My *marines*.

"Good." Gus nodded. "I knew I could. Sorry to be a hard ass all the time."

Then for no reason, Gus got to giggling. How the hell could the captain keep such a grin on his face for so long? That had to hurt.

What about Roxanne and her gang?

The question killed his giggles and Gus had to think for a moment before answering. "Come springtime, when the snow goes away, I'll see what's what. If the bodies are still there, I'll burn them again. If not, maybe I can wheel some dirt to the edge and dump it over. Cover them up. They not goin' anywhere at the base of the cliff."

How are you doing with, you know, Roxanne?

"Don't go there, okay?" Gus slurred, feeling the vodka do its three-punch magic. "Bitch almost killed me. Her buddies fucked up my doors. And you saw what they did to Uncle Jack. You were next to him. Exploded his ass. Right there in the kitchen. I mean, Christ almighty, you try to be friendly and look what it brings you."

The captain agreed. That made Gus feel better. Whatever he might have felt for Roxanne had rotted in him, turned bad, and was presently marinating in hate. Thinking on how she had deceived him, he wished he had shot her a third time. The memory left a bad taste in his mouth, and he reached for the vodka to wash it away.

"Nasty shit," he hissed and regarded the bottle at arms' length. He placed it back down and looked at the captain. The old sailor was the only friend he had in the world, and the memory of Uncle Jack being shot jarred something in him.

"Y'know," Gus said, picking up the bottle and wiping off the label with his fingers. "I think it's time to get you into some body armor. How 'bout that? Hm? You're as vulnerable as a baby's bare ass."

Suppose it wouldn't hurt.

Gus was glad that the sailor approved. He got out a roll of duct tape and covered every inch of the bottle, with the exception of the decal of the smiling captain. He applied two thick layers and molded them to the contours of the glass. Once finished, he inspected his work, gave it a slap, and nodded at the officer.

The captain nodded back, pleased with the new protection.

Needing to replenish his gas supplies, Gus decided to head down to the highway to pop some tanks one morning in mid-January. He remembered the Western Oil storage facility on the other end of the city, but there wasn't any way to channel the contents of the tanks. In the end, it was simply easier to get what he needed from the cars. He suited up, opting to leave his helmet behind again, and went about gathering the items he'd need. A minute later, he was at the gate. His ribs still bothered him, and although the regular doses of Tramacet—boosted by regular shots of rum, whiskey, and vodka—cut away a lot of the discomfort, he suspected he had to be careful when doing anything heavy. He got the first timber down with a grunt, placed a hand against his ribs, and took short shallow breaths. The pain sparkled dully, and even just turning made him ache.

"Fuck," he grumbled and sized up the remaining four thick pieces of wood bracing the gate. "Fuck."

Put your back into it! He heard the captain call out from the cab of the pickup.

Gus rolled his eyes. All he needed was a gay illustration on the front of an empty booze bottle telling him what to do. He backed up, then looked down briefly and realized the snow was up to his ankles. Grimacing, held his side and stepped back from the gate. His breath floated before him, and he imagined with his scars and missing teeth, he probably looked like a fright. Taking a breath and preparing himself for the pull, he got his hands around the next beam. He intended on doing a one-two count, but even the practice pull sucked the strength from him.

"Fuck again." He decided then that he wouldn't be going anywhere in his condition, not until his ribs healed.

"You got me," he whispered and shook his head. Still holding his side, he turned around and looked at the house in all of its frosty glory. The sun seemed to have taken off, leaving clouds hanging miserably in the sky. Gus squinted at them. They were dark. Medieval dark.

The wind picked up, as cutting as jagged glass against his bare skin. He dismissed the gate with a wave of his hand and got back aboard the pickup. Even as he closed the door to the vehicle, flakes splatted against the windshield with a fury that made him pause. The captain, in the passenger seat beside a half-empty bottle of vodka, smirked.

Something's coming.

"Yeah," Gus agreed, sizing up the snow. "I think you're right. Somethin's comin' down the pipe."

He turned the truck around and parked it in the garage, next to the van. He'd already parked the snowmobile in front of the beast, making the garage seem fuller than usual. There would be no harvesting of gas that day and, by the looks of it, perhaps not for a while. Gus lowered the garage door. The wind snarled savagely against the windows, making the entire frame rattle.

"Jesus," Gus muttered, peering out at the snow. He hoped the solar panel for heating the house would function. It had last winter, during the fiercest of storms. There was the fireplace in the living room, but he didn't have any wood chopped for it. At worst, he'd have to throw extra blankets on the bed, get shitfaced, and crawl in under it all for the night to ride it out.

Get shitfaced. Get medicated. He had to admit the idea had a nice ring to it. Losing interest in the gathering tempest outside, Gus made his way deeper into the house.

Isolation, he knew, could fuck a person up. He just didn't believe it could happen to him. But since the shoot-out—more precisely, after Scott and Roxanne were gone—he had felt as if his sanity was slowly coming apart, like a jigsaw puzzle, one crusty piece at a time. He wasn't sure if it was the constant boozing, the drugs, the solitude, or even the lack of sunshine that had started to warp his reality. Maybe it was the conversations with the empty, duct-taped bottle of rum. That sure as hell couldn't be helping his frame of mind.

But when the captain had started talking *back*, and Gus wasn't sure it was himself doing the talking—a displaced part of his own subconscious fabricating and giving the bottle a personae—he knew, *really* knew, he might have a problem. He'd have to watch himself.

And the bottle.

January rolled out like a huge creaking snowball, the kind you would do to construct a fort of historical proportions. Snow fell on and off, the sky throwing down more than Gus ever thought possible. The winter before had been mild in comparison to the frozen hell being wrought outside the house. Twice, he went outside and cleared off the panels, and once even dared fate by climbing a ladder to the roof, thirty feet above ground, and cleared off the panels up there with wide, shaky swishes of an arm. Monstrous drifts filled the yard, as if ancient ice serpents had lain down inside the walls and wrapped themselves around the house. Gus realized he was using the word *monstrous* to describe a lot of things. Worse, the captain seemed to take a liking to the word as well. With a woolly toque on his head, he patrolled the estate with weapons ready, stopping and vigilantly watching the lay of the land beyond the wall. He monitored the rise of any *monstrous* snowdrifts that might take away the defensive advantage the outer barrier once had.

No gimps approached, making Gus feel both disappointed and relieved. He had to admit, some mornings just seemed to start better by blowing away a zombie.

Using ladders to get over the wall, he shoveled snow on the other side, taking frequent rests and refraining from overexerting himself. His ribs were healing. He could take slightly deeper breaths without feeling that stretch of paralyzing agony.

His nose had healed up, but remained somewhat off kilter. Not that it bothered him too much. The pain was gone, but he had something of a whistle, especially at night when he breathed through his nose. His unruly beard framed his toothless grin and grillwork scars like black and silver moss. The hair on the sides of his head was growing out, too, but he couldn't be bothering with cutting it.

It gives you character, the captain told him.

"Fuck off," Gus flatly informed the old sailor.

For the month of February, the Christmas tree stayed up and made merry. He didn't want to take the thing down, and since he was the only guy around—no offense to the captain, he pointed out—he left the tree where it was, casting that part of the living room in a soft multi-colored glow just right for getting sloshed.

When he went outside, he kept the solar panels cleared, shoveling snow when he could. He continued to heal. His face and mouth no longer stung when he ate, and toward the end of the month, he found that he could take deep breaths and twist his upper body to the left and right without crumpling to his knees. He worked a little longer each day. He opened the gates and dug his way through the packed snow, creating a single corridor just wide enough to get the truck through. It took him three days to dig himself out, creating trenches in the snow.

And every so often, he would stand on his deck and take in the silent husk of the city.

One late evening, Gus bent over the kitchen island with the Benelli's and Ruger's guts exposed. After several attempts of trial and error and puzzling over the slide and takedown levers, he managed to take the pistol apart, brush it clean, apply a little lube, and reassemble the weapon. He squeezed the trigger in a dry fire test and was rewarded with a satisfying click. He worked the slide a couple of times more, squeezing the trigger until he was confident the gun was in working order. Then, he went to work on the Benelli.

You seem to really enjoy fingering those guns, *the captain commented.*

"Fuck off."

The old sailor lapsed into silence.

When he finished his weapons and magazines, Gus left them on the island and wandered into his living room, carrying the captain by his neck. Beyond the window, the valley appeared as a black void framed in the dark material of the curtains. Gus left the curtains open most days, as if daring anything down in the city to do something about it. Nothing did. He suspected that the corpses down there were probably too frozen to do anything.

And he liked that.

"You know what day tomorrow is?" he asked the captain.

Don't know. What?

Gus thought about the last few weeks, the building pressure he wasn't sure was an acute case of cabin fever, along with all the other stuff he was feeling. Sure, he was having conversations with an empty, duct-taped booze bottle, but he was pretty much healed physically, healed enough to feel confident about doing something he badly wanted . . . no, *needed* to do.

"Start of fuckin' hunting season," he said.

The old sailor didn't say anything for a moment. Then, Gus could have sworn the smile on the old officer stretched just a little wider.

The captain approved.

The next morning, Gus opened his locker and took three swallows of Canadian Club. Then, he suited up for safari.

He pulled on the Nomex pants and coat and slapped the hard plastic elbow pads and knee pads into place. He got into his neck brace and pulled on his ninja mask and motorcycle helmet without any pain. Viewing the world through the black visor relaxed him to no end. Nothing felt so very *right* at that moment than wearing his armor.

He tucked away his weapons and opened the garage door. A blast of frigid air filled the garage, and Gus basked in the pearly glare of the morning. The sun greeted him, finally showing its face after what seemed a very long time. The path he had cleared to the gate beckoned. Gus paused, thinking. He considered the beast and the truck parked next to it. The beast was out of the question. The truck with its four-wheel drive would be better suited.

However . . .

Gus studied the snowmobile and felt the smirk on his face spread.

The sheath for his bat had enough room for the Benelli, and he had placed four boxes of shells in one of the snowmobile's saddlebags. A filled bandolier crossed the sheath's strap, making an X on his chest. He even packed a lunch—a can of spaghetti with a bottle of water and a bottle of rum. Once all was in place, he got aboard the machine, inserted the key, and pushed the electric start. The machine grumbled to life, green and silver lighting up a speedometer and other instrument dials. Gus studied the illuminated panel and got a whiff of exhaust from the red creature. It smelled nice. Old fashioned somehow.

"You and me," Gus spoke to it, "are gonna have a lot of fun."

The snowmobile growled back.

"Fuckin' A." Gus squeezed the throttle.

The machine jumped from the garage, and he immediately had to brake. The controls were simple, but getting used to controlling the vehicle was another matter. Gus didn't worry about it. After being holed up in his house for almost two months, he just wanted to get out there and *do* something other than watch movies, read, and shovel snow. The machine roared through the gates, jostling him in the seat even though the shocks absorbed most of the impact. Gus could tell Russell had paid top dollar for the rig. As the snowmobile rumbled over the buried road, he knew he had chosen correctly in taking the smaller vehicle. Snow smothered the mountain road and bordered the edges all the way down to the highway.

Gus slowed and turned onto the main road, looking around, awed at the extent of what the winter storms had done. Snow covered everything in a knobby white blanket that sparkled in the sun. He weaved in and around cars with only the upper parts of their roofs visible. Sahara-like dunes rose like finely sculpted waves about to crash. In places, he rode high before dropping into dangerous dips. The road was too bumpy for a smooth ride, and it would take a few runs to flatten everything. Or another snowfall to fill in the hollows.

It took him an hour to get into town. He felt the cold in his limbs. He also had a slight ache in his arms from steering and in his lower back from riding out the dunes. On the main street, storefronts and houses had been buried to the point that Gus felt he was driving down a ceramic half-pipe.

He continued until he came to one of the parking lots of the shopping mall in New Minas. Once there, he moved off the road and circled the area several times before coming to a stop on a bed of snow perhaps three feet deep. He stood up on the machine and gazed around, spotting the tops of several trucks and SUVs. The sun reflected off some of the roofs that weren't covered.

Gus killed the engine and dismounted.

He pulled the aluminum bat from its sheath and flexed his fingers over it.

"I'm back, fuckers." He waded through the snow and smashed out the windshield of a nearby truck. The sound echoed over the desolate expanse, but attracted no attention. He laid into it again, his knees level with the hood of the truck as he punished the body of the vehicle, making considerable noise.

After a minute he stopped, quietly admitting that he needed to get back into shape.

He took off his helmet and screamed, roaring obscenities every bit as cold as the air on his gloveless fingers, until he could shout no more.

"They've fuckin' gone deaf," Gus said. He climbed onto the roof of the pickup and looked about.

There.

Crawling from the entranceway of the mall, a single figure came his way. It struggled in the snow, fell over, got back to its feet, and continued.

Gus almost felt bad for the thing.

Four more followed it. Apparently, the front door to the building was either smashed out or somehow wedged open. They walked unsteadily across the parking lot, black on glittering white, totally out of place in the daylight. He could hear them as they got closer. They came at him with hissing glee.

Then, he could smell them. Foul, decomposing juices, ripe and half frozen, percolated throughout the dead flesh, emanating a putrid odor that only got stronger. Before the world went into hell's handbasket, the smell reminded him of old, raw waste disposal sites, open and festering like rotting meat in the sun. Even in the frigid open air, the smell assaulted his nose and eyes, repulsing him to the point where he took one deep breath and held it.

Like long-lost relatives wanting a hug, they shambled toward Gus. Some of them kicked up snow with bare feet. He thought about the shotgun for a moment, but eventually settled on simply bashing in their faces.

The lead zombie got to within ten feet of him, moving much slower in the cold. It was a mall janitor wearing a white T-shirt under an orange vest. It looked like an ordinary dead person, except the thing's eyes appeared to have been plucked from its head. Gus felt a pang of sympathy and revulsion as it got closer. How he'd ever been scared of the things for so long was beyond him.

Winding up, he bashed in the monster's face. The clayish crack of its skull speared the air, and the deadhead fell over onto its back, shivering as if finally realizing how frightfully cold it was outside. Gus smashed it twice more before it stopped moving. Black blood spurted. He finished the job in time to meet the next one.

A teenage boy dressed in blue jeans and a brown wreck of a leather coat reached for him. Gus pivoted at the hips when he swung, taking off the zombie's head and startling the hell out of himself. The body collapsed to the ground, and Gus smashed the nearby head. Crushing a head in snow, Gus discovered, was a lot harder than he would have thought. The rotten skull sank when hit, requiring a few strikes before he could finally finish the job.

"Two," Gus counted, preparing for the next Dee coming within range. With a huff, he cracked the bat across a salesman's jaw, driving it to the right and causing it to sag to its knees. An over-the-head strike killed it. Then came a restaurant server. It hissed, exposing a black cave of a mouth. The bat took the thing across the face and sent it stumbling to the left. He casually evaded the final zombie until he dispatched the server with another over-the-top swing.

With only one remaining, Gus faced the final corpse.

It had been a woman, dressed for the summer in short shorts and a tank top with the frilly edges of a soiled bra peeking out. The dark hair was stringy and black, as if washed in motor oil, while its sloughed midriff sported a puncture wound that looked big and ghastly enough to stick his hand into. The creature shuffled toward him, its features hanging and pitiful, dead marble eyes hinting at an agony endured with each step.

Gus changed targets at the last second and smashed out the creature's knee.

The zombie felt over, bone punching through the decomposed skin. Its hissing face came up from the snow. Gus killed it with one heavy blow. Breathing hard, he pulled the bat out of the dead thing's head and grimaced at the crater he'd made. Brains. He could see the off-white brains. Movement caught his attention, and he leaned over to look closer. Horror bloomed in him as he spied the little things that moved within the brain matter.

Worms.

That image straightened him up and made him look away. That was the last thing he needed to see, but he saw it nonetheless, and he knew he'd be drinking later to cleanse his memory and to ward off nightmares. Gus stepped to the snowmobile and threw open the saddle bag containing the booze. Rum. He needed rum. His hands shivered, and he hoped it was because of the cold. Just a swallow. He snapped up his visor and clawed at the saddlebag's contents. He opened the bottle and took four mouthfuls, snarling at the last shot and realizing darkly he hadn't meant to drink so much. But it tasted so good.

Standing on the bright expanse of the parking lot, Gus took a moment to gaze around, swirling his bottle and making the amber liquid within slosh. Five. He'd put down five undead. A good start, but he wanted more.

He started the snowmobile and drove deeper into Annapolis, hunting for the dead that had hunted him for the last two years. He scoured the streets filled with snow. Noise attracted the dead shits, so he burned through the avenues and side streets three or four times, hoping the roar of the machine would bring them into the open. He sped through the main drags, weaving in and around abandoned cars and trucks, the engine growling loud enough to wake . . . well, the dead. If he reached an area too choked with vehicles, he turned around and retraced his path, moving even faster, laughing out loud and feeling good for the first time in a long time.

Nothing came for him. Nothing attacked.

The sun approached its zenith overhead, and Gus grew impatient. An idea popped into his head, and he quickly altered course, heading back to the Home Hardware superstore where he had picked up the building supplies and the Christmas lights. After having driven for a couple of hours and getting a feel for the handling, Gus felt confident enough to whip the machine around in a doughnut, stopping only a dozen strides from the opening of the store.

Swearing loudly and hooting, he got off the machine and adjusted his gear. All set, he marched into the store with bat at the ready. He rooted around in the dark aisles, wishing he'd had the foresight to bring a flashlight until he finally located one with a working battery. It was a long watchman's light coated in rubber, the kind that could also double as a club if needed. Gus thumbed it on and continued his search.

Noise. He wanted to be noisy.

He found what he wanted.

He wanted the dead fuckers to *know* that he wasn't about to stand down without raising some hell. That he was through being scared. That he was going on the offensive.

He emerged from the store and sounded the air horn, delighting in its heavy blare.

"That's right, cocksuckers. The fuckin' Loveboat just pulled into port."

He blasted the horn again, his cheeks aching from the size of the grin on his face.

"Wooo!" Gus threw his arms wide and howled. He felt like a gladiator, ready to take on all comers. "All aboard!"

He went to the snowmobile and rummaged through the saddle bag once more. Finding the rum, he steeled himself with whatever was left. He finished the bottle with a ferocious yell and dumped the empty back into the bag, intending on converting it into a firebomb. Seeing as he was in town, he figured he'd scoot on over to the pop-shop and get some more beverages. He wanted more rum—or anything else—to keep his own motor running.

Gus, the self-proclaimed Loveboat, left the store and cruised toward sunnier ports of call, goosing the air of Annapolis with deep prodding toots of the new found horn.

8

He hunted.

The snowmobile's thunder echoed harshly through the city of Annapolis, announcing the hunt in grunge fashion. The air horn blasted the already stirred-up stillness, causing the dead not fully frozen to move mindlessly toward the bleating sound. Just as Gus wanted them to do.

Feeling better than he had in a long time, Gus zipped along roadways, avoiding the close confines of snow-choked alleys and narrow streets. Sometimes the dead wandered directly into his path, causing him to steer around them. He would park a short distance away, dismount, and lay into the corpses with aluminium fury. Gus had no problem dodging near-skeletal hands or slow-moving limbs, bobbing and weaving through several deadheads with half-drunken grace. It was more than easy to dispatch the things. His counterattack became a massacre the likes he hadn't seen since the initial outbreak of zombieness or the siege at his walls. His mind warned him of the creatures' one weapon—mass attack—but the weather was his ally. Whatever evil powered the dead's icy bodies into motion had been crippled by two months of sub-zero temperatures. For the first time in a very long time, the living had the edge over the dead.

Gus killed more than two hundred of the shambling creatures that day. Actually, he had lost count, but he believed that over two hundred was a fair estimation. He retreated to his home in the waning hours and celebrated modestly that night. He didn't want to be so hungover that he was immobilized the next day, which would allow the dead a brief respite. He didn't want them to regroup in any way, if such a thing were possible. The thrill of the hunt excited him, and he looked forward to heading down into the city.

The next day, Gus rose before dawn, got ready, and timed it such that he entered the expanse of Annapolis just as the sun broke free of the mountains. He raced up and down the streets, the snowmobile grinding forward like a warhorse. When the dead appeared, he put them down with his bat, never once having to resort to using ammunition, which he wanted to spare if possible.

After a morning of killing, he steered the snow machine into a fast food takeout that had snow piled up to its smashed-out picture windows. He parked the machine on a huge drift that ran through one corner of the restaurant, making an effective bridge from one window to the other. Dismounting his ride with a moan, Gus examined the interior of the restaurant. The place looked like a bomb had detonated under its roof. Most of the tables with their attached seating were almost filled in with snow, the walls were dented, and pictures were smashed. The large plastic menu hanging over the counter had its face shattered, and loose wiring and the broken light bulbs underneath lay bare. The kitchen area was draped in gloom. Gus walked over and kicked the checkout machine, sending it spinning away with a rattle.

No reaction from within.

Gus went back to the snowmobile and threw open the saddlebag with his lunch. Grabbing a can opener, he sat on the machine and worked the lid off the tin. A moment later, he removed his helmet and dug into his spaghetti and meatballs. He ate in silence, peering out at the cityscape and watching for movement. Halfway through the can, something warned him to look over his shoulder. He spotted a shadow against the dark inside the kitchen area.

The shadow walked unsteadily into the light, followed by half a dozen more—workers in their uniforms and as solemn as monks. He forked another mouthful of spaghetti into his mouth. The seven figures dragged their feet into the serving area and filled the area behind the long counter. Pasty arms sought purchase to haul their bodies up over the counter. Black skin tags and sores clustered around their mouths. Gus stopped chewing. How the hell could anyone eat with the likes of *that* staring at them?

He placed his lunch to one side, pulled the silenced Ruger from his boot, racked the slide, and took aim at the first takeout employee. One shot through the forehead and the corpse dropped to the counter with a hard slap. Gus looked around, checking his flanks. Seeing all was clear, he sniffed, and took up the gun in two handed fashion. *Pewp-pewp-pewp.* The shots threw the deadheads back against a counter filled with to-go containers and coffee machines. One of the remaining zombies stood up and moaned loudly enough that Gus thought the thing was about to beat its chest. He shot out its eye, and the body fell behind the counter. The remaining two gimps fell just as fast, each taking a bullet to the forehead and collapsing behind the counter.

Gus waited for more, but none appeared. Placing the Ruger on the seat, he finished his lunch. Once done, he tossed the can at a nearby trash bin and got it in on the first try.

He started the snow machine. Not liking the service at the takeout in the least, he vowed to never eat at the place again.

By the end of the day, Gus had killed at least another two hundred undead things. He returned home in a whorl of exhaust and blowing snow and got pleasantly buzzed.

But something troubled him.

"Something's not right." He directed the comment at the captain, who sat at the other end of the sofa, tucked between Gus's feet and a cushion. The Christmas tree glowed at the other end of the living room, and Gus alternated between looking at its hypnotizing pixie lights and the duct-taped captain.

What?

Gus didn't care if he was slipping into deep bat shit crazy by conversing with an empty bottle. He needed the company.

"I've put down a good many undead critters in the last two days, and I haven't seen the mob that pinned Scott and me in the attic that one time. That was an army of 'em. You know the ones I'm talkin' 'bout. Nowhere to be found. There ain't many places for 'em to hide, and there was a *lot* of 'em. *Too* many of 'em. I don't even think a stadium could shelter 'em all, and they're . . . brainless. I mean, they ain't goin' *'Holy shit* it's cold out. Jesus, it's cold! My fuckin' arms are dropping off here. We better get the hell inside!'" He shook his head.

And your question is?

"Well, where the hell are they?"

Maybe they're still back at the cul de sac. They're tidal. Maybe they didn't get a chance to move before the cold took a dip.

"Hmm. You're smart. For a bottle. I'll get on it tomorrow. I'll be takin' out some of your boys for this one."

Be careful. It ain't small bunches you're heading after here. You're going after the mother lode. Remember what happened the last time. In fact, I don't think you should hunt for them at all. It's an army of undead, after all.

"Yeah? Well, I'm an army of one." Gus smiled sleepily at the bottle. "Goddamn right, I am."

The captain let that one go.

The captain's idea—Gus gave credit where it was due—was solid, or so Gus thought. Zombies were tidal. There were stragglers, some groups even large enough to be considered packs, but the really big packs, the mobs, the hordes, drifted from place to place like kelp caught in a current. If one of them caught scent of something and started walking, alerting the rest, the entire swarm would follow. And if they found something, they might linger in the area for a bit, before being pulled in another direction.

Thus, as the captain pointed out, if Gus really wanted to wage war on the bastards, if he really wanted to kick them in the collective rotting balls, he had to go to the last place he had encountered them and simply make noise in that general area. If they were still there, they would answer.

The dead feared nothing.

And that would be their destruction.

The next day, Gus packed the saddlebags with another tin of spaghetti, a can opener, and eight Molotov cocktails, ready to roar.

You taking the Benelli?

Gus stopped pulling on his Nomex pants and frowned at the old sailor watching from the workbench. "What do you think?"

The captain didn't have anything to say to that.

"Honestly, man, times like these, I remember you're just a bottle with a face on it. 'You taking the Benelli?' Fuck a monkey, I'm takin' the Benelli. I'd take a fuckin' elephant gun down there if I had one. Or a sniper gun. That'd be cool. Can you imagine that, eh? Snipin' gimps a mile out? Wouldn't mind tryin' that. That might be the safest way of doin' things. By the way, you ain't comin' on this one. You get to stay home here. Watch the fort."

Why?

"No room for an empty bottle on this trip. Only got room for eight of your marines as it is. Your boys ready?"

They're ready. You're taking my finest.

The captain's finest. Or so *he* said. Gus could have made room for the duct-taped officer, but space *was* limited on the snow machine, and there was no way he was going to endanger his only companion by lugging him along. But he wasn't going to flatter the bottle by telling *him* that.

Watch yourself out there.

"What are you? My mother?" Gus huffed in exasperation as he pulled on his helmet and batted down the visor.

Just wishing you well is all. No need to be snarky about it.

Gus realized the captain was right. He gave it a thumbs-up as apology and adjusted the X of bat sheath strap and full bandolier across his chest.

Finished with his preparations, he mounted the snowmobile and started the machine, filling the garage with the smell of exhaust.

"Love that smell," Gus said, savoring it for a moment.

Give em hell out there, the captain said in a serious tone.

Gus regarded the bottle one last time. "You got it."

And he was off.

An hour later, he drove through the car-filled streets of the city, heading to the cul de sac where he and Scott had been trapped by the undead. He didn't know if they were *all* of the remaining dead, and they probably, most *certainly*, weren't, but if he killed as many as he could, it would go a long way in making Annapolis safe. Zombie free. If such a thing was possible.

Not remembering the exact location of the cul de sac, he took a few wrong turns before finally coming upon what he believed was the right one. The house where he and Scott had taken refuge was at the end, smashed windows leering like a broken smile. Snow snaked up and over the picture windowsill, flowing into the living room. Gus stopped the machine, gazing at the place where he had hidden for three days. Or had it been four? The aftershock still muddled his memory.

Gus studied the cul de sac area, his machine resting on perhaps feet of packed snow. He stood up, rooted around in a saddle bag, and brought the air horn to bear. The blast ripped through the morning quiet and made him smile. It was almost too much fun. He squeezed off another couple of blasts, then waited. There were plenty of residential areas where he knew the corpses still roamed. If he couldn't summon the dead there, he would check the other places.

Gus switched off the engine. In the abrupt choke and death of the motor, he inhaled, feeling nary an ache from his ribs. He studied some of the other wealthy-looking houses. He cleared his throat and listened.

The creaking of his seat.

Wind. Rising and falling, like the breath of a sleeping animal.

White ghosts blew across the front of some houses, misting their colors.

A gray arm punched through the surface of the hard-packed snow, startling him. Gray fingers clutched at air, then dipped and scratched at the snow. Another limb joined it, devoid of any fingers at all, a fleshy spade stabbing into the air, flexing. The subtle sound of shifting snow, a soft grainy hiss that might have been the hitching escape of air from a puncture tire, captured Gus's attention. Other hands and arms burst into view, some extending from the icy surface just past the elbow, others appearing as twitching digits as long and frightening as spiders' legs.

The snow near the first arm shook, bulged, and broke. A gray-black head struggled to free itself of the drift. It turned, and black cavities where eyes had once been captivated Gus for a moment, rooting him to the spot. The snow around the skull shivered, and another head rose near it, like a curdled knob in a vat of milk. Its jaws opened, and Gus knew if he were close enough, he'd hear the joints creak.

More figures fought free of the snow, working their way to the surface until the scene resembled something from a horror movie where the deceased occupants of a cemetery decided to rise for foul reasons. The mob he'd been seeking *had* come back to the cul de sac. In fact, they had evidently fallen and frozen in place. With the presence of nearby meat serving as a tantalizing stimulus, the dreadful power that animated them in the first place surged within their decomposing cores, powering them to extract their bodies from the deep snow.

The first zombie, grinning malevolently at Gus, dug itself out enough so that its upper body was visible. What was worse, however, was that three more heads appeared around the fractured snow of the zombie, sifting through it like creamy quicksand.

Christ almighty, Gus thought, as a fresh sliver of fear rammed through his core. *They're lying on each other under the snow.*

Right below him.

Gus stabbed at the starter button of the snowmobile. He pulled the machine hard to the right, spinning out a circle and sending snow flying in his wake, running over lumps he knew weren't snow. More zombies appeared in his tracks, coated in particles of ice and writhing stupidly. Some reached for him. One broke through the surface directly in front of the machine, and Gus bounced in the seat as he rolled over it, the bladed treads raking the flesh from the dead thing's face in an instant and crushing the weakened skull a split second later. Gus held on, keeping control of the snowmobile, and charged for the throat of the cul de sac. All around him, zombies rose, moving like automatons in need of grease.

Gus gunned the engine, blasting for the entrance to the cul de sac. Limbs reached and flailed at him, but were bashed aside by the fiberglass snout of the machine. Wasted fingers slapped the windshield before spinning away behind him. Decomposed faces flashed by, all seeming so glad, so *very* glad, he had taken the time to find them. More figures stood on the edges of his vision, but Gus plowed through the mob, thinking only of escape.

With a high-pitched roar, the snowmobile shot up and over a low rise, escaping the cul de sac and speeding toward less zombie-populated areas. The idea of stopping and flinging a few Molotovs back at the mob occurred to him, but Gus decided against it. The firebombs needed a hard surface to break against, and the snow wouldn't do it. Thick elms zipped by in his peripheral vision as he focused on the intersection ahead. It would be better to retreat a bit and watch—

A rope snapped up before him, pulled taut and dripping snow. Gus clenched the brake in reflex. He couldn't stop in time. The rope snapped against and over the windshield and took him across the upper chest, yanking him from the seat. He landed explosively on his ass and the weapons strapped across his back. His head whipped back, but the helmet and hockey vest underneath the Nomex coat absorbed much of the impact. It did nothing to alleviate the burn across his upper biceps.

He heard the snowmobile crash into something, while the sounds of running feet punching through the icy surface of the snow grew louder.

Voices.

Then, someone was on him. Weight pinned his shoulders.

"Whooowheee gotcha you fucker!" a wild face preened in mad delight. Hands gripped him by the shoulders. "Gotcha. Ain't no one told you this is a quiet neighbourhood? Huh? You stun sumabitch! Been listenin' to your ass buzz all over town for the last couple of—"

While the man prattled on, no doubt believing his prey effectively stunned by the rope, Gus lifted his left leg and extracted his Bowie knife. Just as the word "of" left his lips, Gus stabbed him with whatever power he could summon. He curled his arm and stuck the knife into his attacker's lower back, through the man's parka, deep enough to take the wind out of his rant. The rough face morphed from joy to agonized shock. The would-be trapper rolled off, wrenching the steel from Gus's grasp.

Gus got to his knees. He looked to his left and saw another attacker—a big brute armed with a bat. The new guy balked—no doubt every bit as surprised as the first trapper.

"You fucker!" the brute snarled.

Gus yanked his Ruger from his other boot. The appearance of the weapon made the bat wielder turn to run. Gus readied the weapon and shot the guy in the back, knocking the man forward in the snow. Gus got to his feet, and a split second later, someone else crashed into him from behind, driving him face forward into the snow. The pistol flew from his grasp. He rolled over, and a fist hammered the forehead of his helmet. Furious grunts punctured the air. Two fists crunched into Gus's midsection, the impact dulled by the Nomex coat and hockey vest. He punched back, grazing a forehead hard enough to give his attacker pause, then bucked, throwing the man off of him. Gus scrambled to his feet, while his latest attacker did the same.

The young man, no more than twenty if a day out of his teens, was broad across the shoulders and dressed in dirty winter outer clothing. A ragged white parka hung off his frame, and his hands were gloveless. A fringe of red hair stuck out from under a black toque, giving him a Special Forces kind of look. The guy hunched over, holding the right side of his brow while bright blood made a stark contrast against the backdrop of snow.

"You cut me, you fucker," the boy whined. "I'll kill you."

In answer, Gus groped for and hauled out his bat.

The youth's eyes went wide.

To one side, the man Gus had knifed moaned, his life's blood spurting out in alarming jets and slashing the snow. "Git him, Wilbur."

Wilbur? Gus almost burst out laughing. He stepped back, mindful of the man he'd shot, who still lay face down in the snow. He didn't see any others.

"I'll git 'im!" Wilbur bared his teeth. "I'll git 'im."

He stalked Gus, mindful of the bat, and having nothing except his size going for him. That, and being pissed off. Gus knew from experience that being pissed off counted for a lot. Wilbur appeared as if nothing short of breaking his neck would satisfy him.

"Gonna fuck you up 'til Tuesday," Wilbur seethed, hands flexing, ready to grab at an opening. Blood seeped down one side of his face like war paint.

Gus raised the bat over his head like a sword. Wilbur watched it go up.

"Git 'immm . . ." The man in the snow moaned, fainter now.

"I'll git 'im!" Wilbur promised.

Cletus, Gus's mind added and giggles rumbled his frame.

But then Wilbur looked to his right, back the way Gus had come. Though he knew better, Gus made the same mistake.

The dead.

The dead were coming. Some shambled, and some crawled, all partially frozen, yet willing their bodies onward, toward the combat, where hot meat battled. They rose up from the distant dip in the road, like a gray tsunami of swinging, twisting limbs where no one shape was distinct from the other. A hissing, moaning, *starving* mob.

A mob that only wanted to bite.

"Jesus," Wilbur hissed.

"Wilburrrr . . ." the stabbed man wailed, the words swallowed by the wind.

While Wilbur's attention was on the approaching mob of dead things, Gus stepped forward and clobbered him across the shoulder. Wilbur somehow sensed the attack at the last possible moment and got his head out of the way. Still, the bat clipped the guy's shoulder, and Wilbur yelped in pain. The boy jerked back, and Gus swung again. Missed. Screaming and holding his shoulder, Wilbur stumbled backward, and Gus whipped his bat across the boy's knee, shattering it.

Wilbur dropped into the snow, screaming as if his testicles had been shorn off with a sander. Like Gus gave a shit. He kicked him across the jaw and hovered over the broken form of the youngster. He heard moans and wasn't exactly certain if they came from Wilbur, the prick he had stabbed, or the advancing deadheads. The Dees were closer, easily filling the breadth of the road. Faces shriveled by the cold spotted the living. Dark mouths opened. Limbs reached and hands pointed at him.

Gus stomped over to the stabbed victim and jerked back the man's head. "Who are you?"

"Whuua . . . ?" The man's eyes looked glazed.

"Who are you?"

"Uhhhhh."

Gus ripped his knife out of the man's lower back. The man sighed when the weapon came out, as if all would be fine. Gus wiped the blade on the back of the guy's coat, then sheathed it. He turned to look for his snowmobile. Dead. Wrapped around a telephone pole. Gus felt as if he'd lost a friend.

"Christ." He stomped back to where he'd lost his gun. The snow had been disturbed and his heart sank. He checked on the dead man, then Wilbur, and the one he'd stabbed. All where they should be. Gus moved around, thrusting his bare hands into the snow, hoping beyond hope he'd find the Ruger. He prodded ahead, feeling, touching, swearing at the three hillbillies. His fingers became raw and red with the cold. Gus was sure God was chuckling, probably laughing his holy ass off and lighting up the cosmos in the process.

He glanced up, up to his shoulders in snow.

The creeping dead were perhaps fifty feet away, stumbling, swaying, and heading right for him, swallowing up the space between them. The whispery sounds of their frayed vocal chords made the hair on his neck stand on end as if he'd been zapped.

Dig! he commanded himself, and he dug, rooting around in the snow and feeling nothing. Then, something . . . "Shit!" He brought up a crumpled aluminum can. He plunged his hands back into the flattened drifts.

Behind him, he heard a more human moan. Wilbur was coming around.

Gus got up and stomped his way over to the kid waking up in the snow. He took his bat and bashed the boy's other knee, cracking it twice and making the youngster squeal in pain. Twenty, Gus had guessed Wilbur's age earlier. He scoffed at the number.

Wilbur wasn't eighteen yet and this time, Gus had the feeling he got it right. He immobilized the youngster's ass and he went back to looking for his gun. Wilbur's agonized cries sawing at the air.

Forty feet. The dead seemed to be closing the distance faster.

Gus made fists, willing heat back into his fingers. He scuffed along and felt his toe connect with something under the snow. He dove on the spot and frantically cleared away the white, uncovering the black grip of the Ruger. He snapped up the weapon and pointed the gun at Wilbur—Jesus Christ, the boy probably wasn't more than *sixteen*. The kid looked over the wrecks of his knees and *begged* Gus to pull the trigger with red eyes and a face smeared in blood. He told Gus to just shoot his ass dead and not to leave him to *that*.

Ignoring the pleas, Gus ran to his dead snowmobile.

"*No, no, Christ almighty, no,*" the boy screeched. The kid knew that a bullet, a *precious* bullet, was far superior to the fate bearing down on him.

Gus shook his head in sadness and frustration over the mess of the snowmobile. He flipped open a saddle bag and took out the can opener, the tin of spaghetti, and the boxes of shells. He opened the other bag and grimaced at the mess of glass shards. The bottles had all broken except—he grabbed the neck of the whole one and extracted it. One of the captain's marines had made it—covered in gasoline, but intact.

"No! No! Sweet Jesus! *Noooo!*"

Gus turned.

Wilbur had dragged himself perhaps ten feet away from where Gus had crippled him. It was twenty feet too short. The zombie at the front of the pack reached out and touched Wilbur, the contact making the boy shriek and thrash like an eight-year-old. Gray hands fastened around Wilbur's coat, and he turned to fight them off, throwing his fists at the wall standing right over him as if he were having a temper tantrum. Zombies crawled on top of him, and one corpse, with a movement that was utterly slow motion, sank his rack of teeth through the denim covering the boy's right knee.

Gus thought Wilbur was wailing before. He was sadly mistaken.

Like a stack of cans falling over the shrieking figure, the tide veered and slowly covered the boy. Some bit, some clawed, but *all* got a piece of him. The dead shifted, piling on one another, reaching, clawing, trying for just a *taste*, just a *taste* goddammit, was *that* so much to ask? The moaning was loud enough to drive Gus just a little more insane. The smell of the dead, like rotting meat in the deepest part of a freezer, hit him and made him wince.

He turned away. The tearing of cloth rose over the moaning, followed by a searing screech of the still-living. Wilbur's voice was muffled by the bodies still piling onto him.

Gus shoved the four boxes of shotgun shells into the inner folds of his coat. He stuffed the spaghetti in there as well. The Benelli was still slung over his back. He looked for the air horn, but didn't see it. One more search of the machine and he turned to leave after picking up his bat. That nerve-splitting squeal of Wilbur's turned into a wet, dying gurgle.

Then nothing.

9

Gus bolted for a nearby house, well aware of the mob's undead tide-line oozing toward him.

Well, a voice chuckled all shucks-like in his head, *you* wanted *to find them. Didn't you?*

Gus ran up the front steps of the nearest house and tried the door. Locked. He turned and cleared the front porch in one leap, landing in snow up to his knees. He almost lost his bat, but managed to maintain his grip on it. The next house was twenty feet away on the other side of a tall green barrier of evergreens. He pushed through them, snow sprinkling down and boughs clawing at him, and staggered to the front steps of the second house. Another locked door. Rattled the knob a second time.

Sweet monkey fuck!

It wasn't a sprint, it was a marathon. The dead could only move so fast, and he hadn't seen any runners. Still, Gus couldn't quite fight the urge to just *jet* from the scene as fast as humanly possible.

He didn't have time to test every door. He charged across a front lawn with small trees that probably were some sort of exotic hedge and pounded up the front steps of the third house. He gripped the knob and tried it. Locked.

He looked at the front window and, making a split-second decision, heaved himself through it.

He landed in a living room, flopping over a low bookcase in a glittering shower of glass and a crackling of wood. He stumbled to his feet and looked outside. He couldn't see the mob, but he could hear it. Whirling, he made his way to the kitchen area, through a short hallway, and into a den, where he spotted a sliding door leading out to the backyard. Gus scrabbled at the lock of the door, almost ripping his fingernails off in his frenzy. He yanked open the door and plunged outside.

His jaw dropped.

The backyards of the houses in that neighborhood had no fences, and Gus had stumbled directly into the path of the zombie tide. Where he had zagged, hoping to throw them off, the mob had kept going straight, heedless of the houses in their path and moving around them as if they were rocks in a river.

Horrified, Gus turned and ran, snow flicking up from his boots as he tore across the landscape. The voices of the dead sounded like a full congregation in mindless worship. He panted as he pounded through deep drifts. He reached the street and crossed it with a gasp, shoulders heaving. Behind him, an embankment of corpses followed.

Gus forced himself to slow down, reminding himself that even jogging was faster than the frozen pursuit of the dead. Cars and pickups dotted the road and driveways, buried in snow to the point that he could spend hours digging them out. He decelerated to a hurried walk, plowing through the snow, feeling the weight of it grinding him down, wearing him out. How far away was he from his house on the mountain? Fifty kilometers? Forty? A twenty-minute drive at eighty would translate into how long treading through deep snow? A day? Two days? He wouldn't make it. It would take a day to clear the city at least, and then another day to walk down the highway to his place.

The road arced left, and when he looked over his shoulder, the houses blocked his view of his pursuers, which meant they could no longer see him, either. That was some small relief. The snow drifts were knee high, and even walking in the tracks of the snowmobile didn't make things easier.

Hide, his mind screamed at him. *You have to hide. An attic. Find an attic like before.*

It was worth a shot. Out in the cold, he wouldn't be able to keep up the pace. But how does one escape a wave?

Get above it, his mind came back at him.

Behind him, the mob seeped into view. The determined ones appeared first, like the first signs of rot around the edges of something good to eat. They pursued at a crawl. He glanced repeatedly over his shoulder as he crossed buried front lawns and popped around corners to hide his trail.

Another house loomed ahead, a two-story old-fashioned deal painted yellow. He ran up to the front door, which had a window set in it, divided into fashionable little squares. As with the previous houses, the door was locked.

He rammed his bat through a pane of the door glass. With a vicious swipe, he cleared away the fragments around the edges, then stuffed his arm inside, felt around, and located the knob. It had one of those locks where he had to press in on the knob to unlock it. He did so and put his shoulder to the door. The door held. Muttering, he punched out another section of glass and stuck his arm inside. There—a dead bolt. He hooked it with his fingers and opened the door with a relieved huff.

Plunging inside and slamming the door behind him, Gus locked it again. He closed the drapes over the front windows, then furtively peeked back out at the street. A hand unconsciously went to his ribs, and he took a deep breath. No problem there, and he thanked God for it.

He looked around the interior of the house. A stairway was set beside a hallway that probably went to the kitchen. The pinewood floor was bare and worn. A living room lay to the right and a small office area to the left. A desiccated corpse sat at the desk in the office, the almost silver face twisted in a rictus of pain, as if the man had suffered greatly. The house was cold, and Gus didn't know if he was looking at a corpse or a *corpse*.

He raised his bat, watching the figure in the chair. Full head of dead hair, perhaps in his seventies. Gold ring on his finger.

Gus stepped forward, cranking the bat up and letting it fly.

One of the eyes creaked open.

The bat split the zombie's skull with a pulpy crack. The impact toppled the dead-head, flipping him over in the chair, feet pointing ceiling-ward.

Breathing hard, Gus studied his kill. Satisfied that it was indeed dead, he went to the only window in the office and drew back the curtain. Outside, the pursuing dead filled the road. He dropped the curtain and stepped back. High ground. He had to get to high ground.

He moved toward the stairway, but something made him look in the direction of the kitchen. He wished he hadn't.

Poised in shadow, a zombie stood. A slow, stuttering hiss issued from the figure, a sound that put Gus's raw nerves on edge just a fragment more.

Taking a batter's stance, he debated whether to wait for it to come to him or to charge it.

Three smaller shadows came into view then, just behind the larger one. Hisses broke the air like leaking gas pipes. Gus lowered his bat. The larger form took an unsteady step forward, leaning heavily against the wall. One of the arms came up and into the light, then a bare belly that resembled a deflated medicine ball. The smell of the four crept up on Gus, and his stomach recoiled from the reek.

He pulled out his Ruger.

The androgynous lead zombie took another step forward, the light revealing a mouth without any lips. Gus shot it twice, exploding its head in a dusky blossom. The children came after, porcelain features marred by grotesque splotches of black. Their eyes appeared as smoky marbles.

Gus fired about five rounds and dropped all of them. He listened, waiting for something else to appear, another family member, but heard nothing.

He went up the stairs. Quickly going through four bedrooms, one of which possessed an inviting bunk bed, Gus established that the upper floor was empty. He found a trapdoor in the ceiling, a rope dangling.

Below, something crashed into the front door.

The sound froze Gus for all of a second before he yanked down the trapdoor. A set of stairs came down with a metallic yawn, and Gus was momentarily impressed. It wasn't the bare wood stairway of the house Scott and he hid out in for days while the dead roamed below; it was something else.

For one thing, there was light in the attic. Two, the stairs, which were painted, slid down rather than unfolded.

Another crash from below got him moving up the steps. In the attic, he was further surprised to discover that the door and steps could be retracted by a rope on a pulley system. Gus pulled on the rope.

More thumps came from below, like multiple forearms and elbows being rammed into the surface of the front door.

Gus saw that the light actually came from a skylight that he hadn't been able to see from the yard. The window was cut into the ceiling and tinted. The slanted roof made him duck, but the attic had been transformed into a fifth bedroom. A comfortable-looking single bed, along with a matching night table, filled one end, while two bookcases and a low desk stood at the other. Walls with shelving hemmed in the lowest parts of the area, and in one section, Gus saw a small oven-sized hatch where perhaps the real attic was located. He thought he'd had enough of attics from the last time, but the room was actually . . . nice.

The thumping on the front door intensified and Gus went to the window. He looked down and spied most of the front lawn area, as well as the road beyond. The sight rooted him to the spot. A parade of undead, half-frozen, but swollen with an unholy zest for life, sifted down the street like the chips and shards of a glacial ice flow. The sight of so many ice-crusted zombies chilled Gus's core, and watching the slow press of the mob severely tested his mental resolve to kill all of the things. He saw *hundreds*, and who knew how many were beyond his field of vision? As he watched, faces lifted skyward, their mouths dark holes, wailing in that eerie, yet pitiful way they had. They were so tightly packed, Gus thought of concert venues in the summertime. Limbs waved above the mass like crooked antennae scanning for any sign of life.

He heard more banging on the front door. A crash of glass made Gus perk his ears, and he cringed at the idea they might have gotten in already. He sized up the skylight and thought about breaking out the glass and going . . . where? He'd probably slip and slide off the roof, only to land right in the middle of the crowd below, like a singer throwing himself into a savage mosh pit. Turning his back on the glass, he focused on the raised trapdoor.

He'd played the waiting game before and never thought he'd have to do it again. Placing his weapons on the bed, he went to the attic door and opened it. He pulled out cardboard boxes filled with blankets, books, Tupperware receptacles, winter clothing, and trinkets. The trinkets he stuffed back into the nook space of the attic while he hauled the Tupperware and blankets out of their containers. The blankets were thick, red and white quilts made for the winter, just the thing to cozy up under. There were four of them and each one went onto the bed. The Tupperware would be for voiding, and Gus knew he'd be shitting at least once up there, perhaps even twice. He looked over the box containing the plastic containers and figured he had enough for six or seven liters. It hooked a memory.

"We could drink our own urine if it came down to it."

"What is it with you and this fascination with consuming your own waste?"

Gus smiled, hoping that wherever Scott was, he wasn't in a similar situation.

Then another thought hit him, sobering him instantly.

He'd just killed three men in cold blood. Two men and a kid, and the kid was the worst. He'd left Wilbur as a wrapped up snack, using him to get away. Three lives he had taken. The realization didn't bother him as much as he thought it would.

They tried to kill me first.

But had they really? Sure, they'd knocked him off the snowmobile, but had they been trying to kill him?

Gus wrestled with that notion. No, they weren't planning on killing him, but he was certain they would've warmed to the notion eventually.

You still killed three men, insisted the voice. Killed them easy.

Lying on the bed and keeping a hand on his Benelli, he eyed the trapdoor as the light outside faded. Gus figured it was going to be a long night.

10

The downstairs thumping stopped a few hours after nightfall, but another disturbing noise started . . . in Gus's head. It had been a good seven or eight hours since his last drink, and he was parched. *Parched*. Aching for a sip of something with bite. The headache had only begun an hour before, but the steady pulse of pain in his frontal lobe and temples made him grimace. A sip. Just a fucking sip was all he needed. He lay in the bed and tossed and turned. He thought there might be something downstairs, maybe in the kitchen somewhere, and if he could hold off until morning, he could check it out. But, goddammit, he needed a drink, and he didn't know if he could wait.

Restless, he got up and looked out the window. He could see nothing in the black, moonless night, but he sensed they were still there. The skylight had a latch and could be opened if he wanted, but that might somehow alert the dead.

So he crawled back into bed, still dressed, boots on, and lay on his back. Sleep came in stingy doses, and he always woke with the headache still working its drill into his flesh. Sometime during the night, he heard the patter of rain against the window and shook his head. Nova Scotian winter—winter one hour and summer the next. The rain grew stronger, and the wind picked up, a nasty soulless howl that *knew* Gus was hiding in the attic, moaning in zombie-speak, no doubt trying to communicate with the undead and inform them that the meat was just above their heads. Gus wiggled underneath his mound of blankets and quilts, trying to keep warm and find peace.

Hours later, light streamed through, and he opened his eyes, wishing for a drink. Anything to get the taste out of his mouth. He got up and stumbled to the window. Rain pelted the glass, and the house was still under siege. Gus sighed when he saw the zombies, all pressed together in wet misery, looking for food. He understood them at that moment, recognizing his own need for a shot of booze. With shaky hands, he rubbed his chin and tugged on his bush of a beard, eyes flicking to the trapdoor. The wind still blew outside, periodically pummelling the glass of the skylight, but he didn't hear anything else below.

Could he risk it?

A sip.

Gus lowered the stairs as quietly as possible, cringing at a deep sounding groan the springs let loose. He paused before letting the steps slip to the floor. Above all, he had to be careful. He had to use *stealth*. He removed his boots, slipped down to the floor, and listened. Hearing nothing except the hiss of falling rain, he crept forward until he came to the staircase and inched his head out to peer below. All seemed intact.

He backed up and let his breath go. His stomach gurgled, and after a short search for the bathroom, Gus emptied both his bladder and bowels. The toilet seat felt cold enough to freeze his ass, and he wouldn't be surprised to see flesh stuck there once he stood up. Half a roll of toilet paper lay on the dispenser next to the can, and for that, Gus was grateful. Having finished his business, he carefully descended the steps, then stayed below the window line of the front door, despite the closed curtains. The door remained shut, much to his surprise, although glass and fragments of wood coated the floor. Making a face at the mound of dead he'd shot the day before, he edged around the broken glass and crept into the living room, bathed in darkness. He peeked out at the world once more before padding off to the kitchen. The pantry shelves were full of supplies, and he found several cans of pork sausages, noodles, and other foods. On the top shelf were packets of juice mixes and other sugary flavours, while four liters of bottled water lined the bottom shelf. He didn't find anything with booze in it, which ignited an irritable slew of soft curses. There wasn't much he could do about that, so he took an hour to transfer the food and water to the attic. Afterward, he returned to the lower level and rooted around in the den for anything remotely alcoholic. He even searched both bathrooms for mouthwash, but found none.

Just his luck, he fumed.

Finding a bag of unopened chocolate chip cookies and not worrying in the least about expiration dates, he retreated to the attic again, but left the stairs down. It was easier to get to the bathroom, and since nothing had breached the house, he felt somewhat safe.

He spent the day on the bed, reading paperbacks, napping when he could, and munching on chocolate chip cookies that had to have been pumped full of preservatives to taste so good. Rain beat against the skylight, running down the glass in rivulets that warped the day.

The day had been a little warmer, but the temperature dropped again at night, while the rain also continued. The dead had milled about below for the entire day, and Gus believed they were even moving faster, as if warmth had somehow seeped into their limbs. Some moaned constantly, soft pitiful sounds that seemingly begged for a bullet, while others let loose much more dramatically. One in particular moaned loud enough for Gus to hear above the rest in the attic—and kept crying out, which prompted Gus to bury his head in a pillow.

Just after the daylight retreated from the room, Gus got up and looked outside, opening the skylight just a crack. Zombies still walked about aimlessly, dark lumps against the greater dark, but fewer in number. It appeared the mob had drifted on again for whatever reasons, and a feeling of good fortune swept through him. It was almost enough to help him forget about his trembling hands or his tormenting thirst that sugared water simply would not quench.

He went back to bed, but sleep didn't come easily.

His very being wanted booze.

The next day, Gus looked out the window again and saw that the zombies had dispersed even more and the snow had melted somewhat. He studied the lay of the land while eating a tin of meatballs and gravy. On impulse, he opened the window so he could listen to the dripping of melting snow. Around early afternoon, the sun eased out from behind a cloud. Snow levels dropped more, and zombies moved even more freely.

By late afternoon, he had become aware of another problem. The stench of the deadheads below had risen to the attic. Gus pulled his boots back on, racked the slide of the Ruger, and jammed it inside one boot. Thus ready, he descended into the upper floor of the house. Plenty of blankets covered the beds, and he thought about taking some and dropping them on the newly deceased. A second thought stopped him— giving the house another look over for booze. That took precedence over the blankets and rotting smell. He crept down the steps to the front door and peeled back the corner of the curtain.

A zombie stood not ten feet from the front door.

Seeing the dead thing startled Gus, and he released the curtain. The material dropped back into place, and he cringed at the sudden movement. He raised his Ruger and took a breath.

Nothing. Had the thing even seen him?

Carefully avoiding the glass on the floor, he stepped in front of the curtains and placed the barrel of the weapon on the broken window sill. Leaning over, he tried spotting the gimp through the crack of cloth. He didn't think he had much time. He inched the curtain up until he spied the monster through the barest of openings. If he didn't know any better, he'd have said the thing was actually mulling over if what it had seen was worth investigating. The zombie was an apple-shaped male wearing a T-shirt and track pants that were soaked to his body in grotesque fashion. A mop of soaked black hair topped off the creature's head.

Gus wouldn't wait for the monster's cry. One squeeze of the Ruger's trigger and a bullet hole appeared just above the zombie's left eyebrow. With a little jump and without a sound, the dead thing fell over backward to land in a soft squish of wet snow.

Gus let the curtain fall back into place and booted up the stairs, forgetting about all else, hearing battle klaxons sound in his head. He climbed the ladder to the attic and hauled it behind him, panting and waiting for the crush of bodies he knew would slam into the house at any time.

Only they didn't.

Puzzled but wary, he peeked out of the skylight and peered down. The unmoving body of the fallen creature lay right where he had dropped it. Other dead things shambled closer and moved around the fallen corpse, but none moved to investigate or approach the house. He'd gotten away with it.

"Oh, Jesus, Mary, and Joseph," Gus whispered and collapsed on the bed. That was the closest he'd come to shitting himself since going on the offensive.

Having had his fill of chance-taking, he remained in the attic for the rest of the day. With the steps raised and a quilt stretched over the trapdoor, the rising smell was somewhat suppressed. Boredom and the need for whiskey or rum or anything containing alcohol did a cruel double team on his senses. He couldn't rest. His hands trembled badly at times, frightening him enough to make fists and clench them until he tired himself out. Cold sweat beaded on his forehead and in his armpits. Reading didn't satisfy him anymore, so he burned time by looking out of the skylight at the street below. The one zombie lay still in the snow, an ugly angel that made him hope for a cold front. The snow continued to melt, and in places, pavement could be seen glistening darkly. Other corpses dragged themselves through the street, and at times, there seemed to be more than others, which kept him stationary for fear of simply not being able to see where the majority of the mob lurked.

He drank water and ventured down to piss in the upstairs bathroom, which was becoming quite rank from his recent visits. He wished he had a drink, wished he'd saved the scant bottle he'd brought on his hunting trip, wished he'd brought *more*. The notion of going to a liquor store entered his mind. It was only a thirty or forty minute walk away, but upon looking out the window again, he decided against it. Gus kept looking outside, contemplating his next move.

Evening became night, and Gus still stood at the skylight. The clouds had rolled away completely, and the moon rose over the mountains. He gazed below and saw that the streets had cleared of dead things. The only corpse down there was the one he'd shot earlier and deposited in a frame of white. The snow gleamed in the moonlight, and the houses with white paint shone. Gus thought again about the liquor store. He could make it. Every pore of his body was telling him he could make it. Make it *easily* and goddamn it, it was *worth* the risk. Gus rubbed his face. He peered up one end of the street and then down the other.

The street was empty. Even the constant dripping off the eaves had stopped.

Then, a noise came from street level.

He barely heard it, yet caught enough that it hooked his alcohol-deprived senses and opened his ears for more. Leaning toward the skylight, he strained to listen.

A rustling.

Gus scanned the road in front of the house, but saw only the ghostly gleam of melting snow and patches of black pavement. Wilting drifts still covered most things, and he would have no problem spotting a deadhead if one were in the street.

Then, he spotted something.

Tracing the lip of the curb was a small dark mound of... *something*. It slipped along the length of the road, pausing every few feet, before continuing. The thing crept along, brushing aside some uncovered debris and giving another barely heard *bump* to the picture.

More of the things came into view, moving soundlessly over the snow and easily visible in broad sweeping swards of moonlight. Gus swallowed, a dry click that sounded painfully loud in his ears. He realized what they were, even as more of the things filled the streets. A dark stream poured into the road, filling it in a lumpy, rustling river of darkness. The mass gradually thickened, moving beyond the rim of the curb and coming up onto the front lawn until the white was swallowed by the tide of teeming night. A growing sound reached his ears, more than the rustling he'd heard earlier, a long, continuous brushing noise that forced him to keep his eyes on the gathering mass below, even though he could scarcely believe it.

Rats.

The street was filled with rats.

Then, a rat found the body he'd shot earlier that day. It fluttered up over the neckline of the fallen zombie, moving in a herky-jerky way that suggested all wasn't well with the creature, and disappeared for a moment. When it came back into view, it perched on the chest, near the chin. More followed the first, milling around the body as if conducting their own investigation, until the zombie was covered in a lumpy mattress of rat hair.

Gus heard the gnashing of rodent teeth and the gentle grind of tooth on bone from two and half floors up. A minute later, an arm raced feet away from the body. A leg went in the opposite direction. Both limbs were halted and swallowed up by more rats arriving on the scene, drawn to the smell of raw carrion. And they ate. The snow became black with rats, infested with the things.

Holy shit, some horrified part of his brain whispered. He couldn't tear his eyes away from the rising flood of rodents moving with the sound of coarse hair rubbing incessantly against each other, as softly as a meadow full of crickets. Dogs. He'd originally thought dogs were taking away the zombies he and Scott put down. But the gloomy vermin of the earth had risen up from wherever they had hidden in the absence of humanity, and found that a veritable all-you-can-eat *buffet* waited for them on the surface. Dead flesh. They were feeding on dead flesh. Had perhaps been feeding on it for years.

The invisible grips of fear around Gus's junk, heart, and *mind* squeezed harder.

What the hell did the virus—or poison or whatever it was that turned folks into starving undead things—do to *rats*?

Gus continued watching as the level of bodies swarmed, covering the street. The numbers seemed impossible, but hadn't he seen hundreds of zombies in the street only a day ago? So why was it so difficult for him to fathom *millions* of silent flesh hunting rodents doing the same thing?

Millions.

The front lawns of the neighborhood slowly winked out of existence in the rising gush of rats. The cacophony rose until it sounded like the low powerful hum of a power station at midnight. The rats crawled over each other to get to the meat they no doubt smelled, becoming almost knee high and rising. Some were big, but others were huge, perhaps the size of puppies.

What frightened Gus most was the scratching he heard at the front door.

11

Blood pounding, Gus hauled back the blanket covering the trapdoor and dropped the steps. He descended and crept down the hall toward the stairs, before reaching the landing, where he stopped and stared.

The front door trembled in its frame while the sounds of scratching on the wood caused the hair on the back of his neck to rise. Except, it wasn't scratching at all that he heard. It was chewing.

"Holy fuck," Gus let out, his jaw dropping. "Holy sweet fuck almighty."

He clapped his hands over his mouth to stop the scream. They'd hear him. The rats *and* the zombies. That thought stuck in his head. The zombies were probably long gone, maybe sensing the invasion of the rats like dogs with earthquakes. *Dogs!* Gus shook his head. It was vermin all the time, perhaps the only living thing besides the cockroaches that would survive a nuclear blast. Horrified, *terrified*, he gripped the bannister and took a few steps down toward the foyer.

In the dim moonlight, the door trembled with increasing violence. Gus shook his head in wonder. Why did they want inside? Then, he remembered the dead lying inside the house. All that decomposing meat, just lying there. He frantically considered heaving the bodies out the window.

Gus focused on the door—wood, perhaps some metal, but not enough to stop the new plague. He came halfway down the steps, feeling incredibly brave to face down his fears in doing so, but incredibly stupid for not getting the hell away.

A shard of wood buckled inward at the base of the door. Gus tensed, ready to bolt. The sliver bent and shivered, and he could see something dark poking through the breach. Teeth flashed, gnawing at the edge of the opening. Furious movement in the dark, more flashes of teeth.

Don't be stupid, his mind told him.

The wood shuddered and finally popped. A dark protrusion poked through, shook, then retreated.

Gus couldn't just stand there doing nothing. He hurried down the steps, crouched at the base, and pulled out his Bowie knife. When the rat's head emerged again, he chopped it off like a knuckle of meat on a cutting board. Blackness spurted onto the floor, like a gob from a squished ketchup packet, marking his first kill of this new enemy. First blood was his.

The rats outside seemed to gnash at the wood with greater enthusiasm. More fragments bulged and split inward, the cracking of the wood dulled by the hum of the creatures on the other side. Multiple snoots speared through in various places, and Gus stabbed back. He heard squeaks of pain and blinked in raw wonder when another rat poked its head through the first hole. Gus stabbed it through the skull.

The door rattled in its frame as if possessed. The Bowie knife flashed and stabbed, but the crackling grew louder. More teeth pulled wood fragments backward, and not just at the base. Points in the wood halfway up the door started weakening. A rat squirmed through a new hole inches above the floor. Gus hacked the thing through the middle; the forward half dropped to the floor. The half-rat thrashed, oozing guts and blood. Gus froze, aghast, and flung himself backward when the rat came toward him, clawing its upper half along in hitching jerks.

He clambered to his feet and stomped on the thing, crushing it beneath his steel-toed boot. The rat didn't move after that, and he felt a burst of relief. The rats were still only small rodents, and took little effort to kill. The problem was simply that there were just too many.

Another rat squeaked into the house. Gus stomped on it, squashing the lower half of the thing. A second boot crushed the remainder. Two more rats got through. He stomped on one and got the tail. The other bolted past him, heading to the hallway. Two more forced their way into the house, and Gus did a heavy dance, killing one with a stomp on its head, but missing the other. More cracking of wood. More squeaks. The rustling swelled, and something made the curtain flutter. He nudged the curtain aside for a peek.

Huge rats pawed at the bottom edge of the windowsill.

Gus drew back in revulsion. The window was five feet from the floor. The things had piled up on the backs of each other.

Splinters cascaded to the floor and the door bulged inward. Holes at the base widened. More rats scurried through and squealed in hungry delight. Gus jumped on them, holding his knife, but doing more damage with his boots. He stomped on two at once, feeling the twisting creatures underneath his soles. With more heavy stomping, he quickly turned the floor into a slippery mess of blood and innards. If he crushed anything but the heads, the rats moved on, answering the question of what feeding on the dead did to them. A long splintering of wood made Gus's heart sink, and he turned to see a small torrent of rats gush inside, moving so close together they appeared like a solid stream.

Glass tinkled, some falling to the floor. Rats spilled inside like great greasy gobs of hair. He jumped back to the staircase, turned and kicked at them with one foot, crushing several into meaty lumps. The rats headed for the small office, and Gus watched the shadowy body of the old man zombie slowly disappear underneath a carpet of feeding rats and white tails.

Gus took three steps back up the stairs, keeping his eye on the front door. The lower part of the door finally gave way in a crackling snap, splitting right down the middle. Rats flooded the entryway, spewing across the floor. They found the corpses quickly and began feasting. The door cracked again as writhing darkness slowly widened the opening and more bodies wormed into the house.

Shaking his head in disbelief, he retreated a few more steps, placing distance between him and the fearsome tide. The door finally gave completely, and a sheet of rats surged into the house. The wood twisted inward, and when it was finally dislodged from the frame, it tumbled without a sound, landing on the hairy backs. It bobbed for a brief moment before the hungry river pouring into the house swallowed it.

Gus turned and bounded back to the trapdoor. Breathing frantically, he climbed the steps and hauled them up, leaving only a crack so he could see the dark hall and the landing.

"How the fuck do I deal with *that*?" he asked out loud.

No answer came, so Gus decided on his own. He grabbed his weapons, but then realized with horror that his boots would do more damage than the firearms or bat. The rats were too small for anything else. Then, he remembered the Molotov cocktail. He'd left it on the night table, along with a lighter. He grabbed the bottle. That was what he needed, but he needed *lots* of them.

Gus returned to the stairs and lowered them. He went almost to the bottom and paused for a moment, listening to the squeaking that had become almost a chorus of nail-on-chalkboard scratches. Nothing appeared in the shadows, so he crept to the landing and looked over the rail.

His breath caught in his throat. He suddenly knew what sailors must feel when ice or some other object pierced their vessel's hull, allowing the mighty sea to gush in. Rats flooded the lower level, climbing over each other to get to the food. A few even reached the seventh and eight steps of the staircase. The sight of a dark, twisting, writhing mass filling the downstairs struck him speechless. And more were entering.

He flicked the lighter, and the flame flashed upward a good inch. He touched the flame to the cloth sticking out of the bottle. The wick lit up, and Gus watched it for a moment before hurling the Molotov cocktail at the wall next to the door below.

Glass exploded, and fire rained down on the mass of bodies. The flames caught the closest rats and stilled them within seconds. The fire clinging to the wall and around the stairway flashed up, illuminating the swarm and casting a ghoulish light on both them and the walls of the lower level. The mass of rats churned like a huge vat of black gruel.

He retreated back to the attic and located his motorcycle helmet and pads. He quickly suited up and checked his equipment, making sure he had all of his weapons on him. The Nomex was layered, the top coat draping over the pants, and Gus feared that rats might somehow get up under there. He hauled out the boxes of winter clothing he had found earlier and went through them, finding thick gloves and several scarfs. He looped the scarfs around his midsection and tied them off. With one last look around, he pulled on the helmet, leaving the visor up for the moment.

He ripped the blankets from the bed and, with his knife, shredded two of the thinner ones down the middle. Knotting the ends together, he made a rope. Last, he pulled on the gloves and took a deep breath.

It was time to get the hell out of Dodge.

Gus descended the stairs with the blanket-rope in hand. He veered away from the burning stairs, toward the back of the house, and ducked inside what he thought was the master bedroom, slamming the door behind him. Tall sturdy looking bedposts greeted him, and he tied the ends of his makeshift rope to one of them. The window behind the headboard would lead to the backyard. He got up on the bed and kicked out the window. Drawing his bat, he cleared the frame of jagged edges before throwing the blanket-rope out into the void. He stuck his head through the opening and peered down, seeing only black, which did nothing for his confidence.

Around the edges of the closed door, the fiery glow grew and flickered. He caught a whiff of smoke and forced his way out of the window. Holding on for dear life, he felt the tug and worrying stretch of the tied blankets. His boots clattered and scraped against the side of the house as he rappelled. In moments, his soles felt ground.

And felt it shift.

Gus looked down and bit back a scream. The rats had come around the house, surrounding it. He instinctively lifted his feet, but realized he had nowhere to go.

He couldn't climb back up the rope. Even if he could, he'd be stuck in a burning house.

Taking a breath and twisting on the rope, he lowered himself down, feeling the pressure of the small bodies against his boots, then his knees, until his soles touched down on the backs of thrashing rats. They clawed at his legs, clambering to get higher. Gus teetered for a moment, slamming a hand against the house for balance. A multitude of jaws fastened onto the Nomex and chewed. He felt them wiggling furiously against his inner thighs. The rats pressed against his feet and lower legs like foam, thick enough that he momentarily thought his limbs had been sheared. Swearing, he reached back with one hand, pulled the bat out of the scabbard, and thrust it down into the mass. Using the bat like a cane, he waded forward, slapping his visor down. The light from the fire inside the house flickered through the windows, emitting a glow. Each step was an experience in loathing and terror. Gus waded unsteadily, feeling as if he were in a blocked sewage system. The rats stayed with him, fastened into the Nomex by the sheer strength of their jaws. Gus started pawing at himself, swatting the creatures off. Something shifted underfoot, and he leaned heavily on the bat to maintain balance. Rats nipped at his gloved hands.

He fell.

A combination of deep snow and writhing bodies underfoot made him sprawl face forward, arms going out in front of him. Rat tails wormed across the visor as furry bodies struggled to get a bite of his helmet. He felt pinches along his hands from a rash of bites at the gloves. The visor stopped the jaws of a puppy-sized rat, and Gus lashed out in reflex, batting the thing away. Hundreds of mouths gnawed frantically on the material, and he felt them all, like forceps trying to get a grip of meat through a rubbery membrane. They wiggled against his neck. They squirmed over his arms and back. They swarmed his legs. His *crotch* . . .

Gus freaked.

With a yelp, he scrambled to his knees, using the bat for balance while swiping frantically at his person, knocking off the rats. He squished the lives from several of the creatures just by grabbing and making a fist, crushing their tiny bones. He struggled to his feet and ran, coming close to falling over twice more before he'd gone two feet. A minute later, he ran into the side of a storage shed, smashing against its metallic shell. Screaming, he rolled against it over and over as if lathering paint onto its surface, crushing the rats clinging to his back. He jigged on the spot, crushing more under his feet.

He looked back toward the house. He'd only managed to travel about twenty yards. Flames flounced and grew behind windows, lighting up the area and revealing the deep tide of the rats. Two lumpy currents flowed around the house, converging into one solid mass which scurried straight for him. Somehow, they knew he was fresh meat.

After rolling his body against the shed one more time, Gus broke away and put more distance between himself and the wave. Knee-high drifts of snow sucked at his feet as he plowed ahead, gasping for breath. He punched through a line of trees and emerged into the backyard of a dark split-level house. He pounded across the yard and bounded up the back steps of the deck, feeling his strength ebb away. He ran to the door and grasped the handle. Locked, of course. He looked back. The rats struggled across the snow, the edge of their mass blackening it in the moonlight. They might have the greater numbers, but he had the longer legs.

Gus raised the bat and slammed it into the window, shattering the glass. He reached in and found the lock. Not sparing another look at what was behind, he plunged inside and slammed the door. Chest heaving, he looked back out and saw the rats scurrying toward the house like a dark wave. But he was inside, and at least he could get a few moments rest.

Something slammed up against him, ramming him into the side of the doorframe and moaning in his ear. Gus squirmed around and came eye to visor with a huge deadhead, perhaps the tallest he'd ever come across. The gimp pressed him against the wall while gnawing on his helmet with almost feverish gusto. Gus saw the lower jaw squeak and grind against his visor. He shoved the thing back a few feet, but the arms of the corpse, long and wasted like bony vines, held onto his head. Gus swung the bat low, making contact with its knee and bursting it like a hard-boiled egg. The zombie teetered for a second before it crashed to the floor, hissing as if surprised to be actually off its feet.

Using the bat, Gus bashed the head open like a bad melon. He straightened only to see two more moaning forms shambling toward him in the meager light made even darker by the visor. Frustrated, he swung hard, pivoting at the hips for extra power, and took one head clear off the shoulders of one shadowy figure. With only one zombie left, Gus dispatched it with weary urgency, smashing the head in with two swings.

He trembled with exertion and struggled to push his visor up, needing air.

Seconds later, he heard scratching at the base of the door.

"Well, fuck me."

Gus made his way hurriedly through the house until he came to the front door. He had no idea where he was anymore, only that he had to put space between him and the pursuing plague. He stumbled down a short set of foyer steps he hadn't noticed in the dark. His arms felt like weighted lead, and his chest ached with each breath.

Staying in the house was out of the question, what with the fresh zombie corpses there to draw the rats.

He looked out the window set in the front door. Attracted by the fire, the sounds, the smell, or just out for a midnight walk, zombies milled in the middle of the street. Gus put his bat away and got out the shotgun. He readied the weapon, unlocked the door, and stepped out into the night. The gimps in the street moaned and balked for a moment, as if startled to find the living amongst them. Gus fired, exploding the night with the shotgun's violent beat. *Boom*, a head blew apart. *Boom*, a body flung backward. *Boom*, another spun about with the top of its skull gone. *Boom*, a face disintegrated. *Boom, boom, boom*, zombies fell and did not get back up.

Click.

The shotgun emptied just as he came face to face with a zombie that had snuck in from his right side. Not feeling particularly sporting, Gus whipped the weapon's length up under the zombie's chin, snapping its head back. He tripped it a second later, and stomped its face in with an eggshell crunch. Ducking and weaving the others, Gus fed shells from his bandolier into the Benelli.

He cut a path through the dozen or so that still stood, killing any that came too close. When the Benelli ran out of shells again, he climbed the front steps of another house, and reloaded as quickly and as calmly as he could in the face of five approaching dead.

Then it came to him. He didn't need to get away from the rats. He just needed a diversion.

He only had four rounds loaded when he aimed and shot the first zombie reaching the steps. The force of the blast knocked the dead thing to the ground. Gus got two more shells into the weapon before the others got too close. He shot them at close range as well, taking his time and destroying their heads. With his back against the house, he pulled more shells from his bandolier and thumbed them into the shotgun. A red glow erupted above the roof of the house he'd just run through, adding color to the night. The fire was blazing.

Gus staggered to the front door. He tried the knob and found it unlocked. He threw open the door, slipped inside, and slammed the door behind him. One quick look out the window informed him that nothing was in pursuit. Yet. He studied the interior of the house and eventually spotted the stairway.

"Hey. Any dead fuckers in here?" He waited. Nothing came to greet him. "Hey! Dead fuckers!" He waited seconds longer before deciding the coast was clear and moving through the house. A few minutes later, he declared the place clean. Only then did he come full circle back to the front door and the staircase. Breathing hard, he climbed the stairs and moved into a hallway, searching for an attic, but saw no trapdoors.

"Fuck it." He moved into one of the bedrooms facing the street. He peered through white curtains and saw the inferno burning one lot over. Open flames licked at the dark and smoke billowed. He watched the street and waited for the rats to appear.

Ten minutes later, they came.

Only a few showed at first, but then the ones and twos became a stream around the house across the way. The stream became two and grew into great black rivers that threatened to sweep everything away. The rats pooled into the road and swarmed over the zombies he'd shot, hiding the corpses from sight.

He thought about the house. There were no broken windows and more importantly, no freshly killed undead lying inside. If all went well, he should be fine. He took a step back from the window, just because it seemed safer to watch from the shadows. The moonlight gave him a clear view. The rats crawled over each other as they feasted. Tendrils of rodents looped away and outward as if in search of more food, only to be absorbed by even greater numbers arriving over the backs of others, the mass thickening and growing impossibly deeper. In places, limbs pointed up into the air as the feeders ripped and tore them apart. Hands pointed to the night sky for short moments before some famished undercurrent pulled it below the surface and out of sight once more. Gus watched in horrified amazement. What did Discovery Channel once say about piranha and the speed it took a school of a certain species to eat a cow to the bloody bone?

It couldn't have been faster than the rats.

Once the flesh was consumed, the swarm elongated in all directions, even moving around the foundation of the house he hid inside. The dozen zombies in the road that he had put down were utterly gone. Even the bones had been eaten. Gus supposed that if the things were capable of chewing their way through wood, a few stubborn bones shouldn't be too much of a problem, especially when he factored in the numbers of the rats. He backed away from the window and looked at the open doorway of the bedroom. Pulling off the helmet, he strained to listen for anything gnawing at the front door. It wasn't deadheads that frightened him anymore. It was the sound of jaws grinding through wood.

After a few moments of silence, he relaxed a little.

He backed up, keeping his eyes on the floor as if he were on a ship instead of inside a house, wary of springing leaks. His legs bumped against the edge of a bed covered in pink blankets, and he realized he stood in a little girl's room. Stuffed animals adorned the walls, some on shelves with what appeared to be shadowy kingdoms fashioned out of stone.

With a deep breath, he lowered himself onto the mattress and unslung his weapons. He examined his gloves for the first time, shocked to discover the outer layers were shredded. The scarf he had tied around his waist was likewise in ribbons and nearly useless. He removed his neck brace and shook his head at the little holes made in the outer cloth. Simply incredible. Gus stretched out on the bed.

He kept one hand on his shotgun, closed his eyes, and listened. His mind replayed the gruesome work of the night, especially the parts with the rats, his mystery revealed at last.

Sleep took a long time to find him.

12

Morning found him clutching a teddy bear to his chest. He cracked open his eyes and drew back a little, but when he recognized the thing for what it was, he sighed, and settled down to listen to the buzz of silence. The thought of how the thing had gotten into his arms crossed his mind, but he left it unanswered. Stuffed bears he could handle. And they were kind of cozy as well.

He sat up, placed the bear to one side, and stretched until he felt his back crack. Rubbing at his face, he moved to the window and looked outside. Tendrils of smoke rose lazily over the house across the way, and the sun had decided to make an appearance. It shone down on a street empty of rats and zombies. All gone, devoured right down to the last scrap. Gus shook his head in pure amazement, reflecting on the night of horror. The pavement was clear of everything, and Gus wondered if it was safe to go down there.

In the end, he went to the kitchen. There was nothing to eat in the cupboards. The wish for whisky or rum or something entered his mind, making him swallow dryly. He thought of the snow outside and melting it to drink, but he scratched that idea, remembering the rats scurrying over it.

He used the toilet, once again grateful for a roll of toilet paper in the bathroom, then went back to the girl's bedroom. Gathering his weapons, outer gear, and placing the motorcycle helmet on his head, he left the house with bat in hand. The air was chilly, but nowhere near the freezing temperatures of the past months, and he was very much aware that winter usually held one final storm for March, like one last boot to the balls. Looking up and down the road, Gus stepped out into the middle and studied the surface. He saw nothing to mark the events of the night before, except the disappearance of the zombie corpses.

The question of where the hell the rats had gone came into his mind, and he answered it straight away. There, on the side of the curb, was a storm drain.

He cautiously moved toward the drain and hesitantly got down on his hands and knees. At the edges of the concrete, he spotted hair—rats' hair, pulled from their bodies as they were cramming below, escaping the daylight.

"Jesus Christ," Gus whispered, feeling a chill that had nothing to do with the weather.

They were right below him, beneath the city the whole time, surfacing when the sun went down and scampering back at sunrise. Never staying in the city after dark, he would never have seen them. But why hadn't he and Scott seen any rats when they had been stranded in the attic? Gus thought about it. He had been out of his mind then, but even when his senses returned, he'd never really looked out of that one small window in the attic. And the rats moved. Perhaps they never took the zombies straight on, when they were clumped into a mob. Or perhaps they were tidal like the zombies and just hadn't surfaced in that area. The more Gus thought on it, the more possibilities came up. Perhaps the things were getting bolder by the day, staying out longer?

How long before they finally began braving the sun?

That thought did nothing for Gus's morale. Two-legged, man-sized deadheads he could handle. Rodents were something else entirely. How the hell was he supposed to deal with a swarm of undead rats?

"Christ," he muttered and got to his feet.

He needed to get out of Annapolis. He needed to get back home.

With that thought, he started walking, staying in the center of the road. He had no fear of single corpses anymore or even small groups. He feared what lurked beneath. The sewer system ran for kilometers in all directions. Who knew how much space they had down there? And from what he'd witnessed from the night before, he dreaded to think there could actually be enough rats to fill the underground pipelines. That thought alone made his heart freeze and sink.

Home. He had to get home.

Cars, pick-ups, and SUVs dotted the road. Most were smashed into each other or into massive tree trunks. He checked the vehicles that were intact, searching for keys. The ones that did have keys had had their gas tanks drained, or the batteries were dead, or they were trapped between other vehicles. He needed a ride like he needed a drink. A drink! The very word set his tongue to tingling. Reaching an intersection, he realized where he was, and how far he was from the liquor corporation. He smelled the dampness on the air and noticed how the pavement had become dark from the melting snow.

Warmer weather meant more dead things thawing.

He checked vehicles as he marched toward the liquor store, hoping he'd find something capable of running. Two more cars contained keys, but the engines refused to turn over for reasons beyond him. He met six zombies and executed each of them with well-placed shots from the silenced Ruger. He left the bodies in the road with the mental message of *"Lunch is on me."*

Around early afternoon, he reached the liquor corporation and practically ran into the dark cave of the entrance. Stopping just past the threshold, he took out his pistol and held it at his shoulder as if about to enter a duel. Shadows coated the interior, punctured in places by single white glares of light stabbing from small windows. As bad as he wanted a drink, Gus held himself in check. It was not the time to get sloppy.

"Anyone in here?" Seconds dragged before he decided all was well with the store. Moving down a dark aisle, Gus noticed that some of the shelves had been smashed. Becoming wary, he crept around the store, looking for signs of what might have caused the damage. No clues could be found, but when he opened the door to the storage area, he knew what the problem was.

Someone else had found the place.

Cases of gin, vodka, lesser quality whiskey—in his opinion, anyway—and other brands had gone missing. Boxes he knew he had left unopened were ripped wide, the flaps left hanging as if someone had been too impatient to use a knife. Gus quietly moved through the storeroom, checking things out and finally deciding the place was empty. Someone had been there, though; that much he was sure of. Someone just as thirsty as he was. The three men who had ambushed him in the street came to mind. They probably had a place somewhere in the city, perhaps even near the cul de sac. Gus thought of the young teenager he'd left to the undead and felt a stab of guilt. Did anyone deserve that? Even three bandits who were probably going to kill him? The thing that bothered him the most was that he hadn't even stopped to think about killing two of the attackers. He had simply reacted, stabbing one and shooting the other in the back. He rubbed his face and pinched the bridge of his nose. It had been pretty damn easy to kill the three of them, even the kid he'd left to be eaten. Gus realized he hadn't even been drunk at the time. They'd tried to take him down, and he had killed them, plain and simple.

No thunderbolt came out of the heavens to strike him dead. Gus didn't like the moral grayness he felt himself passing through, or perhaps he was already through it.

If anyone came at him with bad intentions, he'd kill them. The coldness of that vow was noted, but it didn't change how he felt.

Gus found a bottle of vodka and opened it with a twist. He took a sip and savored the burn. Lord above, it tasted sweet. He took another shot and sighed, glancing around the dark room and listening to the buzz in his ears.

Times had just become a little more dangerous. He drank vodka until he felt pleasant again, and his black mood had lightened. If there were other folks about, he'd deal with them sooner or later, if the rats or deadheads didn't catch up with them first.

Leaving the bottle he'd opened and stuffing two fresh ones into his coat, Gus stepped back out into the light. He'd pick through houses until he found something to eat, but the trouble was, he'd already been through this strip of the city. Deviating from the current path meant going into another residential area, and without any wheels with him, he felt oddly put off by the task. Home called, along with the protection it offered. Slapping his visor back down, Gus got to walking.

For the rest of the day, he walked perhaps twelve kilometers, killing about a dozen zombies and dodging groups too large for him to confront. He emptied one magazine and made a dent in a fresh one. None of the cars he came across would start, and some of them, he realized, had holes punched in the tanks for their fuel—done by his own hand. The idea that he'd be stranded in town without a vehicle had never occurred to him at that time, but it was certainly biting him in the ass.

He crossed over what was once the New Minas-Wolfville neighborhood border. With the sun sliding off the arc of the sky, he stopped for the night just off the main road, in a two-story house he remembered clearing out months ago. The door was still unlocked, and the windows intact. He went through it upstairs and down, minding the corners and wary of rats. The house remained uninhabited, and he locked and braced the doors and checked the windows. After that, he retired upstairs and stripped the blankets from three beds, heaping them onto a queen-sized delight that would be his sleeping quarters.

As night came on, Gus lay in bed and sipped on vodka. The alcohol filled his stomach and calmed him. A single window with red curtains faced east. Wallpaper, dark with pink roses, plastered the four walls and left him thinking old folks must have once lived there. In the gathering silence, he listened for the moans of the dead or, even worse, the rustling of untold millions of coarse-haired bodies rubbing against each other while searching for something, *anything*, to eat.

13

Sunlight crept across the floor, scaled the bed, and touched his face. Smacking his lips, he considered the bottle of vodka on the night table. He threw the blankets off and winced, weak from hunger and dehydration. He shrugged out of his Nomex coat and went to the bathroom. He peed a few drops, and that was that. The throbbing of a headache started around his eyes as he rumbled through the house, smelling its stale air. The living room had a dark set of furniture, worn but comfortable looking, placed around a white rug of thick, imitation fur. He stopped in front of the picture window and looked out while scratching his nuts. Nice day out there. Good day for walking. The ache around his eyes seemed to intensify, ruining an otherwise peaceful morning.

Despite the good weather, he discovered he was reluctant to leave the house. Perhaps it was the headache or the lack of water in his system, but he had to force himself to get moving. He suited up and stepped outside, taking in a great gulp of cold air and holding it, as if it might give some nourishment. Melting snow blanketed the area. He considered it and shrugged. Rats or no rats crawling over it, he needed something in him. One shrivelled drift appeared cleaner than the others, so he dropped to his knees, landing harder than he intended, and scooped up a handful. The drift lay in the shadow of a large elm whose scratchy bark calmed him for some reason. The touch of snow on his tongue made him close his eyes for a moment, just savoring the water seeping into his parched throat. He got to his feet and munched on a handful as he walked. He had a ways to go. Somehow he had to get through town, sneak by the hospital, the university, and about three residential areas. There was a golf course, as well, and he briefly thought about stopping in to play a few rounds.

With the sun out in force, the snow pulled back from the road. The snow water helped alleviate his thirst, but Gus felt his midsection starting to tighten again, needing something more. Thinking about all of the great goodies back at the last house didn't help any. He scolded himself, heated curses that stung, saying he should have kept one house prepared in the city in the very case of what was happening. It had actually happened *twice*, but mulling it over, he thought the first time with Scott didn't really count. They hadn't had any choice in that case.

Mid-morning, Gus stopped on a half-buried sidewalk in the shade of some pine trees, very much aware of their woodsy scent. He also became aware of something else. He turned around.

"Well, shit."

Not sixty feet behind him, and following like puppies, were three gimps. Two were dressed for the summer, in beige dockers, button-down shirts, and rags that Gus realized were supposed to be ties. The other one was dressed for camping in a light windbreaker, hat with ear flaps, dark denims, and hiking boots.

"You fucks." Gus seethed, not wanting any part of the undead this morning and getting them anyway. That was what he hated about dead folks. They showed up whenever you least needed them, always looking to bite off your head.

Gus stood there, watching them stagger toward him at a gait that was probably the same speed as his own. *They* didn't suffer, however, from vodka headaches or an empty gut. Well, he reconsidered the last bit. Maybe they did suffer from an empty gut. His head pounded, and he blamed the dead for that as well. It was too goddamn early in the morning for such thoughts, and the very thought of *that* made him even madder.

He didn't have the energy to swing the bat. He dug the Ruger from his boot, worked the slide, and took aim. The pain around his eyes made concentrating more difficult.

His hand wavered a moment, then he lowered the gun. They were sixty feet out, and he wasn't going to hit them at that range. A sharpshooter he wasn't. He took a breath, parted his feet, and waited for them to close the distance.

"C'mon then," he said, glancing around for others. "C'mon, you goddamn dead bastards. You walkin' shit-stains. Come to Papa so he can blow your goddamn heads off. Jesus, you pricks are slow. *Slow*. And stink, too. *Christ*, I thought I smelled bad. You guys shower in shit or something?"

Forty feet away, their glazed eyes regarded him as if he were a tender morsel. Moans cut the air. Each step raked on pavement and grated on Gus's nerves. One of them wore a sneaker that had its sole detached, and every step made it look like a set of great flapping lips with toes. The summer ones had bites which were easy to see. One wore a wound on the shoulder, right through the shirt that must have soaked up every drop of blood, and the other had a hole in the thigh, the cloth around the wound shredded to the knee. The camper didn't have any obvious wounds, and Gus couldn't tell if he'd been bitten or not. Perhaps it was something the old guy ate. Or breathed.

Thirty feet and Gus felt they were close enough. He brought the pistol up with both hands, squinted one eye shut, feeling the thump of blood in his temples, and fired. The pistol spat, snapping a forehead back and collapsing the zombie to the wet asphalt.

The other two came on.

"That's right," Gus said, taking aim again at the second summer one. "What's there to fear? Just me and this—" He fired and exploded an eyeball of the second man. The zombie fell back hard, slapping pavement in a crunch that sounded painful, meshing with the tinkle of the spent casing. "Sound-suppressed Ruger. Nothing to break your balls over."

The last zombie smacked his lips. The thing had no nose, just two holes delving deep into its sinus cavity, below eyes that were bulbous and staring.

"Didn't like that, did ya? Huh? Well, too fuckin bad."

He aimed at the forehead of the creature. Its hands came up, clenching eagerly. Gus fired.

Twang!

The metallic sizzle of a ricochet startled him for a second, and he stood there, gaping at the old hunter twenty feet away.

"The fuck?" Gus aimed again, licking his lips.

The sound of the silenced bullet *pinging* off the old geezer's head woke Gus up, and he stood there, blinking at the zombie closing the distance. The hunter's hat had fallen off on the second shot and flaps of dead scalp skin hung off a forehead that gleamed.

"Well, fuck me."

The dead fucker had a steel plate in his head.

Ten feet away, the hunter's arms came up. His blackened jaw opened, and dark grayish fluid spilled over his lips. Gus took aim and squeezed.

Nothing happened.

The zombie closed in. Gus pulled the trigger again, but the weapon wouldn't fire. Something had jammed it. Or he'd run out of bullets. He jerked backward, attention divided between making the pistol work and the nearing gimp who appeared pretty sure of itself at the moment.

It lurched for Gus.

He let out a yelp and ran until he was well out of its reach, the hunter tracking him while flexing its jaw and teeth. That one charge was the dead's last trick it seemed, and it eyed Gus's retreating figure while conveying the message of *"Son, I am so gonna take a bite outta your ass."*

"Oh, I hear you, you old bastard," Gus said, composing himself and bending over as if about to pitch a baseball.

The hunter closed in.

Gus slapped his visor down and stuck the pistol down his boot. The deadhead's shadow fell over him, black fingers curling into claws. The fingers grazed the Nomex covering his back, gripping the material in a bunch.

Gus straightened and stabbed the Bowie's entire length up under the jawline of the undead, through its rotten brain. He twisted it with as much torque as he could get. The force of the jab straightened the zombie for a split second, then it dropped to Gus's steel-toed boots without so much as a twitch.

"Weren't expectin' that, were ya, huh? Stupid unawares ass chewin' *fuck*."

He pulled out the blade, wiped it off on the back of the corpse, and sheathed it in his boot. *Breathe*, he told himself, and took a series of deep breaths to clear his head and just taste the air, having had quite enough excitement for the morning. The ache around his eyes didn't seem so bad anymore.

Shaking his head, he turned and got back to walking.

"Just my goddamn luck to wake up and get the fuckin' *terminator*."

Mid-afternoon, his luck changed for the better. He found an open parking area filled with cars, paint gleaming in the sunlight and snowmelt sliding off the hoods. Gus crossed the street and surveyed the area, spotting five zombies lurching around the cars. The parking area was next to a rise of small cottages which he knew were sometimes rented out to students during the academic year. Blowing away any of the five zombies might attract more. Stealth was needed.

Slipping around several large elm trees, he stayed off the snow for fear of crunching noises. He crept along the road and approached the rear of the garage, keeping the corner of the building between him and the zombies. He didn't want a full-out bat-swinging fight. He gripped the hilt of the Bowie knife and extracted it from his boot.

From what he could see, no other zombies were moving in the area. He placed his back to the garage wall as he snuck closer. Reaching the corner, he peered around it and located the zombies. Still only five.

Even as he looked, one of the heads hissed and turned in his direction.

Gus swore and jerked back out of sight. He'd forgotten about their ability to smell. Though he was covered in Nomex, obviously there was enough of a scent for something to hook their attention.

The sound of dragging footsteps approached. A moan. Closer. Gus placed his shoulder to the wall and waited with the Bowie. He'd have to make it quick. He didn't want to use the Benelli.

The gimp moaned again and turned the corner as Gus flashed out his hand and grabbed the back of its rotten head. He pulled the zombie forward as the Bowie knife stabbed up under the chin, through skin, tissue, and finally brain. Gus caught the corpse before it fell to the ground and dragged it out of sight of the others. He deposited the body in a nearby ditch, shivering at having made contact with the dead thing.

That was one.

Getting back into position, Gus cleared his throat as loudly as possible. He kept on until he heard number two making its way toward him. The zombie's shoulder popped into view, and Gus again stabbed up under the jaw, snapping the mouth shut and twisting the blade hard enough to scramble its brain. The gimp dropped as if stepping onto a trap door. Gus kept low as he pulled the carcass by its armpits over to the ditch, gasping at the stench of the rotting flesh.

He put down the third one in the same way, and his confidence was riding high by the time he killed the fourth victim, grabbing the zombie in a headlock and stabbing it through an eye. He didn't bother dumping the last one into the ditch. Keeping low, Gus entered the garage. He lay flat on the floor and spotted the bare, decomposing feet of the remaining zombie, three cars over. On hands and knees, he crawled to the rear of the garage, past the cars. Rising to his feet, but still hunched over, he moved, stalking the final zombie.

The gimp stood beside the last car in the lot, and when Gus reached it, he tapped the fiberglass rear, attracting the thing inside the garage. He waited until he heard the rustling against the length of the car, and at the last possible moment, tripped the creature. The zombie clattered to the cement with a hiss. Gus sprang on its back, twisted its head completely around so he could see the face, and stabbed it through the face with the strength of both arms. The creature seized up with a snap of cartilage and bone before slumping.

Exhaling, Gus went to work on the cars.

He located a red Kia two-door compact with the keys in the ignition. On the third attempt, the motor turned over, and Gus saw that the car had a quarter of a tank of gas, more than enough to get him home. He pulled out of the garage and onto the main road.

Snow still covered the highway in places, and twice, going uphill, the tires spun, seeking traction. But in the end, it got him to the base of the mountain. The road leading to the house looked icy and lumpy, and he doubted the little car would get him up the slope. He parked the vehicle on the far shoulder, got out, patted the roof in thanks, and started hiking.

The sky had deepened into a dark blue by the time he got home. When he staggered through the open gates, he felt the urge to weep, but suppressed it. It wasn't his fault things had gone into the shitter while he was in the city. It was the fault of the three he'd killed.

With trembling hands, he went to the front door.

14

For the next few days, he stayed close to home, recovering, eating, drinking, and doing little things to improve his defenses. He unjammed the Ruger and made more firebombs in the garage. One afternoon, he went out in the truck and harvested gasoline from the cars on the highway. All the while, the ghostly images of the three men he'd killed in the street haunted him. Especially the boy. That one bothered him. Just as he thought he'd forgotten the whole incident, that wall of hungry gimps came back and pounced on the youngster in agonizing slow motion, making Gus pause in his work and wince.

One evening, with his work done and feeling good about it, he relaxed on the deck and sipped amber rum with the captain in the other chair. Both faced the dark, moon-scarred surface of Annapolis. The last two days had been warm, and much of the snow had disappeared. Moisture laced the air and made it smell fresh. Spring approached, but instead of thinking of romance and open fields finally blooming, Gus leaned back in his chair and mulled dark thoughts of fucking up every last zombie within the city limits.

"A missile strike is what I need here, Captain," he said to the duct-taped bottle.

The captain agreed.

"Fuckin' A," Gus growled and practically inhaled a quarter of the rum. "Fuckin' A," he muttered again. The bottle stayed nestled in his lap for easy access.

"Trouble is . . . I don't have a fuckin' missile. Wish I did, though. Something non-nuclear, but with enough pop to clear the surface down there. And then, and then something like the Americans' daisy cutter. That's the one that . . . that penetrates the . . ." He belched. "'S'cuse me. Penetrates the ground. Get down in there and scour the drain system. That'd be best, but I don't got anything like that."

Gus stopped and mulled some more, fingers playing piano on the bottle in his lap. "I ain't goin' down there, either. Not the storm drains. Too damn tight. Never have a chance. Haveta be able to get them above ground to kill 'em all, and then there's just so . . . goddamn *many* of the little shits."

Can't be that many, the captain muttered.

"You didn't see 'em, man. You didn't. If you did, well . . ." He trailed off, chortling and nodding emphatically that the captain would very much be impressed by the new foe. "I could leave here. And just go. Pack up the beast and fly."

But that idea didn't sit well with Gus and even as the words left him, he knew he wouldn't do it. It was *his* problem—his responsibility—because there was no one else. He supposed he was expendable. After killing living people in cold blood, perhaps it would be an equalizer if he took care of the rats. Something like that couldn't be allowed to go on feeding and multiplying in the valley. He had to do something. Maybe it would tip the scales back for him, bring him back on better ground spiritually.

Why do you care?

He didn't know. Couldn't answer, but it felt like a good thing to do, the *right* thing to do. If he left and drove west, the rats would just . . . what? Stay there? Follow him? He chuckled at that, shook his head, and took a sip of rum.

Kill 'em all, he thought, but how to do it? The firebomb had worked. Trouble was, it destroyed the house. Firebombing the whole city wasn't a good idea.

Why not? the captain asked.

Gus stared at the bottle. He suddenly didn't feel so drunk anymore. There wasn't anyone left alive in Annapolis. Who would he be hurting if he burned the whole city? Razed it to the ground.

The rats would stay underneath until it burned itself out.

Gus knew they'd do exactly that, *unless* he could toast them underground, fricassee the little furry shits right in the storm drains. But how could he do that? How could he torch them underground? He'd have to stuff something into the drains. He'd have to . . .

Holy shit.

The gas tanks. *All* of the gas tanks. The gas stations all had underground tanks. All of them were probably empty, but still dangerous. They all had fumes, and fumes were where all the magic happened. If he could explode each of those stations, that would certainly be . . . a start.

But he needed more gas.

Then, the mother lode struck him. At the west end of the city, in the Kentville area, the Western Oil storage facility had maintained eight huge fuel containers, each capable of containing half a million liters of ethanol and gas—potentially four million liters of burnable liquid and certainly explosive under the right conditions. Gus knew that the gas stations in the valley had been emptied, but how many people, in their panic, had actually thought about the Western Oil facility? He didn't think there were too many. He hadn't even thought of it much, as just popping gas tanks and draining them was more manageable. He knew they were there, but the pipelines were too big, too much trouble. But if he were only unleashing the fuel with no other intent other than to torch the city. . . .

The dark face of the city gleamed evilly at him, knowing he was on to something. Gus leaned back and smiled at Annapolis. He exhaled, feeling the rum's magic. It helped him think.

Fire. Purify the place with fire.

He rocked in the chair, not feeling the cold, and stared into the distance. He had the beginning of a plan in his head.

Firebomb Annapolis. Burn it all down.

That thought burned in his mind like a single bright candle.

He would do it. The final decision made him blink and almost brought him back to sobriety. The city made no sound, wary of the course of action he'd decided upon.

"Have to do it soon, 'cause I have a theory. I think them little bastards hate the cold just as much as their two-legged cousins. Slows them down. Keeps them underground where it's warmer. I've seen rats—live rats—scamper around old storage sheds and garbage sites, but these move like something's wrong with them. Either the cold or the virus or whatever. Spring is comin', though. Might come a time when they'll be above ground all the time. The sun won't keep 'em down. Not for long. Certainly not forever. But one match at the right time and I could potentially nuke the whole fuckin' bunch of 'em."

He thought more about it, feeling in his guts that it was the right thing to do.

"You're not sayin' much," he said to the captain.

And the sailor didn't respond.

The next morning, Gus woke up in miserable condition, nauseated and flooded with diarrhea. His bones and joints felt as if someone had thread wire through them during the night and was currently jacking him up by yanking on the ends. He spent the morning on the bucket in the bathroom, and later meditated on the outhouse throne. He swore he'd never drink again. It was the booze, his old love, leaving him stricken with the morning light. He'd had enough. He didn't want to see another bottle. But by mid-afternoon, the thirst became so bad, he gave in without even a curse. He went back to sipping on Jack Daniels, needing just one bottle for comfort. It helped him control his shaking hands. His supply of that particular brand of whiskey was dwindling, and he hoped that maybe he'd find some in the city soon.

While it was still there.

He wrote the day off, drinking equal amounts of water with his whiskey, and stayed home. He took it easy and watched the snow melt. Once, he wandered outside to look at the city. He thought he heard the sound of children playing, but when he stopped and strained to hear, the kids became coy and didn't make a peep. He stayed out there, though, shivering in the early spring air, listening anyway.

The day after that, he felt in better health. He got up just before dawn, got dressed, ate, checked his hands for shakes, and performed a once-over check of the truck he'd prepped the night before, transferring most of the equipment over from the beast. He covered himself in Nomex gear, tightening a leather belt around his mid-section. He located some hockey gloves and tossed them on the passenger seat of the truck. Those would be for heavy combat, he figured, and went back to the fingerless gloves he preferred when heading out to town. The Nomex gloves would stay behind. He cracked open a fresh bottle of amber rum and took a long, steady drink, lowering the bottle only once for a breath and an unseeing look at the wall. The half-empty bottle went back on the shelf.

The pickup made its way down the mountain side, feeling out every knob and rut in the road and rocking Gus to an irregular beat. When he got to the highway, he thought maybe winter would be over early this year. The pavement looked dark and wet under the dreary daylight, fringed in gobs of white. He slowed when he came to the body in the road. Curls of snow dressed the dead man, but he was still in place. The rats hadn't taken him yet.

"You're my marker," Gus said grimly and motored on.

Halfway through the drive, the sun turned the dark sky orange with all the subtly of a lit match scorching paper. Watching the road with leery concentration, he unconsciously checked off the familiar sights of the junk left and plundered as he passed them—an old truck charred to the metallic bone, gutted trailer of a semi stabbing a billboard straight through the gullet, motorcycle on its side as if the rider had been clawed from the seat. Yellow foamy innards spilled on the pavement. All landmarks. All old acquaintances. Unmoving, unchanging.

Uncaring.

The full bottle of dark rum rolled and nudged his leg with every movement of the truck. Next to that, the captain rode in the passenger seat, in all his duct-taped glory, grinning and obviously happy to be riding shotgun. With the captain were three of his Molotov soldiers, his marines, loaded with gas and primed with a cloth wick. Gus had wrapped them in a blanket to keep them safe. He was glad the bottles were there. The bottles were on *his* side.

He stayed on the main roads upon entering the city. The sun rose above the mountains, turning on its bright charm. Houses thickened into residential areas. Lanes split into two. Hulks of abandoned shopping malls and super stores lay silent, snow still covering their parking lots. Looking down side roads, he glimpsed the occasional slouched figure, but he didn't engage. He wanted to avoid confrontation until the very last moment. On the far side of what was once known as Kentville lay his objective. He was going to start at one end of the city and work his way back, *burn* his way back. He'd brought all the supplies he needed in the back of the truck, vowing never again to be caught in the city on bad terms. He had tinned food and bottled water, enough for a few days, and he'd thrown his mountain bike into the back. If he lost the truck, he wouldn't be walking home.

He'd burn his way back.

Jesus Christ, he thought and suddenly felt the need for a very long drink. Was he actually going to do burn the city? He took in the streets and the trees and everything that was once good.

He took a deep clarifying breath.

Yes, he was. Goddamn right, he was.

Little furry fuckers had tried to *eat* him. He couldn't have that. Word might get around. That notion made him giggle.

Twenty minutes later, he turned onto the forested street that led to the Western Oil storage facility. The place had been built outside the city limits for safety. But the concrete and steel rash that was the city had crept up on it, leaving only a thin veneer of forest around the area. To the east, an industrial park pinched off any expansion. Beyond the industrial park, a twenty-year-old subdivision snaked around the entire works. So much for safety. And Gus could not have been happier for it.

He slowed at the wire fence that enclosed the area, a mesh ten feet tall and topped off with barbed wire. A checkpoint lay just inside in the form of a red and white bar running the length of the road. A gatehouse stood to the left, and Gus couldn't see anyone inside. The vertical tanks loomed perhaps forty feet high and at least that wide, gleaming like barrels of ivory in the morning sun.

Gus put the truck in park and got out, studying the treeline. He walked to the gate and eyed the steel padlock. When the world was still the world and folks weren't eating each other like slabs of Japanese sashimi, there was an old show called

Mythbusters on the Discovery Channel. The purpose of the show was to debunk questionable stunts and feats found in movies and TV shows. The one segment he remembered was where the guy shot off a padlock with a gun. He couldn't remember the make of the gun or the type of padlock, but he did remember it not working, as it so often did in the movies.

Flipping down his visor, Gus took out the Benelli and flicked off the safety. He braced the skeleton stock against his shoulder and took aim through the scope. Checking to see how far back he stood from the gate, he sniffed and fired, blasting open the lock.

Mythbusters was full of shit, he thought as he unhooked the wrecked lock and tossed it into the nearby trees. With a metallic squeal, the gates swung inward with a push. Flipping his visor back up, Gus went to the gatehouse and studied the box and motor that would lift the blocking bar. Electrical. He pushed a black button, jabbing it impatiently with his thumb. Nothing happened. Placing the Benelli across his shoulder, he supposed he'd have to do it the hard way.

Bending low enough to step under the bar, Gus entered the storage facility. Wary of any lurking gimps, he approached the tanks, which were surrounded by a concrete dyke wall that came up to his waist. Equidistant from each other, the tanks were connected by a network of pipes and metal stairwells. An opening in the wall allowed Gus to move between the tanks, and a lattice of pipes and hoses threw snake shadows on the white ground. Western Oil didn't have any tankers on site, and a quick look informed him that the small office built off to one side probably didn't hold much of interest. Gus stepped up to the first one and, with the barrel of his shotgun, tapped its side. The connection echoed dully and told him nothing. He didn't know if the thing was full or not.

He walked along the base until he came to an oversized red pipe with yellow markings. A large valve with a yellow handle stood on top. Another metal padlock and chain kept the lever in place. The mouth of pipe was large enough to stuff a grapefruit inside of it. He gripped the lever and pulled it to the right. The padlock and chain kept it from turning.

Gus took a deep breath and looked at the little office building. Painted in gray and black, with windows on all sides except in the rear, the structure appeared glum under the sun. A huge load of orange sand bags were stacked behind it, like a collection of heavy bean bags. A stack of fire hoses, coiled like great green serpents, lay to the side of a hydrant. He walked to the front door and peered through a window. Charts and notepads covered the back wall, along with a blond model, topless, showing off a little more than her tan lines.

Tapping the glass with his plastic elbow pad, he smashed it on the second try. In seconds, he was inside the office and rooting through the one desk. He found a set of keys, but a quick search informed him there wasn't anything else of interest. With no power, the box with a bunch of switches and levers was useless, so he exited and returned to the first tank.

Fingers trembling, he found the correct key and removed the padlock and chain with a yank. Steel crinkled and rasped on steel, and he tossed the length to the ground. He wrapped his hand around the valve lever, and after a dramatic pause, he pulled it.

And couldn't budge it.

Best use a crowbar, the captain called out from the truck.

"Don't need no . . . crowbar," Gus growled through clenched teeth.

I'm telling you. Use. A crowbar.

"Lay off . . . with the crowbar."

The sailor didn't comment again. Gus strained with the valve and failed to make it move. Panting for air, he inspected the metal for rust and scowled. Grunting, he returned to the truck and fished out the crowbar.

"Not one goddamn word," he warned the captain.

The old sailor kept his thoughts to himself, but the smile gleamed.

Gus went back and applied the crowbar. After almost a minute of wrestling with the valve and lever, he opened up the lines. Greenish liquid squirted out, splashing onto the ground in gulps. Amazed, Gus pulled harder on the crowbar, fighting the crankiness in the valve. He moved it another notch, and more gas splashed onto the ground, pooling at his boots. He wondered why they left the entryway for the tankers open. Perhaps they had something like sandbags to seal the opening if there was a spill. In any case, Gus didn't mind. He stood back and became mindful of where the gas pooled. It interested him for only a few more seconds before he went to the next tank and repeated the process. More gas splashed down, its smell pungent, sharp, and not at all bad. He believed the second one was filled with ethanol from the urine-like colour, but wasn't sure. He knew there were plenty of octane-spiking additives that went into engine fuel, and there were probably more beneficial ones he wasn't aware of, but none of that mattered as long as it all burned when he put a match to it.

He opened the remaining tanks, but only four had fuel in them. The valves spat fluid onto the concrete as if vomiting. Gus looked around for the storm drain, but couldn't find one. The grated hole wasn't anywhere inside the compound either, which puzzled him even more. Had he missed something?

Moving back to his truck, he studied the sides of the road. No storm drain. His stomach lurched. He knew things had been going too well. Holding the Benelli in one hand, he marched down the length of the road, eyeing the thawing forest on either side. At one point he stopped and regarded his pickup, about fifty feet away. Feeling exasperated for not checking on such an important part of his plan, he jogged back to the truck. Fuel oozed out along the concrete, moving away from the tanks and toward the gate where it would go . . . nowhere.

"Goddamnit." Gus started the truck and made a three point turn, turning it around and driving slowly down the road.

What's wrong? the captain asked.

Gus didn't answer. He searched carefully, hoping to Christ he hadn't just wasted all that fuel.

Then, he spotted it.

Stopping the pickup, he slapped the machine into reverse and backed up to the iron grate set into the curb. Only one opening, but it was all he needed. He jumped out of the truck and sized up the storm drain. He looked back toward the Western Oil facility and figured he was perhaps three or four hundred feet away from the nearest tank, away from all that glorious flammable goodness.

"Oh, man," he muttered, reaching up and clasping his hands together over his helmet. "Oh, man. Oh, man."

He glanced at the captain still sitting in the passenger seat. "Not sure it's goin' to get here."

The captain swore a particularly surprising oath coming from a bottle.

"Yeah." Gus watched the road, hoping to see a tide of gas heading his way. "Shit, what can I do?"

The captain had no advice on the matter. In the ensuing silence, Gus reached inside the pickup, unscrewed the top from the bottle of rum, and took that very long drink he needed. Standing in the middle of the street with a bottle in his hand, he shook his head and felt his anxiety rise.

"Shit." He replaced the cap on the bottle. He got aboard the truck and turned it around, heading back to the tanks. Parking the truck outside the gate, he got out and found a huge pool of gas flowing almost to the gatehouse, but it was headed away from the road, following the barest of inclines.

Gus looked toward the office and saw the answer just lying there. The sandbags. He splashed through the widening pool and got to the stack of sandbags. If he could build a low wall and divert the flow to the road outside, the curbs would channel the gas to the storm drain. Filled with new purpose, he grabbed one large sack, perhaps weighing ten kilograms, and lugged it over to where the dike wall stopped. He dropped the back, pushed it firm against the wall, and watched as the gas lapped against it, flowed along its length, and around.

More sandbags.

He spent the next two hours building a low wall of sandbags which channelled the gas past the gatehouse and into the road. With the sandbags in place and stacked two layers high, the gas bled steadily into the street and followed the curb, heading towards the drain. Gus walked unsteadily on the long line of sandbags until he reached the gatehouse. Exhausted, he sat in the back of the truck, watching the gas flow by. He opened a can of beef stew, ate it with a spoon, and washed it down with equal sips of water and dark rum. The gas streamed by the truck tires, and Gus had an image of all four catching on fire. He didn't get up to move the truck, however. The only thing moving his ass for the next little while would be deadheads, and he wouldn't mind their company in the least.

An hour later, Gus started the truck. He drove slowly and stopped when he reached the drain on the right. Gas disappeared into its depths. On the left side of the road, the stream continued unabated. He drove on until he came to a second storm drain on that side, further down the road. He'd missed that one completely, but the gas trickled into it, too.

Gus drove a hundred feet before stopping and gazing back. The gas kept moving down the road and funneling into the storm drains. That sight filled Gus with a sense of hope and awe. He'd have to be very careful on that section of road right up until he finally dropped a match. He had no idea how long it would take for the fuel tanks to empty, or how long the flow of gas would take to reach the inner parts of town, and he wasn't going to stick around to watch.

He had other things to do.

15

He pulled into a shopping mall parking lot spotted with deserted cars and melting snow. Backing up to a set of glass double doors, Gus killed the engine. He got out and breathed deeply of the moist cold air. Fresh air, he thought, couldn't be beat. The zombies he'd put down a few days before were gone.

Gus looked for a handle on the doors and realized they were the automated kind. The main entrance had regular doors, but the set he stood in front of gave direct access into the E-Mart store. He had no intention of wandering in through the main doors and then walking the hundred meters or so through a dark shopping mall to get to E-Mart. But after lifting sandbags for a good chunk of the morning, he didn't feel like smashing in the door with his bat, so he got back into the truck, slapped it into reverse, and slammed the rear through the doors with a resounding crash of glass and metal. A minute later, Gus stepped through the wrecked opening, with the Benelli loaded and ready. Fragments of debris dropped from above, tinkling as they landed on the floor.

"Anybody in here?" After a moment, he returned to the truck and got out a flashlight, sheathed the shotgun, and pulled out the Ruger. Crossing his wrists as he had seen cops and FBI agents do in movies so they could point the weapon in the same direction as the light beam, he stepped back into the mall store and flicked on the flashlight.

Moving quickly, Gus walked into the dark interior of the massive shopping store. He moved past checkout counters and empty display racks and headed down an aisle filled with gaming consoles locked behind glass display cases. He stopped at a junction and looked up to read the department signs—*Household*, followed by an arrow. Once he got his bearings, he stalked off in a straight line. He found the bedding section and took an armful of packaged cotton sheets. After a brief struggle to balance the sheets, gun, and flashlight, he retraced his steps.

When he emerged from the entrance, he tossed the three packages of sheets into the rear of the pickup. The image of the boy being consumed by a flood of corpses crossed his mind. He reached into the truck and found the bottle of rum. Taking a healthy shot, he stared at the parking lot. The booze made him forget about the boy.

He got aboard his truck and returned to the storm drains. Gus got out and inspected the steady stream of gas flowing underground. The sight of it, like a shallow summertime brook, made him smile. He climbed up into the back of the pickup and pulled out the Bowie knife. He cut open the first package and opened up the sheet. Yellow summer flowers in a swirly pattern covered the material. Gus sawed the knife downward and cut a narrow strip from one end of the sheet to the other. Tying the strips together, he made one long fuse which he rolled up like an extension cord. Once done with the first, he got to work on the other sheets and made ten long lengths.

Once the fuses were all cut and rolled, he got down from the truck and unceremoniously dropped them into the combined flow of gas and ethanol, saturating the material. He tossed the soaked wads of cotton into the back of the truck. He wasn't sure if dipping the lengths in the mixture of flammable goodness was a good idea or not, but he was willing to chance it. What was the worst could happen? He'd be blown to hell and probably not even know it. When faced with that or being feasted upon by something that should rightfully be dead, the choice was pretty clear to him.

An hour later, the back of his truck was filled with the soaking masses of the cotton sheet fuses. Puddles of the fuel mixture seeped onto the metal floor. Gus got aboard the truck and drove away. He wanted to start blowing things up *right then.*

Driving back into town, Gus thought his nerves were becoming a little twitchy. The sky turned red as he stopped the truck perhaps fifty feet away from the first gas station. He pulled over on the opposite side of the road, with his truck pointed away from the station and ready for a fast escape. He got out, took a deep mind-clarifying breath, and readied the shotgun.

Was he really about to blow up a gas station? Eight stations, all chosen because of their locations. Once destroyed, the blasts would corral the rats to the center of the city, right where the drainage system converged.

There were other buildings nearby the first station. One was a windshield-repair place; another was a mom-and-pop take-out restaurant. A few houses stood beyond those. Bare trees leaned in between, as the valley was ever so blessed with the huge elms and a few stalks of spruce and pine. Gus thought they would all burn like afterburners once lit.

The streets were devoid of gimps. He walked across the pavement and reached the overhead canopy displaying, *Frank's Gas Stop and Service Station,* in bold-faced red lettering. One of the doors to the garage bay stood open, and Gus momentarily stopped and pondered. He looked around and saw that the streets were still clear.

He went around to the left of the station and searched the ground. He didn't find what he wanted there, so he headed for the other side. Passing in front of the open bay door, he saw something that immediately captured his attention.

A sledgehammer on a workbench.

For some reason he couldn't explain, he wanted that sledgehammer. Images of bashing in the skulls of deadheads flashed through his mind, then the zombie faces morphed into the face of the boy. He shoved that image away and stepped warily into the shadowy bay. Several tools hung from the wall, but he wasn't interested in any of those. He placed the Benelli on the bench and gripped the handle of the sledgehammer, grunting when he hefted the thing. Heavy and unwieldy, the reality of the tool dismissed any notion of actually using it in combat.

Still, it was going with him.

He hurried back to the truck, glancing up and down the streets for zombies. The sledgehammer went into the back, and he returned to his search, finding what he wanted only minutes later—the manhole cover to the underground tanks. With his crowbar, he wrestled the cover off and gazed down at a gaping hole big enough to plug with a two-liter pop bottle, used when tankers brought in their loads to refill the tanks. A telltale wisp of gasoline tantalized him. Staring down that black eye caused a shiver to shoot through him, and he balked, thinking of the ramifications of what he intended to do. Only for a few seconds, however.

He retrieved one of his dripping fuses from the back of his truck. Getting down on his knees, he found it was difficult to stuff the strip any distance down the opening, but another quick search of the garage produced a sixty centimeter dipstick made of wood, no wider than his thumb. He jammed the fuse into the hole, pushing it as far down as he could with the dipstick. Once that was done, he paused and waited for a few seconds. When he realized he was still alive, he stood and backed away from the hole, unravelling the fuse all the way back to the truck.

He had perhaps a sixty foot length of fuse which ended right at the pickup's driver's side. He dropped the sheet once its limit was reached and took a lighter from the truck. He lit the end of the fuse and watched the flame lick up the gas soaked cloth. It moved quickly, and Gus suddenly realized where he was standing. Cursing, he jumped into the pickup and started it. He looked over his shoulder and saw that the fuse had already burned halfway to the hole. Slamming his foot down on the accelerator, he peeled away.

He got four truck lengths down the street when the fuel container ignited and exploded. The crash of sound and flash of flame made him hunch down in the seat. He divided his attention between the road ahead and the image in his rear view mirror as he kept driving.

Reaching the hundred meter mark, Gus slowed to a stop and got half way out of the truck to look back.

"Whoa," was all he could say, facing the burning station. Black smoke curled and flowered into the air, obscuring the road and everything around it.

Chunks of debris began peppering the road and houses, trailing wild streamers of smoke as if they were dying meteors. He heard glass shatter somewhere, a splintery smashing of wood, then a slab of smouldering pavement the size of his foot landed ten feet away from the rear of the pickup.

Gus remembered the remaining fuses, exposed and soaking fuel. He jumped inside the truck and got going, cringing and waiting for that one superheated rock or fiery piece of debris to end it all. In his mirrors, he saw chunks, both big and small, sizzling down from the heavens, while black smoke continued billowing from the station.

Another blast startled him, distracting him from the road, but he wouldn't slow the truck. A glance in a mirror showed a fireball, partially obscured by a wall of smoke, rising into the air, before dissipating in glorious fashion.

Gus made a turn, and the scene left his mirrors. He kept his foot on the gas until the fear of being hit by something eased. He finally pulled over in a dark section of town and looked back in the direction of the explosion. Sounds of smaller blasts perforated the stillness like distant fire crackers, and the bank of black smoke hung in the air like something from hell, unleashed and hungry.

"Christ almighty." Gus was just beginning to fully understand the destructive energy he'd set off. "Christ on a stick."

He couldn't imagine what the station looked like, but he knew from the periodical stabs of flame in the distance that other things had caught fire. A soft rumbling rolled over the rooftops, as if the earth itself had taken a sabot round in the ass and was none too pleased about it. He got out of the truck and stood beside it, gawking at the distant area, half-ready to get the hell further away if needed. The smoke continued to rise as whatever combustible material near the site ignited and burned. The sky became darker, and the sun was nowhere to be seen.

SAFARI

And in the fiery afterburn of the blaze, Gus smiled.

He reached for the bottle on the seat and drained it, hardly even reacting to the burn. Once empty, the bottle went back into the cab, next to the three firebombs. He'd fill that one up later. He wanted another drink. With the sky darkening, he knew he should head home, but the rush of the explosion combined with the booze already in his system made him feel powerful, invincible.

And the liquor shop wasn't that far away.

Ten minutes later, he pulled the truck into the liquor store parking lot. He switched on the high beams as he stopped in front of the doors. Time passed, and impatience tapped on his nerves and brain. When he could wait no longer, Gus got out and picked up his flashlight. It would only be a quick stop. Just the wink of an eye.

He wandered in, the light from headlights illuminating everything. He wandered past the empty shelves until he got to an open case of white Bacardi rum. He pawed at the cardboard, making the bottles inside rustle and tinkle against each other. He pulled a forty ouncer out of the box. There was nothing quite like a full bottle of booze. Gus compared it to holding a tank shell. He unscrewed the cap and took a pull out of the bottle, snarling just a little when he lowered it. He wasn't much into white rum, but he supposed he couldn't be particular under the circumstances. Sniffing indifferently, he took out two more bottles, tucking one underneath his arm while holding the others by their necks.

With thoughts on a late supper and a bottle of Bacardi, and even more thoughts on the pyrotechnics of lighting up the remaining gas stations, he went back to the truck.

Waiting for him on the threshold stood a man.

Gus halted in his tracks.

He initially thought the figure was a zombie. Then he noticed that the newcomer held a bat in his right hand.

"Howdy," Gus said, frowning and placing his bottles on the nearest checkout counter.

"Howdy." The gravelly response froze him in his tracks.

Gus blinked, holding a hand up to his eyes.

"Where'd you get the truck?" the voice asked.

"Found it," Gus answered after a moment.

"Where?"

He took his time answering, mulling over if he should say anything at all. "Won't lie to you. That truck was parked on my property. Belonged to a man who tried to kill me."

Silence. The shadow didn't move. "That man have a name?"

"Didn't get it."

"I got it."

"Yeah?"

The shadow paused, then with dramatic flair, lifted the bat to his shoulder as if he were about to walk away. "Jonathan."

"Oh." Gus shrugged. "Don't know him."

"If you saw him, you'd recognize him. Big man. Shaved head. Last time I saw him, he wore a hockey helmet."

Gus shrugged again. "Lotta guys walkin' around here like that."

The newcomer's head tilted to one side, as if the statement either amused the hell out of him or pissed him off. Gus couldn't be sure which.

"Last I saw of him, he and about seventeen others got in their cars and trucks and went off to rescue a woman. *His* woman, to be precise."

Roxanne.

Oh, Jesus Christ.

"Uh-huh." Gus squinted, sizing up the figure and estimating him to be a little taller than himself, but shorter than Scott. Bulkier, too. "Good women are hard to find these days."

"I don't give a shit what happened to them."

"I killed them."

Shocked silence. "You did?" The man's tone was doubtful.

"Yeah, I did. The whole works of them." Gus shook his head. "They were trespassin'."

"*You* . . . killed them all?"

"Yeah."

"Didn't talk things out?"

"Hard to talk things out when folks are shootin' at you."

"You killed them."

"Yeah." Gus nodded, looking to one side then the other, in case he had to dodge the bat.

"That'd make you a dangerous man."

"Baddest I know."

The shadow didn't respond to that. After a moment, the shadow hissed, "Jonathan's dead?"

"Uh-huh. Dumped off a cliff, too."

"Shit," the man said. "You did me a favor. Would've done it eventually. Jonathan was a prick right through. I was only bidding my time when I could take him on. Much appreciated."

It was Gus's turn to be surprised. "You're happy he's dead?"

"He *is* dead, right?"

Gus nodded. "Yeah. He is. Shot him through the head."

"Shit. Good riddance then. Owe you one for that. 'Cept there ain't no gang left over on account you killed most of them. When did this happen?"

"Couple of months ago. Around Christmas."

"Yeah, that's when they all went missing. Went up the side of a mountain and never came back."

Gus shrugged. "How was it you weren't with them?"

"Fuck 'im. I didn't care for the man. Didn't care that he turned our people into what they were. My boys and me were left waiting for him to get back. To mind the camp."

"Your boys?"

"Yeah. My boys."

"Where are they now?"

"Figure dead, too."

"Oh."

"Went out searching houses one day and never came back."

Gus suddenly didn't like where the conversation was heading. "Three men?"

Guarded hesitation. "Yeah."

"One was a teenager? Big blocky kid?"

"Yeah."

Gus tensed. "Was."

"How'd you know?"

"Saw him get eaten," Gus said.

"You saw him?"

"Did."

"And you didn't do anything to save him?"

"Hard to do when the boy was tryin' to take my head off with a rope."

The shadow straightened. "*You're* the asshole on the ski-doo."

That made Gus pause. "Was the asshole . . . got the truck now."

More silence. "That boy . . . was my son."

Well . . . shit. "Wilbur." Gus sighed.

The shadow charged, screaming, bat raised.

Gus stepped back into the shadows, past the counter, and heard the hiss of the bat somewhere just behind him. Something shattered. The father roared in both fury and grief. Gus darted to the right, down a dark aisle. The father smashed the bat into something behind him, making one length of shelves shudder. Another roar, and the stomp of pursuit.

Gus whirled and bent to get out his pistol. A monstrous shade rose up before him, and as he pulled the pistol from the ankle holster, the bat cracked it from his hand, sending it spinning into the dark. The father jabbed with the bat, hitting Gus square in the chest. He fell backward and bounced off a metal shelf. Something swished by his head, and Gus lunged forward. He punched and connected with the guy's midsection, feeling the thick cloth of winter gear. He punched several times more, getting a solid four punch combination into the bigger man's body and making him grunt. An elbow smashed into Gus's helmet, spinning him around and disorienting him. He instinctively dove for the floor. He heard the swish of the bat where his head once was, rolled away, and got to his feet. The bat came down and cracked into the floor with a heavy sounding *clunk*.

Metallic. Man's got an aluminum bat. Gus ran deeper into the shop, cloaking himself in shadow.

"He was only fourteen," the father growled. "Hear me, fucker? You killed a *boy!*"

A big boy who squealed like something wild when the dead ate him, Gus thought, hating his mind for thinking it. He wanted to shout out that he didn't really kill him, that he only knocked out his kneecaps. Then he realized those words would drive the old man into an even greater rage.

Gus cut through the store, moving as quietly as possible, straining to control lungs that wanted to gulp air. He circled around the back of the shelves, listening for the wheezing of the father's breath. Gus shook his head. He'd had to kill Wilbur to make a diversion for the deadheads, so he'd have time to get away. If he hadn't, he'd be just as dead and gone. Just as eaten.

Just like Wilbur.

The lights. The headlights of the truck. Gus headed back toward the entrance and made it to the truck. He yanked open the driver's door, then stopped.

No.

He wasn't going to leave the father behind, not after leaving his son. He didn't think there was enough booze in the whole of Annapolis for him to forget that. He reached in and pulled out the Benelli. The shotgun was more than an equalizer.

He saw Wilbur Senior in the glare of the headlights. White-faced with eyes slitted. Older man, perhaps late forties, with a week's unshaven stubble on his face.

"Got a gun, I see." The man's shoulders heaved, his bat held across his pelvis. He wore a blue and red padded jacket and a lumberjack cap. Blue jeans and bare hands.

"Always had it."

"Then you better use it, y'fucker."

Gus kept the Benelli pointed at the ground. "No." He tossed the gun into the cab. Stepping away from the truck, he dragged his own bat from its sheath. He held it like a sword. "You know about the rats?"

"Yeah."

"The rats got your boy, I figure. Got the others, too."

"You fucking *cocksucker*."

"Yeah, well, I'll make it up to you." Gus moved to his left.

Wilbur Senior mirrored the movement. "Yeah? How?"

"I'm still here, ain't I?"

Wilbur Senior charged, swinging his bat at Gus's head.

Gus jumped out of the arc of the swing and whipped his own bat at his foe's head. Wilbur Senior ducked and swung again, connecting with Gus's stomach and knocking him a step back. The man screamed, brought the bat up over his head, and brought it down onto Gus's helmet, knocking it askew. The chin strap held it on.

Gus lashed out with his own bat, trying to drive the other man back, but Wilbur's father charged in again, gouging the head of his bat into Gus's mid-section. Gus bent over with a huff. A second later, the bat crashed across his back, collapsing him to the pavement.

Wilbur Senior stomped on Gus's lower back, and Gus watched the man line up the bat with Gus's head like a mallet about to nail a lawn ball. Gus tried to move, but the booted foot held him down. A split second later, he heard a murderous crack as the bat smashed into the side of his helmet, knocking his head to one side. Gus fought for breath. He saw stars and felt his consciousness leaving.

Another blow shattered Gus's visor. A boot crushed his side, practically squashing his kidney. Another boot went into his ribs and flipped him over.

Over the lip of his helmet, Gus saw Wilbur Senior standing over him, expression hateful, bat poised at its apex to stab downward.

Gus realized he still had a grip on his own bat, and he plunged the head of it into the man's balls.

Wilbur Senior staggered back with a throaty gasp, bat dropping as if suddenly too heavy for him. Gus achingly got to his feet. He watched the other man hunch over at the hips, spitting and holding his crotch.

Gus winced simply thinking of that pulsating, nauseating pain. It would be easy, easy to step over and break open the man's head like an old ceramic piggy bank.

But he didn't.

Gus righted his helmet and pulled away the broken pieces of his visor.

Wilbur Senior panted and bared his teeth. He glanced over at Gus, then dropped to one knee, cupping his balls.

Gus figured he'd nailed the guy in the nuts pretty damned good. He should just get in the truck. Or finish the man. One or the other, but he shouldn't simply *wait*.

But he did just that.

A solid ten minutes later, Wilbur Senior asked, "Why?"

What could Gus say? "For your son. That's why."

"I'll . . . kill you."

Gus shrugged. "When you're ready, get up, and we'll find out."

Wilbur Senior slowly got to his feet. He bent over and picked up his bat. Then, he faced Gus and pointed the bat at him as if it were a sword.

Gus did the same. "You ready, then?"

No sooner had the final syllable left his mouth when the big man sprang at him, whipping his bat back over his shoulder and swinging for the fences.

Gus stepped back and swung his own bat with murderous intent.

The faster bat connected.

Gus smashed the other man's head with a meaty thud, snapping it over at an altogether wrong angle. Wilbur Senior's bat left his fingers at the last possible second. It grazed Gus's helmet with enough force to back his head up on his shoulders, cracking his spinal column like a fat whip.

Both dropped to the pavement.

Gus rolled over a moment later, groaned, and sat up. He turned his head to the left and right, testing his neck. Nothing seemed to be broken and his head was still on his shoulders, but the headache and stabbing pain in his neck didn't feel right. Gus knew he probably should've just shot the bastard and been finished with it, but oh no, he had to make an *even* fight of it, in guilty memory of Wilbur. He gazed over at the other man, who lay on his back, face up and eyes open. A squashed ear oozed blood. Gus heard a long hissing breath erupt from the man's chest. He couldn't be alive. Could he? Not after *that*. The man's eyes remained open, unblinking.

Cringing, Gus got to his feet. He felt he won the fight fairly, if he didn't count the shot to the balls.

That was a move of desperation, *the captain informed him from the truck's interior.* Perfectly acceptable. And you allowed your foe to recover, which was more than fair.

Gus didn't feel that way. He staggered over to where the man lay and tried closing his eyes. Contrary to what he had seen in movies, the eyes didn't close easily. He snapped his fingers over the man's face. Gus reached down and brought up his Bowie knife. He put the tip of the blade under the man's stubbly chin. One cut, and the episode with the family was over. One cut.

Gus adjusted the blade and stabbed the man up under the chin and into his brain. He twisted hard. Blood welled around the metal, bursting forth when he pulled it out. It drenched the front of the dead man's coat in a blackness that gleamed in the headlights. Gus drew back, falling on his ass. He watched the man bleed for a few long seconds, still somewhat dazed by the crack to the head, despite the helmet.

Wilbur's father had been *strong*. But he was dead, as dead as Gus could make him, and he wasn't being left for the gimps.

Gus absentmindedly cleaned the knife off on the dead man's denim-covered leg. Putting the blade back down his boot, he stood, stumbled for a moment, and reminded himself that the Ruger was still somewhere inside the liquor corporation.

Gus stooped and picked up his bat. He checked to make certain it was his and not Wilbur Senior's, because that would be weird. In pain, he made his way around the truck to the driver's side. He crawled inside and pulled the door closed. The headlights annoyed him, so he switched them off.

Then passed out.

16

Darkness moved, shifted, and seeped whispers that dragged him back to consciousness. He awoke feeling lightheaded and achy. He was distantly aware of something not right. Something bothered him, and it wasn't the sudden glaring pain in his neck. He groaned and stayed still for a moment. He realized he was staring at the ceiling of the truck. He'd passed out, keeled over, and landed painfully over the automatic gear stick. Groaning again, he pulled himself up onto the seat. He wasn't dead. Far from it. He looked out the window and saw that the night was moonless. The dark bunker of the liquor store lay in front of the truck like a massive brick and mortar tomb. He wondered if the fires were still burning. He gripped the steering wheel with one hand and leaned forward to look into the blackness beyond the hood of the truck.

Something moved.

Frowning, he started the engine and flicked on the headlights.

The abrupt blaze of light was still enough to surprise the rats and send the writhing mat of them scurrying in all directions. Gus screamed and thrashed in his seat. The headlights cleared the rodents down to the blood-soaked pavement, where Wilbur's father lay in a half-devoured heap. Stark light bleached bare guts and bone. Gus screamed again. With the position of the body, Gus could see into the exposed ribcage . . .

And the dark things that rustled within.

Shrieking, Gus slapped the gearshift in reverse and stomped on the gas. The truck lurched in its one-eighty turn, crushing two lines in the coarse carpet of rats. He drew breath to scream yet again when he saw the scope of what the headlights illuminated.

An ocean of the black creatures spanned the empty parking lot, layer upon layer, searching, no doubt, for the bloody corpse of Wilbur's father. Gus placed the truck into drive. A primal loathing threatened to overcome him, and he gripped the steering wheel an inch from having his knuckles explode from his flesh. The rats struck at the metal chassis, and as Gus drove forward, the truck bucked and jumped over the bodies underneath, fighting for traction and automatically shifting into four-wheel drive. The creatures tried to avoid the oncoming truck, but the wheels mashed droves of them flat before they could get out of the way. There was so goddamn *many* of them. Gus believed that if he stepped out of the truck at that very moment, he would be up to his knees in the squirming things.

The pickup plowed through the masses, as thick and viscous as lumpy oil. He yanked the steering wheel hard to the left, the headlights touching the edge of a road. Rats scurried away from the oncoming machine in that little hop-a-long way they had of moving. The truck burst out onto the street, and Gus gunned the accelerator, spinning the rear tires and sending a mashed spray of meat and bone up into his sight through the rear view mirror. The wheels finally caught pavement, and he shot forward, bumping up over a curb and into a smaller parking lot. He hauled on the steering wheel again, slowing to better take the turn as the vehicle wheeled about. The headlights flashed over the ground, revealing a swarm seemingly bubbling from the night. Gus felt his nerves freeze. Completing a full turn, he thumped violently back onto the main road and pressed on the accelerator once more, crushing a pathway until the ride smoothed out and the wheels were on pure pavement.

He sped for about a block, making sure the rats weren't following, if such a thing were possible. Realizing he was on the road to home, he decided to go there. He didn't like driving at night, but he sure as hell wasn't going to stay anywhere in Annapolis, not with the skin-prickling image of rats crawling over each other in the blaze of headlights.

Dawn hadn't broken by the time he reached the outer gate of home. The shock had left him, but the memory clung. Once inside the wall, he parked the truck, got out, and closed the gates, then shone a flashlight beam under the frame of the truck. Shredded pieces of fur and flesh hung from the chassis, enough to make him want to throw up. He'd leave the truck outside for the night, as there was no way he was parking it in the garage with the gas-soaked fuses in the back of it.

He entered his house, tired, aching from his fight with Wilbur's old man, and mentally frayed from the sight of the rats. The climb to his bedroom drained his remaining strength, and he passed out on the bed, not even bothering to remove the Nomex.

Dawn found him twisted uncomfortably amongst the numerous blankets, as if he endured nightmare after nightmare during the remainder of the night. He wondered for a brief moment if his fight with Wilbur Senior and escaping the rats had been only a dream. He hoped to God it was, hoped that all was actually well with the world, and that Tammy was waiting for him when he opened his eyes. They could argue about who was going to make breakfast.

He peeked through slitted lids. No Tammy. No smell of bacon wafting through the apartment. He was in a stranger's house that he had claimed as his own, waking up in a stranger's bedroom, after killing the father of a boy whom he had murdered in cold blood.

He just kept right on crossing lines.

Shoving back the blankets and kicking his legs free, he rubbed his bare head and combed his fingers through the rug that was his beard. Water. The thought made him smack his lips. Preferably water mixed with some scotch. He wasn't a scotch drinker, but the combo sounded better than coffee. Peeling off his Nomex coat, he went downstairs. In the living room, he paused and gazed out a window toward the city.

Coils of black smoke marred an otherwise sunny morning.

"Holy shit," Gus muttered, blinking. "Thing's still burning."

After a rushed breakfast and morning dump, Gus suited up in full gear and walked out to where he had parked the truck. He checked the fuses, his weapons, the captain, and the Molotov cocktails. His Ruger was missing, and he remembered losing it in the liquor store. That brought a brain scratch at the notion of having to return there. He remembered the bottles of white Bacardi he'd left on one of the check-out counters as well. Then, the rats came to mind, along with the half-eaten lump that had once been a man, a man he had personally stabbed through the brain, even though the guy hadn't been in danger of rising as a deadhead.

Kicking at the ground, he realized he'd have to return to the parking lot. A quick stop. He'd stop no more than a few minutes, just enough time to find the weapon. The gun was too important to leave. Once that was done, he'd blow up the remaining gas stations before setting off the big one.

Going back to the garage for gas for the truck, he wondered how he would save his own ass. Then, he wondered if his ass was even worth saving anymore.

Mid-morning, he pulled into the parking lot of the liquor store and let out his breath in a whistle. The crawling sea of rat flesh was gone. The parking lot lay bare, and amazingly, not even the rats he'd crushed under his truck remained. He stopped the truck in front of the main doors of the liquor corporation and slowly eased out from behind the wheel, wary of even putting his feet onto the pavement. The only thing left of the man he'd killed was the aluminum bat. Gus wondered if the damn things had even eaten the man's clothes and shoes, but that was probably impossible. Things that couldn't be consumed had probably been dragged off into the night or simply borne away by the sheer numbers, like something caught in a riptide. He avoided the bat, not needing a second one and thinking it bad luck to take it.

A gust of cold wind blew past him, reminding him he was relatively sober. That was something he fully intended to correct. He went to the doorway of the store and unsheathed his bat, swinging it ever so slightly at his hip. Wary of the dark interior, he saw the three bottles of white rum on the checkout counter and smiled. How could it be bad when it was the easiest thing to find?

"Anyone here?"

When no answer came, he wondered how much time there would be before the temperature started to rise and the dead were no longer half-frozen slabs of meat. He stepped around the counters to the area where the bat had knocked the Ruger from his grip, searching just beyond the rays of sunlight. He shone his flashlight across a white tiled floor marked with thousands of scratches and tufts of hair. Rats. They had come inside, no doubt looking for food. Just the thought of them crawling around sent a shiver through him, and he was suddenly thankful for the Nomex. He wore his old fingerless gloves, however, and shook his head in distaste at the notion of touching anything in there.

After mucking about in the shadows for a few long moments, he spotted the butt of his Ruger lying underneath a shelf. His knees cracked when he dropped down, and just as he was about to touch the grip of the weapon, he paused, envisioning undead rats running over it. Gingerly, he scooted the thing out from underneath the shelving unit with his covered wrist and studied the thing in the gloom. There didn't *seem* to be anything wrong with it, and that thought almost made him smile. The five-second rule didn't apply to firearms, he reckoned, nor germs or viruses that could reanimate the dead, but he didn't want to be holding a gun that had had millions of undead rodents crawling over it either.

Gus returned to the truck. Taking the Bowie, he sliced a shred off one of the cotton sheet fuses and returned to pick the gun up off the floor with it. As he walked past the checkout, the three bottles of rum caught his attention as surely as a woman baring a shapely leg.

"Answer's all around me." Gus grabbed a bottle of one of the brands of whiskey he didn't usually drink. The label on the forty-ouncer read *Red Rye*, complete with a blooming rose.

"Red . . . rye," he said in a creaking voice, imitating the kid from *The Shining*. "Red . . . rye. Red . . . rye. Red rye. Redrye."

He studied the label at arm's length, not caring what it was called as long as the alcohol content was forty percent. Cracking open the bottle, he quickly washed his hands in the whiskey, then dribbled some on the gun and the bottles of rum. He wiped it all down with the rags smelling of gasoline and ethanol. Having hopefully sanitized everything, he carried it all out to the truck. After stashing the rum, he racked the slide of the Ruger and pointed it toward a far-off house. Wilbur's father had knocked the gun away with a bat. It was all he needed to be in a situation and not know if the gun would misfire.

A tingling in his head stopped him, and from the shotgun seat, the captain piped up. *Didn't you just wipe the weapon down with a rag soaked in gas?*

Gus supposed he had. He decided to just pull the trigger anyway and let God sort things out.

The sound of a suppressed shot punctured the stillness and the tinkle of a casing on the ground sounded as pure as a single piano key. He regarded the gun fondly before jamming it down his boot.

It would be noon shortly, and he had gas stations to explode.

Driving deep into the city, Gus avoided contact with any walking corpses and focused on the much more important task ahead. Engaging gimps would only delay the end of the city. So he drove by all the gaunt shadows standing in the road or on the sidewalks.

The second gas station was situated in front of a smaller shopping plaza in the lower end of Kentville. Whoever owned the place had built it on the main road, right in the middle of everything. Gus drove around twice to make certain he got the attention of any deadheads in the area.

He did.

About twenty of them emerged from various nooks, crannies, and doorways, stumbling along as if bullied by Satan himself. Some wore full suits, others the casual clothes of summer. Two were children, a boy and a girl, their ghoulish features made bright by the overhead sun. The little boy horrified Gus when he realized the child's eyelids and a good chunk of scalp were missing, as if someone had gotten a hold of his head and simply clawed. As the little one stumbled and lurched across the parking lot, reaching for the circling truck, Gus could see the extent of the wound—gristle black on white bone, shining in the sun.

He didn't get out of the truck to dispatch the zombies. Rather than shooting them, he simply drew them out into the middle of the parking lot and ran them down. He felt nothing as the tires crushed skulls and snapped bones.

After dispatching whatever dead things had lurched onto the open pavement, Gus turned his attention to the station. Ensuring he had an escape route, he found the manhole covering the tank. As before, he stuffed the damp fuses into the access pipe, using a straightened clothes hanger he had thought to bring, and returned to the side of the pickup. Hunkering down and feeling his knees crack, he ignited the ragged length of cloth. It caught fire with the barest of hisses, sending him scrambling back into the truck.

He'd traveled perhaps a hundred meters when the station went up. The muffled explosion jolted him behind the wheel as if he'd been goosed. A quick check showed the rear windshield remained intact. Gus slammed on his brakes, slid to a stop, and opened his door to lean out of the pickup. Behind him, thunderous black smoke punched the sky, rising, curling, and twisting on air currents.

It was all he could do not to just stay and stare. He felt *righteous* detonating the stations, as if he were administering a sweltering blast of concentrated chemo to the city's cancer. Grabbing a bottle of rum, he got out of the truck. The bottle wasn't the one he'd already opened, but he didn't care. Twisting off the top, he guzzled a quarter of the contents, gasping when he lowered the bottle.

"Redrye," he whispered.

Six to go.

The sun had just passed its zenith when he blew up the next station in a roar of flame and a trembling of earth. Bits and pieces of debris cascaded down like smoking meteors, bouncing off the asphalt as he thundered down the street to the next gas station. He'd lingered at the third until a handful of zombies had come out from some nearby houses, reminding him to get in his truck and focus on his task. Gus drove the length of a football field, then stopped to gaze back at the dark figures still pursuing him, walking along at their own speed.

A monstrous gout of flame blurred them away.

On the south side of the city, near the infamous cul de sac where Gus had almost cashed in his chips twice, stood a dilapidated gas station with a built-on convenience shop and diner. As he went about setting the fuse, he looked at the nearby houses and roads, searching for the mob of zombies he'd encountered twice. Not one deadhead showed itself, which made Gus more concerned than anything else. He would have liked catching the entire crowd in a blast of flame as payback.

He polished off another bottle of rum as he pulled away from the doomed station. Moments later, the earth shook, and flames shot skyward like demons escaping hell. Black clouds of smoke hid the damage, but Gus knew it had to be massive.

The fourth and fifth stations, really nothing more than gas bars, were more like carefully studied experiments as Gus drove only as far from them as he believed necessary after lighting the fuses. He parked the pickup close enough to witness the underground tanks of the fourth station explode spectacularly. He glimpsed the earth erupting from below, flinging up chunks of asphalt, dirt, rocks, and even tree roots to rain down half a kilometer away. The fifth station went up with just as much force. He felt the breath of the blast through his visorless helmet. The explosion was strong enough to make him fear again, and he steadied himself against the pickup, staring in mute awe at the uncoiling blooms of smoke blotting out the once blue sky. He even heard occasional explosions from parts of the city where the other stations had gone up earlier in the day. Apparently, the fires were spreading.

The increasing smoke veiled the sun, and Gus felt daylight creeping away from him. There were the remaining two stations he had to get to, and he felt a growing need to destroy them before he left the city that night. He didn't understand exactly why, but he believed the element of surprise was gone. The dead knew what he was doing, and he sensed something was hunting him in an attempt to stop him from further destruction.

"Red fuckin' rye!" Gus screamed in the crumbling aftermath of the third station's explosion. He sped away from the bubbling black smoke and raging fire.

17

The second to last gas station was part of one of the smaller, independent hardware shops Gus had once visited long ago. Trying to compete with the larger chains that had invaded the valley, Rodmell's One Stop had had its business slowly sucked away until only the older, loyal customers frequented the business. Al Rodmell had been an old codger with a reputation as something of a bigot, someone not to cross, as well as a solid mechanic. It had been a year and a half ago, give or take a month, since Gus had last visited the One Stop, which sold gas, ethanol, and hardware and serviced vehicles, including the larger transports trucks. Gus remembered old Allister preferred to work on the big vehicles as, in his words, "That's where the money is."

At that time, Gus had found old Al and two of his sons, still in their blue work coveralls, turned into gimps. The three men had been some of the first gimps Gus had to put down.

Across from the One Stop was an out-of-place duck pond and sitting park, nestled between two great forested hills covered in melting snow. He parked his pickup in front of the duck pond, a little closer to the station and its tanks than he had the others. He got out of the truck with his Benelli in hand. The roads and immediate area were empty of zombies, and he saw nothing but smoke in the sky, even faintly tasting it on the air.

He quickly located the small manhole cover that gave access to the underground tanks and pulled it off with a crowbar. Standing and catching his wind for a moment, Gus realized that he was next to a hardware store and that old man Rodmell just might have carried motorcycle helmets. He didn't like walking around without a visor, as he remembered all too well the incident where he thought he'd swallowed some deadhead's fleshy matter. A dark time that was, probably the darkest, and he sent a silent thanks to Scott for saving him.

Uncapping the pipe, Gus jabbed the end of the bed-sheet fuse inside and walked the other end back to the truck. When the fuse ran out with ten feet or so to spare to his pickup, Gus walked back to the station. On the side of the building that had two bay doors for the service and repair department, Gus eyed a number of tall green and gray cylinders. The cylinders lured him away from the hardware shop, pulling him off his intended path like iron to a magnet. Some of the containers had numbers and letters stamped on the sides, but Gus didn't know what they meant. He did know what was in the cylinders. Studying the dozen fuel containers, he remembered a conversation with a buddy who worked in propane. The guy had told him that the gas was stored as a liquid in cylinders, and a person could pour it out onto the ground. He didn't know how many liters were in a standard cylinder, but he did know that one liter equaled two hundred and seventy liters of vapor. Vapor was what he wanted, where all the magic was.

And there were a dozen of those cylinders lined up in front of him. A grim smile spread across his face. He'd found a much more potent firebomb than mere Molotov cocktails. He reached out and caressed a cylinder, fingers grazing the metal shell. Finding them was a good omen if ever there was one. He paused only a second longer before running back to his truck.

Backing the truck up to the cylinders took only a few seconds, but loading them into the bed proved much more difficult. Keeping the first container upright, he rolled it on its base to the lip of the tailgate before almost breaking his back lifting and finally pushing the thing into the bed. He climbed in behind it and moved the mountain bike and remaining fuses, taking care with the tip of the cylinder, which wore a protective metal cover over the valve that dispensed the gas.

It took him ten minutes to load one cylinder. Figuring he could only lay three more in the back of the pickup, he took the next half hour getting them packed. When all was done, he had four green torpedoes aboard the truck and felt ready for war.

"Hey!"

Gus froze as if he'd just been caught stealing. A good fifteen meters away, across the street and partially obscuring the duck pond, a beat-up, red, four-door sedan was parked. The driver of the car stood on the other side of it with only his shoulders and head showing. Not able to see his features, Gus didn't know what to make of the man who suddenly waved at him.

"Hey!" the stranger repeated, arm pausing over his head as if wondering if all was well.

Gus jumped over the side of the truck and took cover, his heart racing.

Who's that guy? the captain wanted to know.

"Fuck if I know," Gus answered as he opened the door to the pickup and slid out the Benelli. "But I don't want him around."

He eased up over the edge of the truck and pointed the shotgun at the stranger. The newcomer became still at spotting the weapon, arms suddenly dropping to his sides.

Gus used the scope and targeted the man's head. The guy was older, with short-cropped silver hair. Gus squeezed the trigger.

The old man ducked a split second before the gun went off. The window on the passenger side of the car shattered.

"Goddamn!" Gus stood up and unleashed the full might of the weapon upon the car. Seven shots punched the air, shattering the passenger door and the windshield, speckling the hood, the two doors, and both windows facing him.

The driver took the hint and jumped into his car while Gus stopped to reload. Five seconds later, the battered car screeched down the road.

Stuffing shells into the breach, Gus ran out from behind his truck, far enough to get a clear shot at the escaping car. When the last shell went into the Benelli, he braced the skeleton buttstock against his shoulder and targeted the rear of the car. Four more shots rang out. The back windshield of the sedan crumbled. The trunk flew up and fluttered. The vehicle swerved out of his line of fire and disappeared down a side road before he could take aim at the tires.

"Goddamn redneck." Gus stared in the direction the car had gone, just in case the driver decided to come back. It would be a mistake if he did. Gus no longer needed booze to shoot a man, not if the fight was being brought to him.

He stood on the parking lot of the One Stop, waiting and watching, before finally realizing it was best to get moving. He had all the propane he could safely carry in the truck, and—

A moan came from behind him. Then, he smelled it.

Gus whirled to see the biggest zombie he'd ever encountered. The thing towered over him, naked from the waist up, with a chest clawed open to several gleaming ribs. Its face was swathed in reeds of congealed grease and hair, with widened jaws filled with nubs of black teeth. Glints of black coal eyes mesmerized him for the second it took the monster to close in. It swung a heavy arm and caught Gus across the helm, knocking him over and sending his shotgun flying. Gus rolled onto his back. The gimp bent down, reaching with fingers that had been worn into bony points. Gus lashed out with one foot, sweeping the legs of the creature that might have been a basketball player in its life. The thing crashed to the ground.

Gus scrambled to his feet and stomped on the zombie's left knee, breaking it with a sick sound. A hand snaked out and gripped Gus's right knee, as if wanting it to replace the one just lost. Gus brought his foot down on its face, destroying the nasal cavity of the beast. Another stomp and the zombie stopped moving.

Gus didn't stop until he had crushed the head into a pulp.

He drew back from the unmoving mass and took a deep breath. The streets were empty, the car he'd shot at long gone. Smoke continued to thicken in the sky, and shrugging off his shock at the attack, he retrieved his shotgun and gave it a quick inspection. Before he did anything else, he plucked red shells from his bandolier and fed them into the Benelli. Thoughts of where the creature had come from, along with who had been driving the car, jammed his head. *Who was that guy?* That was all he needed. Another human pain in the ass. He didn't need to be looking over his shoulder for living predators. The dead ones were bad enough.

None of it mattered in the end, he supposed. He might have missed the man in the car, but he had driven him off and put down one more dead thing. And the best part was, Gus was only getting started.

He went into the store's hardware section. The place had been ravaged, but there was an amply stocked motorcyclist's department, and within moments, he found a generic black motorcycle helmet. He pulled off his ruined one and tried on the new helmet, grunting at the snug fit.

"I'll take it," he announced, patting the new helmet. He didn't have the time or the inclination to search any further in the store. Jogging back out to the truck, he checked the propane again before jumping aboard and driving out to where he'd left the fuse. Moments later, the fuse burned to its explosive conclusion while Gus raced away, heading toward the middle of town.

The blast still made him jump in the driver's seat.

One station left, he told himself in the fiery afterglow. *And then the grand finale.*

18

The sun started slipping toward the mountains as Gus parked his pickup, pointed away from the final gas station. He got out and studied the building he'd come to destroy. Irving's Gas Bar and Convenience, a red sign declared, and Gus remembered rooting through the place about two years ago. Located on the main drag of the city, just before the numerous shopping malls and superstores, the Gas Bar had been a first stop for several panicking individuals back when the zombies were taking over.

"Dark days," Gus muttered, and the captain agreed. Gus looked at the sky filled with storm clouds of smoke. *All because of him this time.* A depressing thought, but ultimately destroying the stations and the city had to be done. War had casualties. Annapolis would be the casualty of his war.

His attention drifted back to the station. Time was growing short, and he had to light the place up relatively fast if he wanted to blow up the Western Oil facility, and he very much wanted to do that before escaping the blazing city. Standing at one end of the building was a large cylindrical propane tank, painted ocean blue and mounted on its side on concrete blocks. The tank probably held the same as two dozen of the smaller ones he had in his truck, perhaps more. He knew it would deliver a respectable secondary bang after the undergrounds tanks went up.

The expanse about the station appeared clear, but he couldn't see very far back the way he had driven because of the smoke choking off the street. He put on his new helmet, grabbed a fuse, and made his way to the tanks. He knelt on the asphalt and wrenched back the cover protecting the pipe. After removing an inner lid, he stuffed the cloth fuse down the hole using the coat hanger.

Gonna burn, baby, burn big.

He unrolled the lump of cloth as he walked backward to the truck, looking around as he got closer to it. With the exception of the gimps he had run down and the basketball corpse, he hadn't come across the mob that had almost killed him twice. Nor had he seen any rats, not that he expected to see any of them during the day.

The fuse ran out at sixty feet, just before he got to the truck. He dropped the end on the pavement and fished out his lighter. Stooping, he thought of bad horror movies, where anything that *could* go wrong *would* go wrong. He paused for a moment, catching the faint smell of gasoline on the fuse. He flicked the lighter, got a tall flame, and applied it to the end. The fuse ignited, and flames followed the fuse to the tanks. Gus went around his truck to the driver's side, leaned in, and started the engine. He checked and saw that the ribbon of flame was halfway to the target, and debated whether he should waste time watching the place explode.

Scratching at his neck brace, he decided it was best to get going. He got aboard the truck and drove off, intending to take a side street around the shopping area and head for Western Oil on the other side of Kentville.

The station blew up, and the land shook in fury. Gus cringed behind the wheel, and stole glimpses in the rear view mirror. He couldn't see the station itself, but fiery chunks of debris rained down on the street.

Another blast split the asphalt open like a flimsy book and enveloped the street behind him in a furious wash of flame. The earth spat black smoke into the air, and for seconds, Gus held onto the steering wheel for dear life. He slowed the truck, twisted around in the driver's seat, and gawked at the scene from fifty meters away.

A manhole cover shot heavenward with an echoing clatter, and fire erupted from the opening. Gus whipped around in his seat just as another manhole cover exploded upward, a gout of flame spearing up from underneath it. *Pong, Pong.* Two more shot into the sky, the blasts approaching his position. Rocks pelted the windshield, cracking it in places. He sped up, hauling the pickup around a manhole erupting in front of it. Fear grabbed him and squeezed. Ahead, yet another manhole cover zinged up and away, blasted from the ground by a pillar of flame.

"Oh, shit," Gus muttered. How long had the Western Oil tanks been emptying? Was it possible that the fuel had reached so far into the city?

Weaving through shrinking columns of flame and abandoned cars, he knew it was. The fumes had seeped far enough into the combined storm drain system to reach even where he was. All it had taken was one flaming piece of debris, probably falling and rolling into an open storm drain, to set off a monstrous chain reaction.

A car flew into the air as if God had kicked it, then slammed back down in the street. Gus turned the steering wheel hard one way, then the other, slipping between erupting fires and metallic husks of derelict vehicles. Ahead, more smoke, periodically pierced by lances of fire, filled the main drag and reduced visibility. He hunched over the steering wheel. Burning debris twirled in the air like birds ablaze. A piece of something plastered itself to the passenger side of the windshield, and Gus yelled in surprise. More explosions thundered. The heat rose in the truck as if he were driving over one monstrous skillet swamped with hot grease. Blazing figures appeared out of the escalating smoke, scaring him and then fascinating him when he realized they were deadheads, staggering along, heedless of the destruction consuming them.

He accelerated another fifty meters before stomping on the brakes. Ahead, storm drains roared like old-fashioned ovens, spewing blinding smoke into the air. Open flames licked the upper lips of the curbs. More blurry shadows appeared on the road, lumbering aimlessly, lit up as if someone had poured gasoline directly over their heads and struck a match. The smoke cleared for a moment, and Gus felt as if Annapolis itself had become hell. Pieces of deadheads lay scattered in the street, their clothing on fire. Legs, arms, and headless torsos lay everywhere, and he realized where the zombie mob had been. They had been right in front of his truck when the storm drain system filled with fumes exploded, blowing the unliving shit clean out of them.

A trench of pavement came into view, the edges blown up and out like terrible wound.

"Red Rye!" Gus shouted and stepped on the gas. The truck surged ahead, running over flaming carcasses and bursting through clumps of gimps, spinning them around while fiery particles flew from their bodies. He ran over dozens, enough to make his jaw clatter, as their bodies crumbled under his tires. The grill smashed dozens of zombies standing as if shell shocked. The roar of the truck's engine filled his ears. What was once a child ran directly at his grill, its small form completely engulfed in fire. Gus wondered if the thing could even see before it was mowed down with a solid *whump*. A flaming head launched itself from the corpse's torso and bounced up and over the hood, causing a jigsaw of cracks to appear across the windshield. Like a springy meteor, the head bounced up and out of Gus's line of sight. More sizzling bodies crowded the truck, and Gus abruptly remembered what he carried in the rear.

Propane tanks!

Something inside him plummeted, and he had the vision of seeing his ass blown away in one great blistering explosion. An intersection loomed up out of the smoke and flame, marked by another smouldering hole no doubt once covered by iron. He veered to the right, crashing into more burning zombies and plastering them against the truck for seconds before they fell off. A head consumed in flame smashed into the passenger window, breaking the glass before rebounding away. Gus screamed, laughed, and drove on, while the captain grinned manically and yelled *OHSHITSHIT-SHITSHIT.* Another lump of fire came through the smashed passenger window and rebounded off the passenger seat, just missing the wicks of the captain's Molotovs, before landing in the foot well. More corpses blocked the road, and Gus plowed through them all, heaving the truck's speeding mass into the blazing forms like a two-ton maul.

The truck swung into a section of road that was clear of debris and cars. Gus took his foot off the gas only long enough to stretch out a leg and stomp on the fragment in the passenger foot well. Behind him, the smoke concealed the land in a thick soup, masking the still burning heaps that appeared like receding glows. He heard more explosions, but he had cleared the heart of it. He'd soon reach the highway that would eventually loop back to his home. He looked into the rear view mirror when he could, catching glimpses of the beast he had unleashed to purify the city.

Purify. Purify was the word of the day. The frantic thought blasted through his adrenaline-spiked mind. Scorched the whole damn lot, he did. Western Oil had probably detonated in the seconds it took for the ignited gas to retrace its destructive flow back to the source.

He gasped for air, as if he'd being holding on to it for the last few minutes. When the truck reached high ground, he pulled over and got out, gazing over the burning bowl of Annapolis. Pops sputtered in the air as unknown flammable containers detonated. He stood by his truck, slack-jawed and staring. Smoke ran through the streets and around buildings like a billowing gray flood, concealing much of the devastation. Fires smouldered like distant beacons, and for a moment, Gus wondered if the land itself would split apart.

He clutched a bottle of rum, but didn't drink it. Taking in the burning buildings below, he believed he would wait until he got home.

19

The city burned.

Like a beast caught in a mighty black cauldron, it thrashed and spat and flickered light and sound. Gus stood on his deck and revelled in what he had created. The fires raged and turned the night sky a frightful orange. Dervishes of heat and wind danced over the rooftops, waving at him with arms of fire. Smoke covered all but the brightest of blazes in a murky, evil gauze.

With one hand on the railing and one on a bottle of Scotch, Gus swayed and stared, red-eyed and perhaps the drunkest he'd ever been. No, scratch that. He was *shit*faced, and his elation at seeing the city burn was every bit as intense as the fires that feasted on Annapolis's flesh and bones.

"Burn, you fuck!" Gus screamed at the city. He raved at the undead and cursed at the rats beneath the city, branding them a frightening cancer that he had *scorched* from the face of the valley. When he finished his first bottle of scotch, he hurled it into the blackness beyond the deck. He returned to the house and fetched two more. The captain lay on one of the lawn chairs, smiling his foppish grin and obviously just as delighted as Gus was at the ending. At the *victory*.

Gus watched Annapolis burn like some triumphant anarchist, alternating between sitting next to the captain and jumping up to lean dangerously over the railing. He had changed from his Nomex gear into his civilian clothes, just to enjoy the show in comfort. He didn't feel the cold, and when the wind did blow, as faint as it was, it carried a sheet of warmth from the valley, like steam blown off something superheated.

He drank until he staggered and vomited over the railing. When he felt ready, he loaded his guts with more Scotch. The liquor spilled on his clothes, and in some cases, he would apply his lips to an arm or the front of his sweater and suck alcohol from the cotton. He drank to Scott, wherever the man might be. He drank to the scorched bones at the base of the cliff. He drank to the memory of Tammy. He drank to Roxanne, despite her being a traitorous bitch who had tried to kill him. With the captain watching him pleasantly and appearing just as smashed, Gus toasted the duct-taped bottle, glad that at least someone he knew was around to see it all through with him.

His senses swam, and reality detached itself from him like a sliced retina. His vision freakishly elongated everything before snapping it back into its original form. He plopped down in the lawn chair, felt the base of his head thump against the padding, and stared at the burning city. Drool hung off his lips and soaked into his beard. The night's cold would chill him at some point, but Gus didn't care as he downed another long pull of the bottle. Annapolis continued burning, the city he had grown up in, played in as a boy, and worked in as a man. Where he met Tammy, the woman who he thought was the love of his life, but who ultimately wasn't. The city burned, removing the places he'd worked on with paint brush and roller, removing the places where he and his friends had drank and laughed on the weekends, destroying the house where he and Scott holed up for days while an army of corpses roamed the hallway below them. Fire consumed the place where he had met Roxanne for the first time, and damned if he didn't even miss her—long for her. Fire devastated the homes of countless people who were already dead and gone, *years* gone, strangers all, yet the very thought of them made his throat constrict, his eyes water, and his sinus cavity fill. Gus's shoulders heaved, his breath hitched, and he cried in the afterglow of the city. He sobbed until he tenderly—or at least as tenderly as a man in his current condition could do—placed the half-empty bottle of Scotch down on the seat beside the captain because he simply didn't want to see another thing break. He wept and watched and sniffed until the emotional pressure was spent, leaving nothing but the long, hitching, body-wracking gasps that came after such an outpouring of grief.

Moaning while wiping his nose and his eyes, Gus eventually got control of himself. He reached, hands trembling, to pick up the bottle of Scotch again. He saluted the captain sitting next to him, and the little bastard saluted back.

He regarded the city. There was one last thing to do, he supposed, and that was to finish the Scotch. And then the next bottle. Then the bottle after that, and the one after that, and so on.

And if he was lucky, if he got it right, *and* if God was on his side, he would finally drink himself to death.

20

He awoke to dusky daylight and stared out at the smouldering gray carcass of a city obscured by smoke. He moaned and shook his head—a mistake, as his head felt as if someone had nailed hot spikes into it. He slowly sat up, cringing as he pulled himself forward, with his legs on either side of the chair, and placed his head in his hands.

"God*damnit.*"

The city was still there, rooftops barely seen through the thick clouds. Here and there, he spied the orange gleam of flames, still feasting on the bones of Annapolis. He looked over and met the steady, smiling gaze of the captain.

"Little fuckin' . . . *pygmy.*"

Shaking his head, he realized he didn't see the last bottle of Scotch. Leaning over, he saw it on the floor, perhaps three swallows left in the bottle. He'd passed out before finishing it. Gus didn't want any more. He was just glad he hadn't broken the bottle.

He inspected himself and sighed in disgust. The crotch of his jeans was wet. He doubted he had spilled booze on his junk, so that left only one possibility, especially since he had no urgent need to take a leak.

"Well, shit."

That was all he needed, waking up—fucking alive—to the world on fire, and realizing that his first attempt at suicide had failed miserably, and that he'd pissed himself in the process. "Goddamnit." He got to his feet, feeling the almost crippling aches in his joints and lower extremities. His stomach lurched, and his senses spun wildly. He collapsed on the deck, cheek to the wood, and gulped air like a dying fish. He pulled himself to the edge of the deck, where his stomach finally rebelled. He started to vomit, but clamped his mouth shut, forcing it back. Trapped between an unflinching sphincter and a closed upper exit, his stomach hurled with even greater force and blasted a stinging gush of puke out his nose. Gus choked, opened his mouth, and vomitus heaved out that way as well, leaving him in a stream of color. Consciousness left him, came back, left him once more, and finally returned. His limbs shook spasmodically, and a weak "god . . . damn" got lost in the barest of breezes.

He squeezed his eyes shut, content to just lie there, and hoped that he could defy the odds and not shit himself as well.

Somewhere in the next couple of hours, he crawled to the door of the outhouse and pulled himself in, not even bothering to close the door behind him. He stayed there for an hour, collapsed against the wall and defecating at an angle, wondering if he could light a match and blow himself to hell that way.

He somehow made it back into the house and into the kitchen. Panting, sweating cold rivulets, he drank water from a jug. He shuffled into the living room, up the stairs, and into the bathroom. He stripped off his pants and underwear, and splashed water onto his privates, cleaning up as best as he could without taking a bath. He somehow got into fresh jeans and underwear. Not wanting to sleep on the mess that was his bed, he descended the steps again. With a *whuff*, he landed on the sofa as if it were a raised oasis in a desert of aches and pain. Lying there, face pressed into the cushions and one eye squeezed shut, Gus hoped that his innards settled enough at some point so that he might be able to have a comforting drink of rum.

With that thought, he passed out again.

He woke up halfway through the day, or at least he thought it was halfway, and listened to the sound of nothing. Outside, the world burned, framed in his windows, but he felt far removed from it. That thought made him smile feebly. It was warm in the house, and he sensed that spring was rushing in. The snow would be melting—very fast down in Annapolis.

In the evening, he rose and got a bottle of rum. The binge from the night before was over, and it was a new night to celebrate. Bottle in hand, he wandered out of the house, noting how the snow had retreated during the day. Patches of yellow grass lay bare in the fading daylight. He walked back to the deck and stood there for a while, watching the fires.

Gus shook his head, wondering if he'd done the right thing.

He sat down and drank. When he felt his body couldn't take anymore, he gathered the captain from the nearby chair and brought him back inside.

Something tugged him back to consciousness. He opened his eyes and stared at the bare, rustic timbers of the roof overhead, gloomy in the dimming light of the living room. The victory party had lasted for what felt like days. At some point, Scotch got left behind, and he'd switched to the more palatable Jack Daniels. Gus remembered wandering through the house on a drunken expedition, staggering to the deck to gaze at the still-burning city, and then going back inside the house. He recalled managing to get down half a pot of macaroni and cheese, the only solid food he'd consumed in a while. How long exactly had the binge lasted? He had no idea.

Drink.

Lord above, he believed he'd drunk a lake in the last little while. He groaned, feeling how his guts felt both empty and tortured. His head rolled on his shoulders, and he stared at the dark material covering the sofa where he lay. He labored to get into a sitting position. The captain rested in the corner of the couch where his feet had been. Across the room, the curtains were open, revealing a dark stew of smoke. Still burning. Annapolis was apparently set for a slow cook. The best roasts were done at such a temperature. That thought made his face split with a hoarse chuckle.

Shaking his head, he looked to his right and met the black gaze of a rat perched atop the back of a chair. Right next to the still-standing Christmas tree.

Perhaps it was because he'd been so blasted in the last couple of days. Perhaps it was because his only companion had been a duct-taped bottle, but the appearance of the rat didn't surprise him. Not for those first few seconds, anyway. The vermin sized him up in turn, its whiskers twitching in the scant light, nose in the air, hairless tail just barely glimpsed behind it.

Gus took a breath. He was looking at a *rat* in his *house*. Realization hit him like a cold spray of water. In his peripheral vision, something moved. He looked and caught the bobbing form of another rat scurrying from a corner to slip around the end of the sofa.

"Where the fuck did you come from?" He looked around for his boots. They lay against the far window, next to the boarded-up sliding door.

Eyeing the rat on the chair, Gus crossed the living room and pulled on a steel-toed boot. Picking up the second boot, Gus noticed something strange about the rodent's side. Yanking on the boot and stamping his foot on the hardwood floor, Gus noticed something else that chilled him.

The rat didn't run at the noise. It didn't even so much as a flinch.

Gus moved toward the rodent, but stopped after three cautious steps, peering at it in mounting horror. The thing on the rat's side was a wound, an open wound large enough that he could see its viscous innards. The dead thing tensed, no doubt sensing, or *smelling,* fresh meat nearby.

"Oh, Jesus," Gus whispered, drawing back in horror.

The rat leaped off the chair and charged.

Gus stepped back, his shoulder crashing against the glass pane. He kicked the dead thing with all the strength he could muster. The steel-toed boot connected and sent the vermin flying. The zombie-rat smacked into the far wall and crumpled in a shadowy heap near the staircase.

A moment later, Gus spotted movement to his right. Another rat scooted across the floor, heading in the direction of the bedrooms. The second visitor appeared around the sofa's upholstered corner, whiskers twitching. Yet another one ran out of the kitchen, its bulk as long as his foot, moving in a zigzagging pattern. The things made no noise. Not even a squeak.

Steeling himself, Gus walked to the sofa and stomped on the rat peeking around the corner. The body flattened underneath his heavy sole and left very little blood. The rat from the kitchen came close, and Gus stomped on that one as well, twisting his heel to ensure the thing was dead. He scanned the living room and spotted three more of the greasy intruders keeping close to the walls. He moved toward the hallway leading to the bedrooms, but several more wandered into the living room from the kitchen.

Gus danced on his attackers, flattening their small bodies under his boots and leaving pulpy stains on the wood. In threes and fours, more rats joined the fray, swollen things with their mouths open, coming from the hallway and the kitchen. They attacked his boots, actually trying to bite through the thick rubber. He kicked and crushed them as they came within reach, no longer afraid of the things, even though some of the rats' bodies were the length of his hand.

He let out a battle scream as he did his plodding jig on the rats. They didn't scamper off. If anything, they came faster, running at him in their odd, scurrying fashion, only to have their bodies squashed before even getting in a bite.

Gus paused and took a deep breath. More rats were coming into the living room, sweeping in like a black jet of foul water. A sick feeling of horror and revulsion made his stomach clench dangerously. The things moved so low to the floor, they crawled over the smears of the dead and dragged little oily rivulets behind them. They poured in from all sides, as if he stood in a shallow basin. He roared, keeping his elbows high as he kicked. He ground in his heels. The floor became covered in a black paste.

Killing by foot expended a lot of energy. He got tired faster than he thought he would. He walked toward the kitchen. The rats flowed toward him, speckling the floor at an alarming rate. Gus kept moving and, once he got to the island, hoisted his butt up to sit on it. Below his dangling boots, rats pooled against the base in a thin, writhing mass. Some placed their forepaws against the wood and craned their necks up at him. He shook his head in disbelief.

They were coming in from every direction, every opening. Running a hand over his head, Gus turned to look outside, but had forgotten that the windows in the kitchen were boarded up. A sound reached his ears, jerking his attention toward the bedroom hallway.

With a huff, he jumped down, squashing the unlife from several rats as he landed. He crossed the floor quickly, ignoring the rats unless they got directly in his path. By the door, he flicked on the kitchen light. The lights came on, but instead of fleeing, the rats seemed to thicken, unafraid.

Gus turned a corner, lighting up the house as he came across the power switches, and stopped in his tracks at the front entry.

The hole the rats spurted through in the base of the door was as large as the toes of his boot. Rats squeezed through and milled around the floor like a cesspool about to overflow. The sounds of claws and teeth scratching and gnawing came from beyond. The wooden door quivered at its base from a terrible grinding pressure being applied from outside.

Something crawling up his leg made Gus glance down. With a macabre energy, the rats at his ankles piled up and over each other to breach the upper lip of his boot. He jumped, shaking the creatures off and sending them tumbling. He mashed them into the floor, stomping on heads and bodies. With dawning horror, he saw that the rats whose lower bodies he crushed lived on and persisted in trying to reach him. As with their biped cousins, the head was the money shot.

The notion that he had to plug the hole came into his head. He needed to block the opening and then brace the lower portion of the door. Once that was done, he could go about the unsavory task of killing the rest of the rats in the house.

With a roar, he soccer-kicked a swath through the invaders around his ankles, bouncing several off the walls. Nearby was a waist-high shoe cabinet, and Gus pulled it from the wall. Grunting, he flipped it up and over, landing it upside down on the floor. He sat on the upended cabinet, crushing the rats beneath it. Using his legs, he pushed the cabinet against the door, satisfied that the weight of the thing would keep them out.

He whirled on the rats at his ankles and tore through them, heading for the garage. They chased him, charged him, and he kicked against their stream, dashing several against walls and flattening others beneath his soles. The second entrance through the mudroom came into view. He reached out and flicked on the overhead light.

The rats had chewed their way through there as well, except three holes were made at the base of the outside door instead of one. Wood chips and splinters flew as a steady pulse of rats squirmed through the opening. Gus looked around, but saw nothing to block the holes. He plodded over to the door leading to the garage and yanked it open. Sweat dropped from his forehead, and for the first time, he realized he was breathing hard.

Once inside the garage, he slammed the door on his pursuers and switched on the light. The garage door was intact and the place appeared empty, but Gus stopped in his tracks, clamping his airways shut for greater quiet. Something rustled against the lower part of the garage door, heavy enough to gently rattle it. Metal comprised the door itself, so Gus wasn't worried about the rats chewing their way through.

Moving hastily past his parked van and pickup, he looked through the rectangular windows set in the garage door. Though darkness was descending upon the mountain, he could still see a black stream of rats flowing from the gate toward to the house. The scene reminded him of old nature shows depicting swarming ants, and *that* thought dried up any remaining spit in his mouth. The rats ran in an ever-widening sheet that reminded him of spilled blood. They rushed toward the house, where their numbers went beyond his angle of sight. He knew where they were—right at his goddamn doorstep, gnawing their way into his home.

He leaned heavily against the door. He thought he'd taken the fight to the rats. By exploding the tanks of fuel, he thought he'd fried the whole lot of them underneath the ground. He'd flooded the storm drains and scorched Annapolis above and below. He'd thought he killed every last one of them.

Somehow, however, they had survived. Worst, they came up the side of the mountain, seeking the one who had set their world on fire. Obviously wanting a bite.

The gate. The gate was the key. If he could seal the gate and stem the flow onto the grounds, he could mop up the rest. Thinking of how he could do exactly that, Gus turned and went to his locker. He wasn't going anywhere without his armor. He wasn't doing *anything* without his weapons.

The first thing he did, as so many times before, was reach for the bottle of whatever he'd had the foresight to stash up in his locker.

There was no bottle.

Downed it when I got in the other day and didn't replace it.

Gus winced, but then shook it off and got to work. He had no time to lament over a lack of booze. He'd drink plenty after he kicked the undead asses of the latest army assaulting him. He hauled on the protective ninja mask and got into the pants and coat of the Nomex gear. After slapping the elbow and knee pads into place, he strapped on the neck brace, the one still damaged from the last encountered with the animated vermin. The motorcycle helmet went on last, as if it were the switch that changed him from Gus to Mean Fucker. He regarded the motorcycle leather he'd worn so often before, wanting to wear it, but knowing it wouldn't last out there.

Then he gathered the tools he would need for war.

Behind him, the door to the house rattled in its frame.

He had two shotguns, but he opted for the Benelli. The bat went into the sheath across his back. The Ruger went down one boot, and the Bowie went down the other. He loaded up the shotgun and bandolier, slinging the belt over his head and shoulder, making an X across his chest. The leather belt went around his waist, tying off any attack if they got up underneath.

Gus stopped and was about to pull on a pair of thick workman's gloves, thinking that he was forgetting something. Then he remembered the Molotovs.

He looked at his workbench and saw them standing there, almost three dozen remaining firebombs, all ready and willing to make big blazing impressions on any that dared assault the mountain.

"You boys ready to fuck some folks up?" Gus asked them.

Hooah, they growled.

Gus got out two lighters and stuffed one inside the elastic of his glove. Another thought brought him up short. The captain wasn't with him. Holy shit. The captain was still out there on the sofa.

That fucking sailor had gone through hell and back with him. There was *no* way Gus was leaving his companion out there.

The door shook harder, and a small section at the base buckled inward. Gus searched the garage until he located an old ruck sack. He stuffed seven firebombs into the bag and slung it over his right shoulder.

The door shivered violently on its hinges. Parts of it buckled and splintered.

"Little bastards want in, boys," Gus seethed to the remaining Molotovs on the bench. "What say we make ourselves known?"

Hooah!

Feeling as though he had enough spunk to fuck up a dozen undead hordes, Gus went to the door and threw it open.

21

Rats filled the small entryway and hall, turning the floor into a writhing surface that flowed around Gus up past his ankles. He shivered from feeling the press of twisting bodies against the rubber of his boots. He fired the Benelli, obliterating a chunk of the vermin and revealing the floor underneath for a second. Yelling at the invaders, Gus shot repeatedly, destroying huge shredded holes in the attacking carpet of tooth and claw. Red plastic casings flew from the ejector. He emptied the shotgun into the mass, then slammed the door, shoved his back against it, and started to reload. He thought better of what he was doing and went to his locker, where he still had a few boxes of shells remaining.

As he thumbed the third shell into the weapon, the door quivered.

"Nobody told you about me, eh?" Gus snarled as he shoved home the last shell. "I got a reputation around these parts."

He pulled the door. With a battle cry, he unloaded the shotgun, wrecking terrible wounds in the tide. No sooner did he kill, however, then more rats rushed in, crawling over the devastated corpses of their brethren and immediately filling the small areas where he'd gotten glimpses of the floor.

Gus stomped, crushing twos and threes with each strike. Each time he lifted his leg, rats fell from his lower shin. The sound of their bodies rustling against each other chilled his blood, that low droning whisper telling him of the increasing volume of vermin in his house. So *many*! There were so goddamn *many*!

He lashed out at them, feeling several behind him now mounting an attack at his calves. He crushed bodies, skulls, and limbs. Rat tails spiked the mass and bobbed crazily, yellow and sick looking. The footing became treacherous as the pulped bodies of the undead rats began to pile up, becoming slippery lumps of mashed guts and flesh. His boot slipped at one point, and he stumbled against the wall. He straightened, surprised to feel a rat clamp onto the material covering the V of his bent knee. More snapped at the Nomex, struggling to climb up his lower legs. Gus violently brushed them off and crushed them underfoot. He grabbed a fistful of tails and whipped three of the creatures into the wall, their heads exploding. That one gesture threw him off balance, and he almost lost his grip on the Benelli. His back slapped up against a wall, and he had to steady himself before shuffling back into the garage, reluctantly abandoning the captain.

He tried to close the door, but rats jammed into the closing crevice. Gus dropped the shotgun and kicked at the rats, but the bodies were legion, and with every boot he gave them, more struggled into the shrinking gap. Crouching and pressing his shoulder into the door, he felt the wood shake from the weight of the onslaught, and darkly realized that he *might* have a problem.

He quickly extracted his Bowie knife from his left boot. He slashed downward, decapitating the heads of several, sawing his way through the rest, still pressing his bulk against the door to force it shut. The rats seem to have no fear of being cut or pinched in half by the closing door, and again a stab of alarm burst within Gus.

With a final shove, he sealed the door, nipping off several heads and snouts. Twitching whiskers lined the wooden seam. Shutting the door gave him no respite as the rats inside the garage still gnawed on the Nomex, gnashing at the protective material sheathing his legs and lower body. The ferocity of their attack momentarily stunned him.

But only for a second.

He did a maniacal jig, flattening the rodents as they crowded around his feet. His strength ebbing, he aimed his boot heel at the last remaining few and, one by one, crushed the unlife from their small bodies with angry grunts.

The door shook from the pressure beyond. Gus reloaded the Benelli, thinking about the outside gate, the house, and the rats that only a door's thickness kept at bay. He held the shotgun at arm's length and realized it was next to useless. His boots were doing much more damage, but he couldn't kill the army like that without exhausting himself. Watching the door crumbling second by second, its base thrumming from the monstrous assault, Gus knew that all the doors in the house would suffer the same fate. That thought alone made his anger and hate resurface, swamping his doubt.

He went to the outer garage door, gripped the bottom, and hoisted it up. Rats crawled in as he looped underneath the gap and closed the door behind him, trapping some inside the garage. The rest came at him, but he kicked them away. In the diminishing sunlight, he jogged across the grounds, toward the wall. The rats coming under the gate flowed toward the house. A few stragglers broke away from the column and came after him, but he ignored them as he stood back and examined the holes in the gate. Gus threw himself at the ragged openings, crushing heads and bodies as they struggled to enter the compound.

"Little shits. Little fuckin' *shits!*"

He flattened an untold number of rats, squishing them as they pulled themselves through the tunnels in the wood. Sweat ran down his face and his sides, but he kept killing. When he directed his attention at one section, rats clawed away the dead and forced their way through. The rats already inside the gate stopped marching toward the house and attacked him from behind, nipping at his heels and lower legs with feral abandon. The Nomex held, and he squashed even more until he looked up from killing and spied a ladder against the wall.

Gus bounded over the furry corpses and scampered up the ladder rungs, thinking to drop his load of Molotovs on the invaders on the other side of the wall. He reached the top of the wall and pressed his chest against it.

And gasped.

A tsunami had come up the side of the mountain. An unholy wave of fur and white stringy tail and tooth and claw surged around the husks of unmoving cars, pushing against the wall and gate. The rodent army reached at least as far back as the treeline, where shadow melted their hides into the darkness. The scope of the assault paralyzed Gus and made his mouth hang open. *Millions*, his mind whispered. *Millions.*

A crack of wood hooked his attention. The base of the gate bulged in places and Gus thought he saw a puppy-sized head spear through the wood in a burst of splinters—a rat's head, a *big* rat's head.

He fumbled at the ruck sack and pulled out a Molotov. He got out his lighter and lit the fuse. Taking aim, he slung at the mass below the wall where it exploded in a wave of flame, illuminating countless rats. He lit another and threw it, the firebomb erupting in a swirl of fire on the road, dead on target.

"Yeah," Gus growled, regaining some of his lost confidence while lighting another. He tossed the third. The bottle shattered, and a puddle of fire enveloped a section of the creatures. The snap and crackle of burning flesh rose above the almost electrical hum coming from the army of rats. He threw the last four Molotovs at the dead in rapid succession, lighting up the night when the firebombs crashed into their targets.

The rats burned. Some of the smaller ones winked out of sight, smothered by the larger bodies of their brethren, while several stopped in their tracks and died in tiny blazes.

Others, however, forged ahead blindly until the gate stopped them.

Gus felt his stomach drop when several fiery corpses smacked into the gate's wooden base and ignited others. In seconds, a fire rose and grew as a steady stream of burning flesh fed the conflagration.

"Oh, dear Jesus."

He couldn't believe his eyes, couldn't believe that his bombardments just might be the key to bringing down his best defense.

And he had inadvertently caused it.

Feeling sick, Gus hurried down the ladder. He needed more firebombs from the garage. His only chance was to lob Molotovs upon them when they got inside the wall. Laboring through the rats already inside the compound, he returned to the house and, with a heave, opened the garage door just enough to get through, then closed it behind him. Once inside, he dispatched the rats that had followed him with his boots, and crushed the ones trapped inside from when he first opened the garage door.

He paused for a few moments to gather his strength, then made his way to the Molotovs and refilled his pack. Once ready, he went to the door leading into the house and placed his back to it. Sounds of the rats' incessant gnawing made him set his jaw. The door wasn't going to be there much longer. They would chew their way through it as they had with the outer gate. *High ground*, blared through his head, and he thought of the attic. The wood pressed against his shoulder vibrated with growing intensity. If he was going to get going, he had to do it right then.

He threw open the door.

Rats fell into the garage, almost knee high. For seconds, Gus could only stand and stare, mouth dropping open at the sight before him. Rats covered everything. They filled the mudroom, the hall, and the floor beyond. They crawled over each other and attacked his shins. The thought of actually pushing his way through that many rats almost made him retreat back into the garage, but that wasn't where he wanted to go. He wanted to go *up*.

He kicked and stomped on rats as he struggled to close the door behind him. Closing the door seemed important, as it was one less place the rats had penetrated. Once he shut it, he turned around. Holding the Benelli in front of him, he waded forward, stepping with caution and placing a shoulder against the nearby wall. The weight of the rats sucked at his boots like quicksand. Twice, he almost fell, his feet slipping from under him and only saving himself by flinging his back against the wall. He got past the mudroom and into the hall, trudged a few more feet, and turned the corner into the living room. The rats covered the floor, and a grinning captain came into view, still on the sofa, as if everything was just jolly *rosy*.

Gus lunged for the stairs, fastening a hand on the railing and pulling himself from the thrashing floor. Rats, their jaws clamped onto loose folds of the Nomex, went with him. He slapped most away and rolled his lower back against the bannisters, scrubbing off any clingers. A quick glance to the side showed him the rodents had toppled the Christmas tree. That infuriated him, and he crushed any trying to scale the lower steps. Seconds later, he turned and fled up the stairs, vowing to return for the old sailor.

He reached the top and saw the dangling string of the attic stairway. He grabbed it and pulled. The door came down with a metallic yawn. He unfolded the steps and bolted up into the attic. He turned to pull the steps up behind him and froze.

Rats were slinking up the stairwell to the second floor. Beyond them and rising like a writhing, black surf were hundreds more of the undead vermin. He quickly brought up the folding stairs, then pulled the chain for the single light bulb. The skylight beckoned, the night beyond beginning to deepen. He threw open the latch and pried open the window. Stars shone through wisps of smoke from the city. The incline of the roof was perhaps forty degrees and coated with red-brown shingles. He twisted around and saw the peak of the roof six or seven feet away. He crawled through the window, then climbed until he reached the apex.

On the other side of the house, the snow had melted enough so that he couldn't distinguish between what was rat and what wasn't.

Then he heard the crack.

He looked toward the gate and saw the glow of the fire on the other side. He heard another snap and felt his stomach lurch. The rats, being undead, were no longer afraid of the open flames, and while a section burned, there were still enough holes in the base for the creatures to worm through.

With another deep crack, a section of timber buckled inward. A virtual deluge of indistinct blackness gushed inside the stone walls. More timbers surrendered to the jaws gnashing away at them; another gout of foulness erupted inside the compound. Flames flickered through the breach and burned at the edges as the second river of invaders merged with the first.

All flowing toward the house.

"You *fuckers*!" Gus straddled the rooftop, pulled off his rucksack, and opened it.

"Ready, boys?" he asked the captain's marines.

Hooah.

He pulled out one of the bottles and his lighter. He lit the wick, and a high flame split the night. He heaved the firebomb toward the gate. Its flame fluttered as it fell about twelve feet in front of the wall. The ground erupted in a flash, throwing back the dark and revealing an area teeming with rats. The fire flickered and dimmed as the invaders ran over them, quickly dousing the fire with their bodies. Gus lit a second Molotov and heaved it. The bomb fell about ten feet short of the gate, but ignited more surface area, and more rats. Some of the creatures caught fire and streaked away from the impact zone, like bright rays from a dying sun.

"*Fuckers!*" Gus lit and flung the rest of the Molotovs, one by one. The fifth one actually made it within feet of the gate, and Gus almost wished it hadn't for it only revealed the army rushing inside the wall. The sight paralyzed Gus for seconds until he shook free of it, lit the sixth firebomb, and sent it sailing through the night sky, the burning wick fluttering. That one landed short, too, but went up with a *whoosh*, setting vermin ablaze.

Too many, Gus thought dismally, *too goddamn many*. He threw the last bomb at the ground, knowing he would only kill a mere handful. Even as his last bomb went up, the second and third fires were suppressed by the sheer unflinching mass of the attacking rats. The seemingly unending torrent ripped through the growing holes in the wall, and he felt a fresh stab of fear. An *ocean* had come for him.

"Jesus." Gus had about two dozen more Molotovs in the garage, if he could *get* to them, but not even that many would stop the unholy force that had come seeking his flesh. The futility of his situation hit hard.

How had they found him? They were fucking dead rats, for Christ's sake!

Then, he remembered the poor dead bastard out on the highway.

"You're my marker."

He recalled the way the rats branched out in search of meat, how they had sniffed him out. They had smelled the meat on the highway, all those corpses he'd left as an experiment, drawing them closer to his home.

The bodies outside the wall . . . He'd left the bodies of the first wave of gimps to rot; the fire hadn't destroyed all of them, then the snow had come. Later, the snow had melted enough for the stench of rotting meat to be carried to the noses of the hungry rats. And when they came, no doubt coaxed on by the burning city, they *all* came to feast, just like a *Connect the Dots* puzzle.

And he was the last point.

While he had been drinking and maintaining his shitfaced high, playing with suicide, the enemy walked right up to his front door and chewed their way into his castle.

22

As he sat and theorized about just how the undead plague below arrived at his house, one riveting thought stabbed through it all and demanded his attention.

What the hell was he going to do about them?

He heard wood whine in the direction of the gate, and knew another piece of it had been weakened by flame or torn asunder by the unimaginable numbers. Even if he got aboard the beast or the pickup and rolled over them, sooner or later the vehicles would probably only spin out, and he'd be stuck. Gus didn't want to find out what would happen then.

He considered jumping off the roof, as it was only a forty-foot drop at the most. Even with his helmet off and diving head first, the cushion of all those bodies might break his fall enough for him to survive. *Survive until they chewed through the Nomex*, his mind added.

Then, he remembered the propane tanks in the pickup.

Four of them, all waiting for him.

One liter of propane equaled two hundred and seventy liters of vapor.

There was enough of a boom lying in his garage to make him smile. Surviving the blast didn't enter his mind. Why should he, with the things he'd done? He'd killed people—living, breathing people—in cold blood. No, there was no point in surviving, and if he had to go, he much rather be blown up than scarfed down.

Swinging his leg back over, he slid halfway down the incline of the roof and hooked his arms into the open skylight. He wormed his way back into the attic and regarded the closed trapdoor.

"Hooah," he muttered unconvincingly.

The door opened with that familiar yawn of springs, and Gus gazed at the landing. It was alive with rats moving in that jerky crawl of theirs. With a kick, he extended the stairs, then he grabbed the Benelli and descended. He jumped the last two steps and squashed several rats underfoot. Others converged on him. Shuffling through them, he got into position to see the main level.

Rats flooded the downstairs up to the second step. There was no way to reach the garage. He was cut off by a lake of vermin. Before his mind could argue, he slapped the visor down, readied the Benelli, and started firing as he went down the steps. Shredded bodies flew, bounced off the stairs by the shotgun's semi-automatic scream. A *huge* rat, perhaps the size of a small dog and the biggest Gus had ever seen, rose above the horde like a monster surfacing from the deep. A stained snout turned in his direction, homing in and baring broken teeth. Formidable, scarred, and battle-ready, it seemed unhampered by its missing eye and lack of ears. Gus allowed it a whole five seconds of existence out of sheer awe before disintegrating its skull with one shot, spraying the rest of the pack in fleshy matter.

The gun clicked dry, and Gus mashed into the tide, the rats rising up above his ankles. He struggled against them, felt their maws bite down on the Nomex. His boot slipped off the back of several large rats, and he stumbled to his knees. The vermin rose to his chest in one frightening wave. Rats assaulted his head, banging off his visor. He brought the Benelli around, pushing off the writhing layers. They bit into his gloves and crawled up his thighs.

Using the Benelli as a crutch, Gus pushed himself to his feet. He stumbled again in the rising swell and crashed against a wall, one arm flayed out for balance. Rats scurried up and covered him, biting and clawing for purchase. He pawed them from his front and shoulders. He punched at the ones hanging off his hips. His hand grabbed one exceptionally large rat and smashed it snout-first into the wall. The garage door lay only ten feet ahead of him, and he pushed against the rush of bodies, heaving and straining, his legs burning from the exertion.

He fell a third time, face first, and a rush of dead animals enveloped him. A multitude of tiny feet scampered up his back while jaws fastened to his neck brace. Gus screamed and released the Benelli, lashing out with his fists. He pulled himself to his knees. Rats clung from the ruck sack by their jaws. It took several punches to dislodge the foul, twisting bodies, and he winced with each connection.

"*Jesus Christ!*" he roared. Only five feet away from the door, he stretched out with a gloved hand, slapping its wooden surface. Straining, he pulled the rest of his body through the ferocious tide. He gripped the doorknob, turned it, and lunged for the opening, balancing the trick of opening it enough for him to get through yet restricting as many of the rats as possible from following.

Vermin and man spilled into the garage, and Gus whirled, dug in both feet, and heaved the door closed with all he had left. Rats wormed through the shrinking gap until getting caught and crushed between the door and the jamb. Black blood oozed and spurted. He yanked out his Bowie and sawed at the more stubborn ones as he shouldered the door, covering the floor in gristly pieces.

With a click, the trembling door finally closed. The lower part bowed inward with a straining whine, already weakened by earlier gnawing. Panting, Gus rushed to his locker and tipped it toward the door. It landed with a metallic crash, and he shoved its weight up against the door, barricading it and buying a few minutes.

The several dozen rats that had slipped in when he opened the door attacked. He got to stomping, and a long, strength-depleting minute later, crushed the body and then head of the last one attempting to bite through the rubber covering his ankle.

Swallowing and wishing for a drink, Gus gazed upon the beast and the pickup. Wasting no time, he climbed into the back of the pickup and felt along the torpedo lengths of each of the four propane cylinders. He gripped the metal covers protecting the valves and removed them, one after the other, exposing knurled brass rings.

Gasping, he wrestled with the first propane cylinder and pushed it out of the truck. It landed on the concrete with a clatter. He upended the second one and let it strike and slide off the first, then did the same with the third. He opened the valve of the fourth cylinder and left it in the pickup. He didn't know if the thing was hissing, as he couldn't hear it over the racket at the inner door and the scratching outside of the garage.

He picked up the sledge hammer and hopped out of the truck bed. With one swing, he took the valve off the first tank with a frightening crack and rush of air. Discovering he was still alive, he knocked the valves off the other two before dropping the hammer. He moved some milk crates underneath each cylinder, allowing the liquefied gas to spurt onto the floor in an ever widening pool. He stood back, smelling the fumes as a cloud of milky vapor filled the garage. There was still time left, and he locked on to the remaining Molotovs on the work bench. He still had his lighter. He looked back into the pickup and saw the last length of fuse.

At the door, the barest of shavings, like drill bits on the verge of punching through, appeared in its surface just above the locker.

The idea popped into his head, and he laughed out loud. A laugh of a person knowing the end was very, very near, and that he was going to make the monsters outside of his door regret marching up the side of his mountain to make war on him. He only wished he had a drink of something to see things through.

The garage door splintered in places. White slivers of wood hung from points where teeth gnashed through.

"Red Rye!" He grabbed two of the assembled Molotovs. He cracked the necks across the bench and shook the fuses away. Glass fell tinkling to the floor.

He held the bottles over his head and doused himself with gasoline.

23

He emptied four of the Molotovs over the fire retardant Nomex before feeling for the lighter tucked inside his glove. He wouldn't light up in the house, remembering the promise he'd made Tammy so long ago when he was given a cheap three-dollar cigar from a friend at work.

He twisted the ruck sack around to his front and packed eight of the Molotovs. The others he smashed on the floor. He got the fuse out of the truck—sixty feet of goodness, enough to get to the house and the yard. He tied one end of the fuse to the nearest propane cyclinder's broken valve, stepping into a pool of the gas and catching a sweet whiff. He tethered the other end to his left forearm, suddenly wishing he still had the Benelli. The door to the house trembled as if a thousand tiny fists pounded upon it. Trailing the fuse from his arm, he went to the door and studied it. Every second he waited, the fumes from the spilled propane filled the garage a little more.

A mixture of fear and anger thrummed in his chest and limbs, and he channeled that new reserve of energy into pulling the locker away from the door. The door bulged; wood fibers crackled and snapped. Whole heads appeared.

Taking a deep breath, Gus opened the door.

Rats fell forward, writhing around his knees and boots. They filled the hallway, an unbelievable thigh-high black carpet of unliving, thrashing sewage. Rats flowed up from the stairway leading to the basement. Gus didn't think about it; he only went forward. It was thirty feet to the windows in the living room, but with the waves of rats, that might as well be miles. The undead, some as large as kittens, embraced him with tooth and claw as he pushed forward into their angry surf. They swarmed his legs, crotch, and lower belly. His balls felt slowly mashed, causing an aching nausea to creep into his guts. He shoved against them, shuffling his feet forward into the mass.

They latched on to his arms, and he swung and crushed them against the walls. He felt some of them climb his back and bite onto his neck brace. Gus violently slapped them off, but more snapped on to his arms and hands. One rat scampered up his arm against a wall and slammed into the side of his helmet. Gus reached up and crushed its head in a fist, then slung it away.

Press forward. It felt as if he were pushing against wet concrete.

This isn't working.

He got out his lighter only by waving his arms around over his head to avoid the maws snapping at him. He reached into the rucksack, pulled out a Molotov, and lit the fuse, intending to throw it.

He spotted the captain's duct-taped ass on the distant sofa, far and away from his intended path. A layer of hairy backs was almost level with the cushion.

They're inside the perimeter! *the captain roared.*

"Wait!" Gus shouted and swung at his attackers. "I'll get you—"

You'll do no such thing! the old sailor returned, and for the first time, Gus saw a look of concern on the foppish officer's face. *Light the bastards up!*

Then, the rats swarmed the captain's armored form, and he was gone in a flurry of hair and rotting flesh.

Seeing his last friend disappear sent Gus over the edge. He lashed out at the rats with all the power left in his limbs, mashing several into the floor and walls.

"You little—"

The gasoline on his upper body ignited, and he transformed into a living torch. In frightened reflex, he smashed the Molotov against the nearby wall, and sent a wave of fire arcing over it like a bright orange stroke from a painter's brush that ended in a mire of vermin. The flames scorched the rats, turning them into fiery lumps that popped and sizzled. A sheet of fire rose up in front of his visor, and seeing unchecked fire that close unnerved Gus and switched off all cohesive thought except for *stupid, stupid, stupid.*

Gus threw himself forward. Adrenalin spiked through him. Instead of shuffling along the floor, he dragged his feet up, using the bodies beneath him as squirming steps. He muscled his way through the shifting sea of rats, gaining five feet almost immediately. Rats *still* clawed onto his back, biting, scratching, digging. The flames scorched them. He reached the corner of the hallway, latched his hands onto it, and pulled himself around it. The fire burned though the thin straps of the ruck sack, and Gus felt them drag to his stomach.

Then, the rest of the Molotovs went up.

Gus felt the bottles break. He felt the heat of the fireball pressing into stomach. His entire body erupted in sweat as if he were melting. Dark fire coated his visor, licking it voraciously, causing blossoms of surreal patterns to explode and expand before his eyes. He screamed and scrambled forward. Another sheet of flame engulfed his head. The temperature rose, cooking him in his own gear. He got his feet under him and pushed into the living room. The fire gnawed through the gloves, licking his hands and making him squeal. A wall of glass loomed in front of him, and he threw himself toward it.

In mid-air, he heard a *whump* behind him and saw a reflection of himself and the living room in the dark surface of the window.

A gush of fire erupted from the hall, howling at its infernal birth and setting the sea of hair and tails ablaze. The very air became flame. Charcoaled lumps flew, consumed in the firestorm as it consumed everything in its path.

Including Gus.

He crashed through the window just as the explosion blew out most of the windows and engulfed the house in a bright fist of orange. He ran blindly, blazing from head to toe, transformed into a shrieking, feral thing, smoking as if dipped into the sun itself. Mindless and insane with agony, he sprinted toward the cliff's edge, not knowing anything except *the painthepainohChristthePAIN!* His visor cracked and dissolved. Flames licked at his flesh, lighting up his facial hair, dissolving the gloves on his hands.

He didn't know where he was going. In his self-immolating state, he didn't care.

Gus screamed one last time as his feet unexpectedly left the ground.

And if anyone were standing below the cliff, looking up, they would have seen a spectacular flash of orange throwing back the dark...

And a howling figure streaking across the star-filled night sky, limbs flailing, like an angry comet crashing to earth.

24

Consciousness came back to him when, really, Gus was happier in the dark. Wincing and feeling a tightness about his face, he tried to push himself up. Agony lanced up both of his arms, causing his eyes to open wide. Moaning, he rolled over and felt something hard at his back. Both of his arms refused to do anything other than shriek and be slabs of meat. He inspected himself through the melted wreck of his visor. The strap of his bat sheath was still there, and he recognized the weight on his back. He lay on the ground, in a shrinking snow drift. The Nomex was scorched to raw fibers. He did an agonized stomach curl and got to a sitting position. Semi-melted slabs of rubber covered his feet. The Bowie knife remained in one boot, but he didn't see the Ruger. Above him, pungent evergreen boughs, snapped in places from where they broke his fall, obscured the sun. Smoke filled the sky, but he could see the cliff's edge where he had fallen. He even saw the deck of his house.

He was below the cliff, just back from the base. Somewhere to the right would be a charred pile of bodies. He still couldn't move his arms.

Broken, *he realized*. Both fuckin' arms.

He struggled to his feet, thankful his legs still worked, but his poor feet tortured him with the squish and pain of broken blisters.

And perhaps worst of all, he badly wanted a drink. Grimacing and grunting in agony, he couldn't see the house. Not sure if he *wanted* to see the house or if he won the battle, but there were no rats around him, and it was daylight. That was a good sign.

The first step he took on his blistered feet brought a yelp from him. The next one elicited a stifled cry of pain. He squeezed into the forest, the boughs whipping him, lashing his broken arms, and several times he almost blacked out from the pain. The agony triggered dry heaves that drove him to his knees. He wept, mashing his forehead on the cold, wet forest floor. Then, he struggled back to his feet. Firmed up. Pushed on. Pain. The pain was everywhere. He collapsed several times, but got back up and pressed on, whimpering and wishing for death.

He walked until it was night, then plopped down against a tree and tried to sleep. The pain was too great, however, and fended away any real rest. The air was full of smoke, cloying and cough-inducing. The temperature dropped, and he felt every descending degree with violent shivers that rattled his arms and tortured him further. He thought of the captain and wept for his friend who had no doubt been consumed in the blaze. He thought of his shotguns, destroyed as well. But the thing that truly got him weeping in pain and grief and self-pity, the thing that almost pushed him to the absolute fringe of sanity . . .

Was the thought of his house.

The place he had found so long ago, that had sheltered and protected him against foes, both human and zombie alike, had undoubtedly been razed to the ground. All of the food, the books, the movies, the comfort of hot and cold running water, the furniture, the power, and of course, the stores of precious booze. All gone.

It was a long time until morning, and Gus sat in the near-freezing wilderness and wished for the end.

At dawn, he lurched to his feet and staggered through the brush. His feet continued punishing him, and he felt as if he were walking on trapped bubbles of water that sizzled and oozed underneath his flesh when he placed weight on them. Hunger wracked him. He couldn't remember the last time he'd eaten. The question begged him why that was, and he answered it with a dry "because I was tryin' to kill myself at the time. Remember?"

His stomach didn't care about that.

And Gus wanted a drink. Just a sip. That would glue everything back together. Just one little *sip*.

In places where there was still snow, he dropped to his knees and awkwardly ate mouthfuls of what looked clean. From time to time he looked back, but the trees stopped him from seeing any great distance. He plodded on; his face stung and itched. Twice, he needed to urinate, and both times, he had to go in his pants, moaning when he let go. The feel and burn of urine soaking his genitals tortured him further.

Night came again, and he sat down against a tree, wishing for death. Every movement hurt. His stomach felt as if it were gnawing at his ribs. Snow helped relieve his thirst to some degree, but not entirely. In moments where his body allowed him a moment to think, he thought of how far he'd come, and how easy he had it at times. Nothing compared to this.

Somewhere in the night, amid the freezing cold, something unhinged in his mind. Gus dozed, waking occasionally when he moved in his sleep and set off fire alarms of agony in his broken arms.

In the morning, it took him a long time to get to his feet. He trudged through the forest, feeling like a zombie himself. Perhaps the virus had finally gotten to him and he was crossing over. Maybe one of the rats had bitten him before he got away. He sure as hell *felt* like eating someone. *Anyone.*

Then, he saw the rooftops. Most of Gus's consciousness had retreated deep inside his head to escape his punished state, but on some level, he recognized what the structures were. Gus limped into the backyard of a white house with a dark, satin green roof. Hard snow covered half of the yellow grass like a tablecloth pulled back. He plodded around the patch because if he stepped in any more snow and fell, he knew he would not get up again. He walked around to the front of the house, where a long driveway led to the street.

He believed he had walked a very long way, perhaps all of ten kilometers, through forest right up into the edge of Annapolis.

What were a few more feet?

With a short yelp, he pushed away from the house, heading to the wet pavement just at the end of the driveway. The driveway was long, with snow pulling back on either side of it and revealing more yellow grass. A line of young trees lay to the left, while the front lawn was an inverted image of the backyard. He focused on placing one throbbing, squishy foot ahead of the other. He didn't care anymore. He was too tired to care. He just wanted . . .

Falling.

Hitting pavement and bouncing all too hard.

Gus lay on his back, blinking slowly, taking in the gray sky. He heard noise to his right and turned his head. A roadblock was set up in the middle of the street. Police in riot gear and black body armor stood with their backs to him, and he could hear them shouting. From beyond the wooden beams of the barricade, a wave of bodies approached. The police commenced firing, unleashing hell and raining spent red cartridges on the pavement. They fired round after round, the reports of their guns sounding like dreamy firecrackers submerged in a fishbowl. The deadheads reached the line and smashed through it. The zombies swarmed the police, forcing them to the ground and devouring them, only visible for seconds before other gimps pushed by.

Tammy appeared—Tammy with her black eyes and pallid face, wearing only jeans and a T-shirt. She saw him, and her arms came up. Gus panted in exhausted fear. She came right at him, through the throngs of other dead things fighting with the cops. Heads exploded, but not Tammy's. She bent over him, her long dark hair fluttering around his head. Her mouth, covered in black-headed skin tags, opened, and maggots spilled out, falling from teeth eroded into moist shards. Closer she came, until their noses were almost touching, and she hissed and he screamed back....

"Well, *Jesus*," a man's voice declared.

Gus finally, mercifully, passed out.

25

They took care of him.

They entered the room when he was awake and didn't ask any questions. The big man looked strangely familiar, and the woman seemed to be the guy's wife. Two children, probably their kids, peeked in at him from the doorway. Gus didn't talk; he wasn't in the right frame of health to talk.

But he was getting better.

His dreams were sometimes turned over by short movies of reality. The couple kept him drugged. That much was obvious, even to him. An IV was hooked into his arm. They had straightened his arms a while ago, an experience that had yanked him beneath consciousness once more. When he had awakened, his arms were straight and white. No, the casts were white. At the end of the bed, poking up from red and white blankets that didn't itch and looked and felt wonderful, were his bare feet. They looked like pink slabs of meat that had been dropped from a very high place.

The people spoke to him, but their words came too fast for him to understand, and their voices were loud enough to make his head pound—like fog horns, only sped up. More drugs, marooning him somewhere on a median of dark awareness and vibrant oblivion. Colors exploded, then went black. Exploded again. Then black. No pain at all.

The captain even appeared at one point, all puffed up in his bright livery, grinning as if he'd been laid multiple times in the last forty-eight hours.

"You made it," Gus rasped, feeling so very glad to see the old sailor, and a little ashamed for having left him on the sofa back in the house.

"I did," the captain replied, beaming at him. "You're doing well, I see."

"Better. Look. I'm sorry about leaving you back at the—"

The captain *tsked* and tweaked one end of his moustache. "Don't mind that. It all worked out, didn't it?"

"Yeah."

"You did the right thing." The captain bent forward ever so slightly. "I saw *everything*. And as God above as my witness . . . you kicked ass back at the ranch. Blew the ranch to hell in fact, but pay no mind to that. None at all. You're in a better place now."

"I am?" Gus whispered.

"You surely are," the captain assured him and inspected the room, nodding. The old sailor became quiet for a moment, content to just wear his smile and watch Gus recover. "Don't worry about a thing, my chap. I've taken care of everything."

"You have?" Weaker now, but fighting to stay.

"I have," the foppish officer said confidently. "The very least I could do . . . for a friend."

Gus tried to say something, but he flew backward, and the captain disappeared. He didn't feel troubled by the old sailor's departure. In fact, he felt pretty good.

The more time he spent there, in that bed, in that place, the more comfortable he felt.

And his sleep was the best of the last two years.

"You awake?"

". . . Mmmuuh?"

"I asked if you were awake."

Drawn out sigh. "Yeah."

"How do you feel?"

"Stoned."

A deep chuckle. Pure and nice to hear. "That's good. Good to hear. We're going to keep you that way for a while, okay? Just so you know."

"In . . . bad shape . . . am I?"

Silence. "Just between you and me?"

"Yeah."

"You were fucked up."

Gus chuckled.

"But you're in good hands now. Maggie's a general practitioner and an ER vet. She knows how to patch people together."

"I . . . needed . . . patchin'?"

"Buddy, you needed superglue and the hand of God."

That didn't sound so good.

"You remember anything?"

Gus shook his head. "Thirsty."

"Oh, just a sec. Here."

Water. As it hit his lips, he felt it restore life into him. The lip of the glass disappeared once the water stopped flowing. "Thank . . . you."

"You're welcome. Found you on the road on the other side of Wolfville. Shit. Thought you were dead. Damn lucky if you ask me. Maggie peeled all that shit off you, set your arms, rehydrated you, treated your burns and your feet. Hell, you looked like a piece of steak flipped off someone's barbeque and rolled around in shit. I mean, *shit*, I've seen corpses that looked more alive than you."

"Nice." Weariness tugged at him.

A pause. "No offense. You're with us now. When you're ready, in better shape, we'll talk again. See about things."

"Talk," Gus exhaled.

And slept.

The sun had just started slipping into evening. Gus sat on an old kitchen chair and looked north, toward mountains that appeared hunched over at the top, like old men huddling. The valley stretched far and away from his chair in the clearing, and clumps of green trees speckled the edges of yellow fields. He absently clicked the casts on his forearms, a habit he'd gotten into to take away the sometimes maddening urge to scratch at the healing skin inside them. The casts would be coming off soon, according to Maggie. She'd done as good a job with him as he could ever have expected or hoped for, with the supplies the group had, and for that, Gus owed them a lot. There wasn't anything she could do about the burns to his face and hands, but Gus could live with that. The scars gave him character.

He shook his head at a mosquito buzzing near his ear. The sky was starting to turn pink. He heard a car engine and turned his head to see Adam's beat-up, red, four-door sedan. Seeing him returning from his road trip—the same silver-haired Adam Gus had taken several shots at in Annapolis—made him feel relieved. Whenever any of them left the farm area, Gus felt he should go as well, but he was always held back by his healing wounds. That would change soon, and he'd go along on those trips when asked. Adam was a good man with a sense of humor. Not all of the twenty-two people living on the farm shared that trait. They knew Gus was the one responsible for the destruction of Annapolis. They also knew why, and while they allowed him to stay while he healed, the jury was still out on whether or not they would let him stay once he was on his feet again. Adam and Maggie knew there was strength in numbers and were sold on the idea. Gus figured that was a start, even though he was divided on the matter himself. The things he'd done in Annapolis had left an invisible brand on his conscience, and he wasn't certain he deserved any of the goodwill they had shown him. Ever since Maggie had taken him off the drugs and he got his senses back, he wondered if he ever would.

They'd done so much for him in the last few months.

For nothing.

The old sedan bumped and jumped through the sea of wheat, and he watched it slow to a stop. Two children jumped out and ran toward him. The car continued toward the little community that was emerging here, nestled amongst a wheat field, a corn field, and an apple orchard. Gus had always wondered and worried about what he would do when his stores of food ran out and whether he could grow his own. The group had already addressed that very problem. For the last two years, they had been at the southwestern tip of the valley, far and away from Gus's mountain, and at the end of a dirt road not easily seen from the highway.

In the world that remained, Gus figured the area was pretty much paradise. Pretty much. That thought stayed with him for a moment, as fresh as the valley air he breathed.

As they got closer, the children called his name, telling him to come to supper.

Gus turned in their direction, smiling faintly as he was conscious of his missing teeth, and held out his once-scorched hand. Steady as a rock. The longing for a drink, just a sip, didn't bother him anymore. Maybe the people had helped that, but he believed being in an area where there was no alcohol probably helped. Having two broken arms probably had something to do with it as well.

He stood up from the lookout chair where someone kept watch for straggling deadheads most of the day and night. Taking one last look around at the goodness surrounding him, he adjusted the aluminum bat slung across his back. The weapon hung in a new leather sheath Adam had made. Yet another gift he didn't think he deserved. Gus stretched until his back cracked and walked toward the yelling, giggling children bearing down on him, making paths in the field.

The two came to either side of him and took his hands. Their happy faces ignited his smile.

The sun in their eyes, Gus and the children made their way through a meadow that shined and swayed ever so gently and wondered aloud at what might be for supper.

About the Author

Keith C. Blackmore is the author of the Mountain Man, 131 Days, and Breeds series, among other horror, heroic fantasy, and crime novels. He lives on the island of Newfoundland in Canada. Visit his website at www.keithcblackmore.com.

Podium

DISCOVER
STORIES UNBOUND

PodiumAudio.com

Made in the USA
Coppell, TX
17 September 2023